To all families—

—in any form love decides

Woodford Harbor is a quaint little fishing village along a ragged stretch of coastal Maine. A timeless sense of continuity runs through the picture-postcard community, and—except for the village picnic in summer, a few ruffled feathers when garden club awards are presented, and the occasional gunshot over the bow of lobster boats caught poaching—nothing of much consequence ever happens here.

And then murder comes to town.

Nothing prepares local funeral director Lizzy George for the unknown corpse she finds on her embalming table one fine spring morning. Where had she come from—and who was she? How had she gotten to Woodford Harbor, and who had broken in in the middle of the night to deposit her here?

Lizzy suddenly realizes that her quiet succession of ordinary days have come to a macabre and rather sinister end. Murder! Right here in sleepy little Woodford Harbor! Surely none of the good folks Lizzie has known her entire life could have done something so evil—or could they…?

With a murderer afoot, everyone becomes a suspect: the town's lobstermen, the village misfit, the doctor's wife, patrons of The Old Port, even the breakfast staff at the local diner. It's up to Lizzy to ferret out the truth.

And so begins a rollicking romp through small-town New England that exposes the deepest, darkest secrets that lie within us all.

Author Betty Breuhaus lives in a small seaside town just south of the fictional Woodford Harbor, and knows full well the kinds of characters about whom she writes. *A Curious Corpse* is her first work of fiction, and the first in her Woodford Harbor Mysteries series. She previously published a non-fiction self-help guide, *When the Sun Goes Down: A Serendipitous Guide to Planning Your Own Funeral*.

ACKNOWLEDGMENTS

Thanks are due the real Pepper, Tommy, Jennie, and Carly; not all fiction is fiction! Kudos to Amy Brown, for figuring out who the murderer was, and to Marty Riskin for the cover design. Thanks also to the many friends who read my various drafts, and let me know when things didn't quite make sense. And finally, many thanks to Margo W. R. Steiner, my editor extraordinaire.

A man can stand anything except a succession of ordinary days.

Johann Wolfgang von Goethe

CHAPTER ONE

I believe it was Johann Wolfgang von Goethe who said, "A man can stand anything except a succession of ordinary days." I was living with this affliction on that beautiful spring morning as I walked to work. Woodford Harbor is a quaint little fishing village on an inlet along a ragged stretch of coastal Maine. The ocean meets our shores in this cove as a lake touches land. The ferociousness of the ocean, though, is mitigated here. The water seems softer and more peaceful somehow. And life in Woodford Harbor follows suit.

We are just east of Portland, and with easy access to the glorious Lakes Region to the north. Entering Maine, you'll notice a sign: MAINE—THE WAY LIFE SHOULD BE. Sounds a bit over the top, I suppose, but it is pretty much how I feel about Woodford Harbor. Ordinary here is idyllic elsewhere. A timeless sense of continuity runs through the town, and even though practically everyone knows one another there is just enough discord to keep things stimulating.

So why this nagging disquiet? I shook it off, and opened the door to the family business—my business now. It was good to be in familiar territory and I looked forward to starting my day until I noticed an unknown stiff on my worktable. Old Mrs. Arthur—DEAD Old Mrs. Arthur—already had a reservation for that spot and this leggy, petite blonde was no Mrs. Arthur! Who was she, and how had she gotten here? This was a most unusual event at the Bainbridge Funeral Home, where generally things run quite smoothly. Instinctively, I called out for Mr. Stanley. He had worked with my father and my father's father before him. He knows everything—everything that needs knowing that is.

"Mr. Stanley!" I called. No answer. I realized then that it was before 8 o'clock. As knowledgeable and dedicated as the man is, he is equally punctual. His day begins precisely at eight—and not a moment before.

I did the next most logical thing then, and called Uncle Henry. He is my mother's brother, and has been Woodford Harbor's sheriff for decades. "I have the body of a young lady stretched out on my embalming table," I told him when he picked up, "and I'm not sure what to do. I don't know where she came from, who she is, or what she's doing here.

"Why me?" I asked rhetorically. "Why Bainbridge? With the exception of a bump on her head she seems unharmed. No identification, either. Oh, dear!"

"Be raaht ovah," he replied, his thick Maine accent providing a measure of comfort. I knew immediately that my long succession of ordinary days had just come to a screeching halt.

CHAPTER TWO

My name is Lizzie George and I am in my late thirties. Really late—my fortieth birthday is next month. I have a somewhat colorful past, and am presently a single mother and a funeral director. A female funeral director might raise eyebrows with some, but to someone brought up in the mortuary arts for two generations it's as natural a profession as teacher, yoga instructor, or librarian. It also happens to be both lucrative and personally satisfying.

How to describe me? I am neither tall nor short, neither fat nor thin. My hair—neither blonde nor brunette—is straight and forever pulled back in a ponytail that I trim twice a year whether it needs it or not. My dress code is simple: black pants in winter, white pants in summer. The only variables are the cut and fabric and they vary according to the occasion.

I wear my clothes on the baggy side; Miss Piggy would say it's because I want to appear to be losing weight. A crisp white shirt is a must, over which I generally sport a crew-neck sweater, a vest, or a blazer. Summer, of course, brings out polo shirts.

People have often commented that my smile is my claim to fame. Wide and toothy, it leaps from my face like a strobe light at a rave. Not exactly seductive, it instead offers welcome and a safe haven. In my business, this is especially important.

Mothers, grocery store clerks, and teachers warm to me instantly. That's not to say the upward curve of my mouth is without charm for the males of our species—any number have been attracted to the promise they think it represents. I cannot lay the blame for the marginal ones with whom I tend to become involved, however, on my smile. I attribute them to my very flawed filter.

Professionally, I have learned to keep a neutral, sympathetic expression. It keeps me grounded and in control during the tough moments. In everyday life, however, my feelings leap off my face with dismaying regularity. When I see someone I don't particularly care for they know it right away; it shows, quite literally, all over my face. In my defense, however, this tendency carries over to folks I am delighted to see as well. I am working on reducing my judgmental levels, but I do seem to have a knee-jerk reaction to people that is not always appropriate.

As smitten as I am with Woodford Harbor today, it wasn't always so. The world is a big place, and growing up my intellect and curiosity made me want out in a big way. After high school I escaped to the University of Michigan. The thousand miles that separated me from tiny Woodford Harbor seemed a world and a lifetime away.

I thrived in the radical petri dish of Midwestern academia. I studied, read poetry, smoked dope, and enjoyed the pleasures of the opposite sex, Following graduation I enrolled in the mortuary science program at Wayne State, knowing I would ultimately step into my father and grandfather's shoes.

Things were going along swimmingly until I had a Mama Mia moment—quite literally. I suddenly found myself with child. Scary as that was, not knowing which of my current infatuations was the father was positively terrifying. Frankly, all of the possibilities were grim. Ever the optimist, though, I told myself that all would be well. Why couldn't I share my crazy world with a little extension of myself?

Charlie was no more than three weeks old when thIs fantasy evaporated and I booked it back to Woodford Harbor to be near family and friends, the support group I so desperately needed. With my proverbial "village" behind me, I finished my courses on-line and adapted seamlessly to my new role at Bainbridge Funeral Home. Sixteen years later, my Charlie is a great little student, a natural athlete, and a sweet soul. She's the apple of my eye.

CHAPTER THREE

Uncle Henry sauntered through the back door looking more inconvenienced than distressed. He glanced accusingly from me to the little blonde. Dead bodies around here were nothing new, but unidentified, random ones were not the norm.

"What goes on here, my dear?" he asked. "I was just headed to The Driftwood for breakfast when I got your call. Pretty little thing, isn't she?"

"I suppose so," I replied with some annoyance, "but she's dead nonetheless and something needs to be done about this." Softening a bit, I allowed as how it seemed all wrong for a once vibrant young woman to come to this.

"She looks to be in her mid-twenties, wouldn't you say?" Uncle Henry circled the table, taking mental notes. "I'm thinking five-five, maybe, and around 110 pounds. What do you call this T-shirt she's wearing?" he suddenly asked, abruptly switching gears.

"Tie-dye," I told him. "Funny. Her short little cut-off jeans and the tie-dye shirt remind me of the hippies I went to school with at Michigan. Her nails are a bit grubby and her hair has seen better days but she's not a bum; just a little sloppy. Maybe she's going through—*was* going through," I quickly corrected myself—"a rebellious period. That little nose ring and the butterfly tattoo—and the whiff of patchouli hanging in the air—are just the frosting on the cake. This poor girl should be handing out pamphlets at a peace rally, not lying here so still and cold and lifeless."

I was reassured having Uncle Henry in the room. Generally I feel I can handle pretty much anything life throws at me, but his presence today was a comfort. He's been beside me my entire life, and cradled me in the crooks of his strong and sturdy arms when I was a newborn. Call me innocent or naïve, but I've always believed that when trouble looms or difficulties arise Uncle Henry will be there—and right now I needed someone else to help me handle this situation.

CHAPTER FOUR

Uncle Henry looks exactly as a small-town, rural sheriff should. So much so, in fact, that I sometimes wonder which came first, Uncle Henry or the oft-reproduced caricature of a sheriff? Had he, over time, morphed into the caricature, or did he consciously create the image? He's slightly round, an affliction brought on not by advanced age but by a surfeit of all things tasty and liquid that pass one's lips. One should not take Uncle Henry's girth as a sign of weakness, though. When the situation warrants it, he is massively strong and fleet of foot. At the county fair each summer everyone wants him on his or her relay team and at the end of the strong and sinewy tug-of-war rope. He never disappoints.

When not in uniform he sports khaki pants, a plaid flannel shirt—make that seersucker in summer—Bean boots in the winter months, and Bean boat shoes when the weather turns reliably warm. His palette is heavy on navy blue. Not much about Uncle Henry has changed over the years. His chubby cheeks glow year-round and his moustache has been trimmed to exactly the same length for decades. As for me, I have never dated a man with facial hair of any kind. Subconsciously, he would remind me of Uncle Henry—and that's just too incestuous for me.

Uncle Henry lived with my parents and me throughout my childhood. He never quite made the big commitment to another human being. He was my mom's younger brother and she some-how felt obligated to be the woman in his life. His bachelorhood was fine with my father, and heaven for me. My parents are great, don't get me wrong, but there is nothing better than an adult who loves you like his own; we enjoy a distance that allows a bit more flexibility.

He's never said it, but I think the one disappointment in Uncle Henry's life is that I didn't enter law enforcement and become his deputy sheriff. He tried; I'll give him that. He would let me in on many of his investigations and I was privy to a lot more inside knowledge about the goings-on in town than was probably healthy for a young girl. He gave me *The Strange Disappearance of Arthur Cluck* when I was still in preschool, and read me Nancy Drew mysteries before I could read and devour them myself.

And he always had my back. As a high school freshman, I had a long affair with cigarettes. Sophomore year, beer; junior year, rum; and senior year, dope. Unerringly, he seemed always to know where I would be, when I'd be there, and in whose company I'd be. Without a word, he'd cart me home before any dire consequences ensued.

Uncle Henry is not well-educated in the usual sense, but when *Jeopardy* comes on he whips everyone in the room. And he has an amazingly calculating mind when trying to unravel a puzzle. As we stood in companionable silence looking at our unidentified casu-alty, I realized the latter would come in handy.

"Morning!" chirped Mr. Stanley as he came around the corner. The ship's clock struck eight bells in salute. "Ah, what brings you here, Henry?"

Uncle Henry gave a nod toward the silent young lady.

"Oh, my, I believe we had Mrs. Arthur slated for this spot," said Mr. Stanley. It occurred to me that we were all being a bit blasé. This table had held countless dead bodies, most of them requiring no reaction whatsoever. But this arbitrary body, I felt, should be afforded at least *some* measure of drama. Perhaps I was being flippant because I desperately needed a coping mechanism.

Finally Uncle Henry assumed his sheriff persona. "How do you think she got in here?" he asked of no one in particular. "Doesn't appear she met her demise on this table. Must have been delivered here. Any sign of a B & E?" It was on occasions like this that I felt Uncle Henry watched just a few too many *Dragnet* reruns.

At Mr. Stanley's baffled look he rephrased the question. "Has either of you noticed any broken locks? How did she get in here?"

A look of discomfort passed across Mr. Stanley's face. I knew immediately what the problem was, as we had covered this ground innumerable times before. Things had changed since my grandfather and father ran the business. Mr. Stanley, however, had not. He had his own fixed ways and they were next to impossible to reshape. Looking at his shoes, my clearly mortified right-hand man could only utter, "My, my. My, my, my. Now who would want to break in here—into a funeral home? Nothing but dead bodies here. Oh dear! Yes…well, I might have left that back door unlocked last night."

Uncle Henry shot me a knowing look that said, 'I feel your pain.' He then suggested that in order to protect the area as a crime scene we lock the aforementioned door, and proceed with the investigation.

Mr. Stanley's slight frame was shaken, but not shattered. I quite honestly am not sure of his age. But I do know he worked for my grandfather for a few years before assisting my father for thirty. Add his stint with me and I am sure he has easily surpassed the appropriate age to retire. I help him out with the heavy work now, so he is mostly left to answer the phone and see to the folks coming in to make arrangements. His gracious, dignified, ageless face, and his quiet demeanor are an instant comfort to everyone. I imagine he has a first name, but having grown up with him I find it impossible to call him by anything but Mr. Stanley.

Uncle Henry pulled out yellow tape and together we cordoned off the room. I was alone with the body as Uncle Henry left to call the state police. Looking at her, I felt a heaviness in my chest. There had surely been times that I was as vulnerable as she now appeared, but luck had been on my side and I escaped real trouble. My own sweet Charlie was not far from this stage of her own life. What twisted roads would she travel in the next ten years? Life is as unpredictable as the tides are true. We need all the good fortune the universe will afford us. This dear creature looked like a girl who was still discovering the world with the irrepressible naiveté of youth.

The initial shock gone, I began to speculate on a host of other questions. Why had someone chosen *my* funeral home? *My* table? Was this a reflection on the funeral home? Should I be taking this personally? Was it an act of compassion to leave her in a spot where she would be cared for—or merely a convenient disposal spot?

Whoever had deposited this lifeless body must have carried it in through the back door. Her weight might be minimal, but dead weight is dead weight. Whoever had brought her to me had to have been in reasonably good physical shape. Then again, how had someone known the back door would be unlocked? Woodford Harbor doors are often unlocked, as small-town doors frequently are, but not funeral home doors. We hold the town's dead, and have an obligation to keep them safe. Had it been mere happenstance that someone found mine unlocked?

Someone had cut this young girl's journey short and I felt a need to right that wrong. The sounds of Uncle Henry snarling as he returned from the back room broke my reverie. "They're sending that self-important, self-absorbed twit, Detective Daniels.

Thinks he's so smart. Too smart by half, that fool is. He is a tonic unto himself. He and Dr. Twittle, the medical examiner, will be here in about an hour." The one thing Uncle Henry's level disposition will not tolerate is arrogance. Indeed, one of his favorite phrases has always been, "Never underestimate the impudence of an impudent man."

We settled in to wait. Those sixty minutes seemed like an eternity. The three of us sat in uncomfortable, subdued silence until we heard the whine of a distant siren that, when it is intended for you, gives you chills.

CHAPTER FIVE

D etective Daniels flew through the door like Superman. The only thing missing was the cape. The larger and more in charge he became, the more Uncle Henry struggled to control himself. I found myself retreating to a corner, trying not to breathe the charged air.

For some reason Daniels decided to accost Mr. Stanley first. He had the poor man backed up against a wall as he rattled off a barrage of questions. That's when Uncle Henry shot forward, putting himself between the two.

"What are you doing?" he barked. "You can speak to me and I will give you all the pertinent information."

"I'll speak to whomever I damn well please!" Daniels growled.

Detective Daniels might well have the cleanest fingernails in the entire state of Maine. Every slate grey hair on his head falls perfectly into a sculpted wave. I have a vague distrust of men—and women too, for that matter—whose hair is so perfectly coifed it looks like a helmet. The detective's clothes were merely an extension of his toilette; flawlessly tailored, with nary a wrinkle. Humility, however, was not his strong suit.

"Easy, Daniels, these are my people and I want them treated civilly. I've already spoken with Mr. Stanley and we have ascertained that the back door was left unlocked last night so we won't be seeing any forced entry. The body has not been touched and is just as it was found. Lizzie came in a little before eight, and found her on the table. She appears to have a bump on her head," he said in summation, "which may or may not be significant."

Daniels turned his attention to me. The intensity of his questions made me feel slightly guilty. Of what, I don't know. But his sharp, accusing eyes made me wonder. I certainly didn't look forward to him interrogating me; somewhat nervously I considered confessing, just get it over with.

"So that's it, that's all you have to say?" Daniels barked at me. One of those overbearing people with a skewed idea of personal space, he was mere inches from my face. Was that the beginning of a blemish next to his left ear? Oh, God, this was all becoming too much for me!

"Well..." I mumbled, "I guess so. I mean, that's all I can think of right now. I walked in, I found her, and I called Uncle Henry."

"If you think of anything else, let me know," Daniels added, turning his attention back to the crime scene spread before us. What else did he think I might know: I saw the cab that dropped her off? I purposefully erased some footprints? I couldn't quite fathom what else he expected me to remember.

After a long, last look around the room the detective seemed satisfied that he had what he needed. Flipping his notebook closed, he stabbed a stubby, well-chewed pencil over his left ear, popped two pieces of Juicy Fruit in his open maw, and prepared to move on.

Margaret Twittle looked up just then from my embalming table. "I've given the body a superficial examination," she noted, "but it will take a thorough autopsy to determine the cause of death. I'll call the morgue, and have them send the coroner's van." She glanced quickly at Daniels. "That is if it's all right with you, officer."

"I don't see that we can accomplish much more here," the detective said dismissively. "Pack her up."

"And just what else would you expect to see going on here, detective?" snapped Uncle Henry.

Really, they were like two little boys engaging in playground turf wars. They did manage to work together when I brought the body bag. Together they lifted her up, laid her inside, then zipped the morbid shroud closed. Detective Daniels and Dr. Twittle left together, he to the station and she to the morgue. Uncle Henry and I looked at each other.

It was then I noticed Mr. Stanley still huddled against the wall. I gave him a smile and said, "Well, I guess that's it for the excitement around here. I think I'll join Uncle Henry in his quest for breakfast, and be back in a bit. While you wait for the coroner's van, why don't you get started on Mrs. Arthur's paperwork?" This piece of normal felt good.

CHAPTER SIX

I joined Uncle Henry at the front door and we started the short walk through town to the waterfront. Woodford Harbor dates back to the 1600s. It has been populated over the years by fishermen, shoemakers, ardent clergymen, and all sorts of courageous heroes: heroes from the Revolutionary War, the Civil War, both world wars, and—today—our young men and women in Afghanistan.

The town turned out in force for one of our own who fell in Afghanistan just a few years back. His service was held at the local Congregational church; so large was the crowd that many had to remain outside. A somber procession accompanied his body through town to the local cemetery, townsfolk lining the route and waving small American flags. The new football field is named in his honor. I'm so proud that in addition to its colonial charm and beautiful coastline and harbor, Woodford Harbor is a town with a soul. I love living here.

We passed the well-kept homes of former ship captains, and continued down State Street to The Driftwood. The houses nearer the water are magnificent if for no other reason than their fortitude; after hundreds of years being battered by fierce New England storms and devastating coastal hurricanes they still stand. Although similar in style, each has its own character. Thankfully, our historic commission has not yet turned Woodford Harbor into a Colonial Williamsburg, replete with acceptable color choices and artificial parameters. People here still make their own decisions, which keeps the town alive and real.

Uncle Henry's duties as sheriff are admittedly not the stuff of action films. An exciting incident here might be when a Prius advocating 'Random Acts of Kindness' collides with a banged-up car sporting the bumper sticker, 'My Kid Can Beat up Your Honor Student.'

"I kind of miss your mom at times like this," said Uncle Henry. "My goodness, she makes the best over-easy egg ever!" I miss both my parents all the time, and for more than the lack of an over-easy egg. Ken and Mildred are what everyone deserves as a mom and dad: hard-working, loyal to each other, and totally supportive of me.

"Oh, I know Uncle Henry. What do you suppose they're up to right now?"

"Can't exactly say," he answered. "I still can't believe they left Woodford Harbor for the winter. But I guess if it's for Captiva, it's understandable."

Captiva is a barrier island just off the coast of Fort Myers, Florida. Mom, Dad, and I went there for February vacations for almost as long as I can remember. Like so many things in childhood, we sometimes take it for granted until adulthood gives us some perspective. Captiva, to my mind, is more akin to a Caribbean island than to the overgrown craziness that is the rest of Florida. No buildings are taller than a palm tree and the restaurants sport names like RC Otters, the Mucky Duck, and the Lazy Flamingo. There's nary a golden arch in sight. The long white sand beaches—colorful shells strewn their entire length—rival any beach in the world.

Each year we had the same two-bedroom rental. It was just off the beach on a funny little road full of overgrown roots and un-kempt natural vegetation. Its neighbors were all like-minded cot-tages. No McMansions here.

Each morning it was up for the sunrise and breakfast, then off to the beach, or fishing, or kayaking for the remainder of the day. Dinners were timed to the sunsets, and were always outdoors at either a funky local eatery or on our own deck.

When I got a bit older, I would bring along some lucky friend. We were allowed to be on our own, and go wherever we pleased. This newfound freedom had only one caveat; one that was quite lost on us. There really was nowhere to go.

When I left for Ann Arbor, my parents started spending more and more time there. Two weeks stretched into three. They made friends, established routines, and found it to have a similar feel to Woodford Harbor, only with palm tress. A few years ago they took the plunge, and bought a little place with enough space to ac-commodate Charlie and me for visits. Mom and Dad have traveled through life together for so long, their priorities seem to evolve simultaneously. I am impressed, and quite envious. I wonder what my father would say about an unknown dead body on his embalm-ing table. It would probably reconfirm that his decision to retire was the right one.

Uncle Henry and I continued our stroll down State Street. The familiar clang of ships' riggings drew us directly to the water. Woodford Harbor is cut out of the coastline in a graceful curve, seemingly by an artist's stroke of genius. The harbor's moorings protect her boats in almost any type of weather and the breeze lines them up pointing into the wind in an orderly fashion. Locals have been known to tell tourists that we have a town employee whose job it is to point them all the same direction.

Approaching the town landing, we noticed folks preparing their dinghies for a row out to their boats; it was perfect weather for a day on the water. Lobstermen were busy at the pier, loading bait and unloading lobster. I looked for Bode among them. Bode and I have been best friends forever, first as playmates and, more recently, as lovers. He's quite simply a man with whom I love to share time, love, and laughs. Charlie and I still live on our own, but Bode completes us. His would be a welcome face right about now.

CHAPTER SEVEN

We arrived at our destination. The well-worn latch on the front door of The Driftwood sounded its familiar metallic clank as we entered and the waft of bacon and eggs welcomed us. Red-and-white-checked oilskin covered the tables and the old red rug showed the indentations and worn spots left by generations of diners. At the counter sat true regulars; some seemed to have almost taken root in their habitual spots. The small tables scattered around the perimeter were nearly all filled with fishermen, bankers, families, and an occasional tourist. We spotted our mutual friend, Pepper, holding court in the corner, and headed over. We definitely needed the distraction she was certain to provide.

"Hey!" bellowed Pepper. "Heard you had a visitor this morning!"

"Now, how are you privy to this information?" Uncle Henry scowled, disappointed he wouldn't have the opportunity to announce the news.

"Aw, Henry, doesn't everyone sleep with their police scanner? Girl needs to know what goes on around here." Pepper is the resident gossip columnist for the local paper, *The Woodford Reserve.* She's also a big bourbon enthusiast.

Woodford Harbor is not Pepper's first rodeo. She had seen the world as a writer in the navy, and looks the part. She has the wonderful weathered face of someone who has lived life full-steam ahead. Her torso is stocky and her wardrobe is not unlike a female version of Uncle Henry. It's khakis in the winter, with heavy woolen sweaters; come summer she brings out khaki shorts and polo shirts. Boat shoes sustain her throughout every season. Her vociferous growl is well-known, and frightens no one. The power of her pen at *The Woodford Reserve* is mighty. Pepper does not suffer fools gladly, nor does she tolerate bad manners. An entire column can be devoted to the blasphemous habit of men not removing their hats indoors—or those among us who neglect to send thank-you notes.

A devotee of food, Pepper also writes a culinary column. How original the recipes may be are questionable, but her descriptions of food are, once again, the stuff of legend. Her description of a leg of lamb with mint jelly could make the most ardent vegan take a stab at it. And butter? There is absolutely nothing that cannot be improved with more of it. Her discipline also calls for a healthy cocktail around five to get things going. Is there a better character to have as a friend? Did I mention that Pepper is Charlie's godmother? If I leave my Charlie prematurely, I want the person with the most influence on her to be full of life, fun, and bravado.

Uncle Henry and I slid into two vacant chairs at Pepper's corner table and I began to focus on my meal. Although I usually order the same breakfast, I still like to think about other options. Often I wait for my companions to order first, on the off chance they will think of something I haven't. If I don't choose what they have I'll usually spend the rest of the meal coveting their food.

Suddenly, I looked up into the friendly eyes of Jenny, who has been serving me breakfast since Charlie was in a high chair. Jenny is one of those people who really never changes. She is always cheerful, even on the glummest of mornings, and even after two kids and a lifetime of waiting tables she retains her wiry physique and adorable butch haircut; it's her own special style. We had played women's softball together back in the day and I'm sure she can still run the bases like the little roadrunner she was then. I might still be able to wield a bat, but my thighs would not hold me in my catcher's position for much more than one inning.

"Small stack of blueberry French toast with sugar-free syrup?" Jenny asked. My smile and a nod completed the exchange. The French toast at The Driftwood is the very definition of comfort food for me. It is neither thick, stuffed, nor covered in cinnamon and powered sugar. It is thin. Flat thin, and squished down hard. Drowned in an egg wash, covered in healthy little blueberries, and grilled up. Everything in Maine, it seems, requires blueberries. It's not a law, but it goes far beyond tradition. I rationalize my some-what decadent repast by planning to eat only three of the four halves of bread that will be served. Combined with the nutritious blueberries and the guilt-free syrup, I know I'll leave feeling I've been quite sensible. More importantly, though, I know I'll leave happy. Life is too short to drink the house wine, or compromise on breakfast.

Order in hand, Jenny walked it into the kitchen for Tommy to prepare. Suddenly his big head appeared in the pass-through win-dow, accompanied by a shouted "Hi!" and a wave in my direction. I could see his Patriots jersey through the opening, but didn't know if he was sporting a Brady 12 today, or a Vince Wilfork 75. Tommy's infatuation with the Patriots is so strong that I'm sure without his wife's intervention his children's names would have mirrored the Patriots roster. Most of us spread our Boston passions among the Red Sox, Bruins, and Celtics, but Tommy lives and breathes Patriots. I brought him tulips once, after a particularly painful Patriots' loss. I couldn't think of adequate words of sympathy, and hoped they would cheer him up. It didn't work. But when he took them home and left them on the counter, his wife was thrilled. And Tommy? He simply smiled and accepted her accolades. It only further cemented our friendship.

Tommy and his two sisters, Carly and Glenda, own The Driftwood, having taken it over when their father passed away. It's so fortunate for the town that they remained to run the place. Tommy and Carly are caricatures of brother and sister. Both are big, happy blonds. Outgoing and fun, they seem to thoroughly enjoy life. Carly does everything there: cooks, serves tables, cleans the bathroom, and shovels the snow. Tommy's the man on the grill. Both Tommy and Carly have kids who might someday run the place. To saddle those poor young things with running The Driftwood in twenty years is a bit of a stretch, but I like to have my ducks in a row on the important issues.

One of their familiar squabbles rang out from the kitchen. "Tommy, you are just going to have to get your butt out of my way," I heard Glenda screech. She is, admittedly, the most attractive of the three. Her trim body reflects her rigorous exercise routine, but it leaves a sharp edge.

"Hey there, now. This butt is creating some magnificent dishes," Tommy good-naturedly called back to her. "The Phantom Gourmet could be out there right now—and so could any number of cooking show scouts! Wouldn't I look grand on the big screen?"

"If any scouts come in here, you can bet they'll be looking for me, creator of the Big Blue," Glenda retorted. I guess we all have to hang our hats on some accomplishment, and Glenda's is her blueberry muffins, the aforementioned Big Blues. Whether they are truly in a class of their own is up for discussion in my world. If large, sugary gut bombs define culinary success then I suppose they're contenders.

Glenda takes care of all the finances at The Driftwood and it's a good fit for her personality. Always a bit of a loner, she's best suited to deal with the cash register and crank out muffins in the kitchen, away from customers. She was married once for about 45 minutes. Her husband was a perfectly nice fellow who took her to Africa for their honeymoon. Glenda slept with the safari guide and that was it. She's been alone ever since, but she doesn't strike me as a truly independent woman content with her single status.

She seems to be trolling for men, and one in particular—one who is not exactly available. Truth be told, word was that she had actually landed this married man at one point—"landed" in the sense of her being his only extra-marital affair at the time. Perhaps I'm being a bit harsh. Sometimes I think I should have a softer spot in my heart for Glenda than I do.

Carly soon entered the conversation. "So, Glenda, you think you might sell that Big Blue recipe to Ina or some other cooking show star?" Oh, that Carly! She just loves to stir things up.

"Well," said Glenda in response, "that's an interesting thought. I wonder what it might be worth? They *are* world-renowned, you know, my Woodford Harbor Big Blues."

The Woodford Harbor High School teams are also known as the Blues. There has always been some dispute as to whether the name came from our local blueberries, as in *Blueberries for Sal*, or from the lovely blue of the lupines Miss Rumpfius planted in the children's picture book of the same name. Of one thing I'm sure, though. It has nothing to do with Glenda's Big Blues. She is indeed a legend in her own mind.

CHAPTER EIGHT

I was finishing up my third piece of French toast when Pepper started interrogating Uncle Henry as he sopped up the last of his eggs with a piece of toast. "So what did you find? Who's the victim? Don't suppose I get to choose," she said, flashing that impish grin of hers.

"Jane Doe. Don't know. She was a pretty young thing, too; a shame to end up in that state. Other than a bump on the side of her head, there were no other obvious injuries. I'm sure we'll learn more from Daniels soon. But I sure would like to identify her," said Uncle Henry.

"Tell me more," Pepper demanded.

"Well, maybe mid-twenties. Dirty blond hair, 5'5", in good shape; could be a runner's body. Looked kind of lost somehow."

"Maybe it's just that age," I interjected. "Such a need to be your own person then, but not really knowing just what that is. The scruffy clothes, nose ring, tattoo. At some point the look is so well defined it's almost predictable."

"There was actually a girl who might fit that description at The Old Port a few nights ago," said Pepper. "At first glance it didn't appear she was old enough to be drinking, but on closer inspection I noticed her face already showed the lines of a difficult life. She was talking with Duke. A bit creepy, if you ask me.

"A girl like that should be nowhere near a drinking, drugging bastard like him. He still owes me a hundred bucks for firewood last winter. And I hear he's been messing with other lobstermen's traps. They all work so hard; it just takes one jerk messing with their code of ethics to make it tougher and more miserable for everyone. He would have been tarred and feathered back in the day!"

Pepper holds strong opinions, but as harsh as this assessment might seem there aren't many who would rise to Duke's defense. A dishonest lobsterman is about the lowest of the low in this little town. They work incredibly hard to earn what they do, which is not much, and they're forced to live and work together with little more than a shared sense of morality governing them. Their buoys float out in the middle of the ocean, with a line connecting them to a baited trap on the ocean's floor, unprotected. With no one in sight, the temptation to pull up another man's trap and grab his lobsters is always there. And the ease with which you can cut another man's line and rob him of his trap altogether can also prove irresistible sometimes. Add a disgusting, immoral, rot-gut character like Duke into the mix and you have nothing but trouble.

"Oh, dear," sighed Uncle Henry. "I guess I'll have to go see what Duke has to say. Can't be good." I thanked my lucky stars that I had opted for the funeral business, and not pursued a life as Deputy Dog. The job couldn't possibly pay enough to be in the same room as Duke.

Just then sweet Archie scooted past our table to clear the one across the way.

"Good morning, Archie," I called out cheerfully to the young man whose face just makes you want to smile. He's been the bus-boy at The Driftwood for five years now, and is the sweetest kid on earth. He was in the backseat of the family car when a semi lost control and ran into it head-on. His parents were killed instantly and, although the twelve-year-old Archie was spared, he had some brain damage that limits him from leading the life he might have had. A prosthesis replaced his left leg, but he was young and strong and adapted well. You're hardly aware of it. He is now a fixture at The Driftwood, where he has many ardent admirers and friends.

Archie's full name is Thomas Archibald Hamilton III. His father was called Thomas, but the third could never carry the weight of a name like Archibald so he is always just Archie. His bright red curly hair is almost overshadowed by his exquisite green eyes; they have a clarity that shines even when he's occasionally confused.

Archie is most proficient at his given tasks. He can balance a plastic tub with dozens of plates, coffee mugs galore, and food scraps of all kinds without missing a beat. He is unobtrusive, but always catches your eye with an endearing smile on his lips and a twinkle in his eye—something not easy for a teenager in the best of circumstances. Archie puts a lot of energy into his life and it shows.

"So, how did the Red Sox do last night?" I asked him.

"Umm…I don't really know. Didn't catch the game," he mumbled, pushing his way into the kitchen. This was totally out of character for the young Red Sox fan who could normally quote practically every at bat verbatim following a game. And I knew we had won, which usually sent the lad up into the clouds. Life throws curve ball after curve ball it seems. Something was not right with my young friend this morning.

Pepper had by now changed subjects, and was pondering the eternal question, 'What's for dinner?' When asked, she always has an answer for that night's menu.

"I'm thinking a nice little pasta dish," she opined. "Get some tasty boneless chicken breasts, and cut them into perfect little slices. Sauté them in good olive oil, throw in some scallions, and add mushrooms sliced painfully thin. Toss in some nice soy sauce, and throw the whole thing over piping hot vermicelli. Of course I'll finish it off with some crusty French bread and a nice little tossed salad. Ohhhhh, won't that be nice!"

"Wine?" I prompted.

"Of course, a chilled Pinot Grigio, I think, and a nice pour of good bourbon to get me through the cooking process." She smiled contentedly.

"Dessert?" someone asked.

"Ah, yes, the incentive to finish all of the above. I think strawberry shortcake on baking powder biscuits with whipped cream. *Real* whipped cream."

Just then the door opened and the place was filled with a presence I felt at once. Bode strode in, his large frame filling the door. The word that comes to mind when I look at Bode is *solid*. He is about 6'2" and weighs close to 200 pounds—each pound solid. He's also, I might add, reliable, honorable, and intelligent. At least I can be judgmental in both directions, I guess. His blond hair and bushy eyebrows frame a large square face wrinkled from sunshine and fresh air. His lips spread into a smile as wide as the harbor itself. Cheerful and positive, he's also strong yet gentle. He does have a temper, though; one that is best left unchallenged. I can honestly say, however, that I have never seen him direct it inaccurately. He was dressed in jeans and a flannel shirt, his spring lobstering uniform.

I was so glad to see him I felt an electric spark in my chest as he approached us. Truth be told, sometimes I don't like the fact that he means so much to me. That I need him. But maybe I do.

"Hey, kids!" he called out, then sidled over to our table and greeted everyone with the kind of warmth only made possible through life-long friendships.

"What brings you back in so early? Giving the lobster population a break?" I asked.

"Actually, I wasn't much past Childrens' Island when I heard the police report about the girl you found this morning. I was a little worried so thought I would come in and see if I could find you here. That must have been quite a shock."

Childrens' Island covers about four acres a mile off the mouth of Woodford Harbor, and hosts a YMCA day camp in the summer. A ferry transports the children back and forth. The kids love it. I always refer to it as Camp Alcatraz.

Bode always sees beyond my flip exterior, and knew that my discovery this morning would be harder on me than I let on. I don't show my vulnerabilities to many people, but Bode has an inside track. It felt good to have a friend who not only knows me so well, but will come to offer comfort and support. I gave him a look that I knew conveyed my gratitude, then shrugged my shoulders for the rest of the world, and said, "Hey, dead bodies are not news to me." I squeezed his knee, and felt the familiar chemistry between us.

"So what are you thinking, Henry? Any clues as to identity? Motive? How bizarre," said Bode.

"Well," Uncle Henry replied, "seems like a cliché, but Duke already seems involved somehow. Guy can't escape himself."

Bode's face darkened. "I had four more traps missing yesterday—and six more with nothing in them. No lobsters, no crabs, no bait, no nothing. Doesn't seem right somehow. Duke is becoming a ubiquitous presence on the water these days—and not a particularly welcome one."

Continuing to exercise my newfound non-judgmental attitude, I piped up. "Now, now, we can't just pin every bad happening in town on Duke."

"Oh, yeah?" said Uncle Henry and Bode simultaneously.

CHAPTER NINE

We all stepped out together, then Bode suddenly turned and went back inside.

"Back in a minute, Z," he said, looking at me. Bode has nicknames for everyone. I am just Z. I love the way he says it. Although not overly demonstrative, Bode's warmth registers in his nicknames. He somehow owns a piece of you when he can give you a personal moniker.

Uncle Henry and I exchanged good-byes with a quick mini-hug. This was not our usual habit, but we had had quite a morning together and I think he was feeling a bit protective of me, this incident being more his line of work than mine. I watched him walk up State Street toward the police station, and wondered if was capable of unraveling this mysterious travesty.

The police station is in the basement of the Old Town House, which dates back to the 1720s. The building stands smack in the middle of the town square, and has seen its share of history. During the Revolutionary War the British confiscated this noble building. In the room over Uncle Henry's office you can still see indentations from the hooves of horses the British billeted there over 200 years ago. It is a grand old building, and is still in use. In addition to housing the sheriff's office, it's Woodford Harbor's polling place.

Bode was out in a minute and we walked down to his lobster boat, the *Lizzie G.* "What time do you think you'll be over for dinner?" I asked.

"Seven-ish? I'll stop and see Mom as soon as we get in, and then come right over. I went back in because I saw Glenda there, and wanted to talk to her. She is a piece of work. I'll tell you about it later. I asked Archie to join us for dinner. Is Lil' Chuck around?" That would be Charlie.

"He must have been thrilled! He seems to count on you more and more as his role model. And yes, Charlie is around. Maybe I'll make some hamburger stroganoff. That always tastes good!" Hamburger and mushrooms swimming in mushroom soup and sour cream, and ladled over egg noodles. That is my way of cooking and no one complains.

Bode gave me an affirmative smile and a whack on my butt, then hopped aboard. Just then Bob raised his head above the gunnels. Sometimes I wonder whom Bode loves more, Bob or me. Bob's furry head got the rub it was looking for and I got a little slobber on my sleeve from the Bernese mountain dog's mouth. I do believe there are some people who truly relate to dogs; my Bode falls into this category. When he and Bob look at each other, or sit together, or work together, there is an undeniable chemistry.

Bode, Bob, and the *Lizzie G* are a real trio. Bode usually pushes off at sunrise, loaded up with pogies as bait, to pull some 80 of his 250 traps. Reaching his traps, he dons his rubber apron and lobster gloves, and is ready for work. As I mentioned previously, each trap is attached by line to a buoy that floats on the surface. In Maine, only one trap can be connected to each buoy, although in other locales there can be a line of up to five traps.

As a means of identification, each lobsterman's buoys have his own unique colors and design. Bode's are royal blue with two white stripes—classic and simple. I had once suggested I could paint them with polka dots rather than stripes, but that was pushing things a bit far with my lobsterman! The traps are spread out within a five-mile radius of Woodford Harbor, and clustered into three separate areas, making it more efficient to check them.

When he's ready to haul, Bode grabs each buoy and secures it to the power lift. This then pulls the trap up next to the boat's topside. He swings it in, and checks it for lobsters. There is a legal minimum size that each lobster must meet to be a keeper. Bode carries the mandatory gauge that measures them from the rear of their eye socket to the rear of their carapace, or shell. The current measurement is 3-3/4". Any less and the lobster is tossed immediately back into the ocean. Female lobsters are also protected, so the next step is to flip the lobster over, and check for eggs. If she has a row of little black eggs, back in she goes.

If the minimum measurement is met, and there are no eggs, the final check is to see if one of the tail fins has been notched. A notch on the tail fin indicates that this lobster has been hauled in with eggs previously, and returned. A notch-tailed female—even one currently without eggs—must still be thrown back.

For each keeper Bode grabs his bander, eases a fat little rubber band onto its end, squeezes to stretch the band, then slides it over the lobster's claw. Only after both claws are banded is the lobster ready to be thrown into a bucket on the boat filled with circulating seawater.

Beyond companionship, Bob is an actual help on the boat; the next step is his forte. Right on cue he reaches into the bait bucket, pulls out a fish, and lifts it into Bode's waiting hand. In what seems like one fluid motion, Bode releases the trap's mesh bait bag, slides the new fish into it, and reattaches the bag. The trap is then ready to be tossed back into the ocean, and begin its next fishing adventure. Once the two are in rhythm, the process is as fluid as a dance. Bode and Bob are inseparable on land as well. When the two of them sit quietly together they create their own energy. They are a package, and luckily I adore them both.

The pair pushed off. I was admittedly jealous, and wished I could hop aboard and avoid my present reality.

CHAPTER TEN

I lingered a moment at the town landing, leaning against the railing and reveling in the sweet smell of the salt air. Our small harbor sports a great variety of vessels: big, small, sail, power, wood, fiberglass, commercial, and pleasure. The real character of the harbor has not changed much over the years. It is the same body of water that protected the *U.S.S. Constitution* from the British in 1812, and was home to beautiful J boats and enormous pleasure yachts in the '20s and '30s. There is a certain timelessness about the water.

Even transitions in Woodford Harbor are seamless. Nothing feels much different now from the way it did thirty years ago when Bode and I were growing up here. We were always fast friends. We played on the rocks, sailed little Optimists, and traded secrets in a very cool tree house we built together. We had dinner at each others' houses many nights, but could never understand why we were denied sleepovers. We were blessedly oblivious to any differences we had.

My parents were more on the conservative side in those days. I was an only child and they were quite devoted to me. Sometimes I wonder if they were a precursor to today's helicopter parents; if so, I don't think I suffered from it.

Bode's parents, however, were much more active socially. Even with three sons they seemed to entertain and be entertained most every weekend. His father had been a heart surgeon who commuted to Portland, and his mother prepared wonderful meals and tended her lovely gardens at home. Bode and his two brothers went to Dartmouth, his parents' alma mater. It's no surprise their house is painted forest green.

Bode, the oldest, lives in this house now. The middle brother, Jonny, is a surgeon and lives in Seattle. Bill is the youngest, and practices law in Boston. Each of them has two boys, wonderful wives, and seemingly happy lives.

Bode was working at an investment house in Boston eight years ago when his father, James, had a sudden heart attack, and died in Canada while on a fishing trip. It was a terrible shock for the whole family, and especially for his wife, Pammy, who had been with him. It had a monumental effect on Bode, though.

He had never married, and came to realize after his father's death that he had never really settled in Boston. The ostensive reason he stayed behind after the memorial service was to help his mother. But as more and more time went by he gradually realized that Woodford Harbor was where he truly felt at home. During high school and college Bode had had a ten-pot recreational lobster pot license, and earned his summer money selling lobsters at the dock. Back in Maine, he had an epiphany when he realized how happy he had always been on the water. Listening to his heart, Bode bought a used lobster boat, fixed it up, rigged it, and bought 100 traps. It wasn't long before he had painted the name *Lizzie G* on the stern in honor of his second epiphany.

The early spring air, along with these memories, filled me with a renewed energy that seems so present at this time of year. Bulbs were popping up in ordered rows and flowering shrubs were adding somewhat discordant colors in front of houses. I am not a big fan of flowering shrubs, although it seems almost sacrilege to say so, and I find so often that the colors clash garishly. I suspect that shrubbers—as I call those who buy them—purchase these things mindlessly in the fall, and are quite pleased with themselves when they inevitably flower in the spring. But have they adequately considered their color choices? Oh dear, I feel more of my judgmental opinions creeping in!

I walked the short mile along the harbor to my house. The homes along the water have been remodeled and spiffed up over the centuries. The outer layers of weathered shingle certainly belie the shiny granite countertops and the stainless steel appliances that sparkle within.

Soon I was in front of my own little house. Originally built in the 1600s for the first minister in town, it is bordered by Old Burial Hill on one side, an old walking lane on another, woods to the rear, and—across the street—the fish market on Little Harbor. It is here where all the local fishermen sell their goods. Our wraparound front porch offers a delightful peek of the harbor. In truth I love this little view, but when it comes time to describe the house to the tax assessor I quickly deny any view of water!

Once home, I hopped in my old red Jeep, and fired her up, ready to head to Woodford Harbor Hospital and my annual physical. If it is possible to love a car, then I do. She has four-wheel drive for the snowy winters, and a top that comes off in the summer. She probably makes me happier than she should.

Perfectly content, I drove the two miles to the other end of town and pulled into the hospital parking lot. Although babies are no longer born here, but rather out of town in Portland's more modern facility, there are still medical offices in the old facility. Once inside I walked down the hall, and into Dr. Wilson's office.

"Good morning, Trudy." I smiled at the attractive woman sitting behind the desk. "How's everything with you?" Trudy is her husband's receptionist, a nurse living every nurse's dream. She got the doctor. A quarter-century ago Trudy had been Dr. Wilson's nurse; she was the one he subsequently chose to be his Mrs. The unfortunate part of the story is this: Dr. Wilson has many other nurses in town. His indiscretions are so careless, in fact, that it's somewhat embarrassing for the rest of us. For Trudy's sake, the townsfolk look the other way, and cut him a lot of slack.

"Oh, I'm fine, dear," Trudy replied in her modulated voice, a voice that emanated from a mouth filled with capped teeth and surrounded by heavily Botoxed scarlet lips. Trudy's façade houses a wealthy, but shallow, soul. Her parents came from money and she has always been one of the ''fancy girls' in Woodford Harbor. She drives an adorable little white Mercedes convertible, lives right on the harbor, and spends an inordinate amount of time on cruise ships. I don't know at what age these accoutrements cease to provoke envy, but I think I am past it.

"My, my! It looks like you have a big birthday coming up next month," she noted. I hoped my return smile hid my true thoughts. Is there a reason I have to like this woman?

"And how is that sweet little girl of yours?"

Please, Trudy, I thought to myself, you were here when the doctor gave her her first vaccination at two months old. You don't know her name? Is it that you don't care or are you just too important to bother with such insignificant details?

Trudy and the doctor have no children. I imagine it's not for lack of trying, as a couple of cute children always add to the perfect pedigree. Young Archie's father was Trudy's brother, but since the accident Trudy has not had much to do with her nephew. Could her affections be lying dormant, waiting for some potentially flawless offspring? Perhaps Archie, being less than perfect since the accident, does not fit into her flawless little world. I fear these are not merely idle speculations, but frighteningly valid facts.

I worked hard to rein in my snarky observations, and focused instead on how well Trudy organizes the doctor and his office. She is obviously in charge of the operation; Doctor Wilson is merely her co-star. The office was clean, the doctor punctual, and the ship moved smoothly. Credit where credit is due, I say.

"I heard there were big goings-on last night in town. An unidentified body in your little funeral home."

It just never seems to end. The woman can even demean my business. Ah, well, "judge not lest ye be judged." I tried to take the aphorism to heart.

"That's right, Trudy. I walked in this morning and found the poor girl on my embalming table. No identification, just a seemingly lost young woman in the wrong place at the wrong time."

"Well, I was home sound asleep last night," said Trudy. Ha! With or without the good doctor, my perverse little brain wondered, sliding right back into its usual judgmental groove. And then I wondered why she had felt a need to note her whereabouts. She was not the member of her family most likely running around last night.

Just then Dr. Wilson popped his head out, gave me a big hello, and embraced me in a familiar hug. That full head of gleaming white hair and the deep blue eyes were stunning; luckily, however, his age kept his charms from affecting me—that and the amount of cologne emanating from his person. It was nothing short of an olfactory felony. Stop, I thought; stop focusing on every little detail about people that doesn't sit well with me. There is far more to the doctor than just these few traits.

He led me back for our annual chat about how healthy I am, but how much healthier I would be if I drank a bit less red wine. The words do not even make a dent on my consciousness. Life is not only too short to drink the house wine, but too short to limit the intake as well.

CHAPTER ELEVEN

After the inevitable poking and prodding I left the office feeling slightly invaded, and drove back to the funeral home to see what was going on. Mr. Stanley greeted me as I walked in. His internal clock is synchronized with mine and he always seems to know when I need food. I find it a sacrilege to miss a meal and I get good and cranky if it looks like I might. He nodded toward the little door to the left of the entryway. It looks like a coat closet, but it holds a set of narrow steps that lead down to the offices below. We descended without a word, and at the bottom he handed me a cup of warm tomato soup. He then proceeded to slather butter on two thick slices of bread and made me a grilled cheese sandwich over our little gas burner. Mr. Stanley has a real maternal instinct. He has never been married and there is speculation in town that he is gay, but that has no bearing on my affection for him.

"Any news on our poor Jane Doe?" he asked.

"Not really," I said, taking the piping hot grilled cheese from him. "Pepper thought she might be a girl she saw with Duke the other night at The Old Port. Last I saw, Uncle Henry was getting ready to go down and see Duke. Never a pleasant experience."

"How do Bode and the other lobstermen abide that fellow? It seems intolerable that his behavior has no consequences!"

"You're right, Mr. Stanley. I guess it just comes with the territory in that business. I like to think that what goes around comes around, but I wonder how long we will have to wait to see Duke get his." I felt badly verbalizing this, but it was what I believed.

"The Arthur girls are gathering upstairs to discuss their mother's funeral plans. Should I tell them you'll be up shortly?"

"Sure, thanks," I said. "Just give me a minute to enjoy this wonderful sandwich—and thanks, Mr. Stanley!"

I devoured every last crumb, and reluctantly made my way upstairs to my office, where I was met by Mrs. Arthur's three grown daughters.

"Good morning, Meg," I said to the eldest. "I'm so sorry for your loss. It's nice you were able come so quickly from Los Angeles."

"I know Mother would want me to be here with the girls," she replied in an officious manner. The 'girls' were both in their forties. Meg was the eldest by a mere eleven months, and had always been bright and ambitious. She was off to Wellesley as soon as she was 18, and then continued on to get her MBA at the University of Chicago. There she met her husband, and never looked back.

She works with a high-tech company now and he's a plastic surgeon in LA which is beyond lucrative They have not had children, and seem consumed with making money. She was dressed in a killer business suit that looked somewhat out of place in Woodford Harbor. Her perfect head of hair was short and sensible, and was fashioned in a style that was a perfect accompaniment to her outfit. She looked well, and seemed pleased with herself.

"I've been back five times over the past year for what turned out to be false alarms," she felt it necessary to add. There had been talk around town of Mrs. Arthur being somewhat consumed with her death; she wanted all of her daughters with her when the time came. As fate would have it the poor thing passed on with none of them there. I guess she cried 'Wolf!' one too many times.

I then took a sobbing Miranda into my arms. "Oh, dear, I really am sorry. It's so hard to lose a mother." She continued sobbing, but took the tissue I offered and seemed to relax a bit. Sweet Miranda was the youngest, and had always been a real girlie girl. With three daughters of her own, the four of them seemed to operate more as a quartet of equals than as mother and daughters. Miranda was rather short and plump, with red curly hair springing out at all angles. She moved with almost a skip to her step, which only served to exacerbate her baby-girl persona. Her three little ones were round little cherubs, too, and all carried the same curly red hair. Miranda was scarcely taller than her oldest. Together, they looked like little American Girl dolls, and all seemed happy.

I turned my attention to the third daughter. "Hi, Josie. I saw you not too long ago with your mother at The Driftwood. You've been so good to her."

"Thanks, Lizzie. I have been spending quite a bit of time with her these past two years. It's been wonderful for both of us." Josie had always been the most down-to-earth of the three. She had gone off to nursing school, and had been in Atlanta when Mrs. Arthur began to fail. She moved back to town, and took good care of her mother, attending to her physical needs and buoying her spirits.

Mrs. Arthur had the odd habit of always saying, "I best keep moving, or they'll throw dirt on me!" She was insatiably demanding. Josie looked a bit more haggard than she should for her 45 years, but then again she was always the one who seemed to do the hands-on work. The lines around her eyes drooped a bit too much, her brown hair was streaked with grey and hung listlessly, and her sensible shoes looked far too worn. There was—fairly enough, I suppose—an air of resentment in her demeanor.

I broached the difficult subject of funeral arrangements, beginning with the selection of a coffin. And—true to form—my long-held observations that people become caricatures of themselves when faced with stressful situations played out before me. The angry become more angry, the sad even sadder, and the assertive—well, they just become bossy as hell. So it was with the Arthur girls.

Meg began with, "Well, I know Mother always liked the best of everything. Nothing but top-of-the-line."

Miranda started sobbing again, and agreed. "I want the best for Mommy. I just loved her so much!"

"Girls," interjected Josie. "Mom and I talked about this and she has written a few instructions for us to follow. At the top of the list is her choice of casket. She didn't want us to spend a lot, and wants a plain wooden box. Her other wishes are right here. She wants to be cremated, and have costs and fuss kept to a minimum. I have made a copy for everyone."

Josie handed out copies and we began a more objective, organized discussion. By taking the time to specify her desires, Mrs. Arthur had thoughtfully prevented countless emotionally charged arguments and irreparable family disputes. In her way she was still taking care of the family.

I felt comfortable going on. "These details make everything so much less complicated. Just letting you know she wants to be cremated takes a decision and burden off your shoulders. She knew what she wanted; it seems like she's still taking care of things for all of you. Next we should probably discuss a memorial service."

"Well, she said no fuss, so maybe we should just be done with it," said Meg.

"If I may," I interjected, "in my experience, the death of a loved one is an opportunity to recognize his or her accomplishments in life and acknowledge what that life meant to others through an occasion of some sort. You will all grieve more thoroughly if you process your loss via a ceremony of some kind."

"Mother had no use for churches," Meg announced with a superior air.

"But we always went to Sunday school," wailed Miranda.

Josie mused aloud. "What church could we possibly involve?"

"There are many alternatives to mark this occasion that don't involve a church. I'm a certified celebrant," I said, "and can help you organize a service and lead it. We can have it anywhere, not necessarily in a church."

A collective sigh of relief filled the room.

"What was your mother's greatest passion?" I asked.

"Her garden!" was the unanimous reply.

"Then let's use that as our theme. Would you like to hold the gathering in her garden? Or would you be more comfortable in one of our visitation rooms?"

"It would be so nice to hold a memorial service in her garden," Josie said. "I planted hundreds of bulbs last fall and they're popping up everywhere." There were murmurs and sounds of agreement from her sisters.

"This event is the last opportunity you will have to share your mother's spirit and personality with those who knew her," I said. "Think about some readings—or poetry or music—that reflect her beliefs and passions. The three of you standing together are living proof of perhaps the greatest thing she accomplished. It would be nice for each of you to be a part of the service. You might also wish to invite others who might like to be involved.

"A written program helps give structure to the memorial event. I can give you a template that might be helpful. A quotation and a photo of your mother on the cover would be lovely. I read a quote the other day that might work perfectly for your mother:

The glory of gardening: hands in the dirt, head in the sun, heart with nature. To nurture a garden is to feed not just the body, but the soul."

"That sounds perfect," Meg said. "Miranda, why don't you look into some nice music, and Josie, why don't you find an appropriate reading? I'll find a poem, and make up a program. Perhaps some of her friends from the garden club will have ideas as well. And, yes, we will have it in her beautiful yard."

Miranda started to speak. "I agree, but..."

Ignoring her sister, Meg continued. "Josie, you're the best one to choose an outfit for Mother to wear. You know the garden club ladies, too, so why don't you contact them? You also have access to her photographs, so get me a nice one to use on the cover of the program. Actually, you know all the printers in town, too, dear, so why don't you just take care of the whole program?"

"There is only one printer in town, so I could point you in the right direction," said Josie.

Without pausing, Meg went on. "It might be nice for each of the attendees to be given a flower as they enter the service. We can ask people to leave them in a large basket in the front of the church as they leave. They'd make a beautiful bouquet. Josie, can you organize some nice cut flowers? And yes, I will find a nice poem of some kind to read."

Miranda and Josie exchanged glances as Meg sighed with exhaustion at all she had just organized. A lifetime of personal interactions filled the room. A self-satisfied Meg, a slightly overwhelmed Miranda, and a long-suffering Josie now looked to me for further direction.

"Mr. Stanley will be glad to write your mother's obituary if you'd like," I said to break the tension. "He does a lovely job of covering all the facts, but adds warmth to the details of a the person's life as well. He will need factual information, and any other thoughts or additions you would like to contribute."

All eyes turned to poor Josie, and she reluctantly nodded her agreement to take on the additional tasks. I suddenly reveled in my only-child status.

I suggested a follow-up meeting the next morning, and listened to Meg parceling out yet more orders. I knew it was not all resolved, but at least there was some forward progress. As I led the chatting contingent to the door I heard a siren, which wasn't common in town. It was not often Uncle Henry drove his squad car above the posted limit. I left my clients as quickly as was reasonably polite, and raced out the back steps and toward the sound.

CHAPTER TWELVE

A s I emerged into the sunlight I was surprised to learn that the siren was from an ambulance rather than a police car. Apparently Uncle Henry had made good on his visit to Duke, as both his squad car and the ambulance were parked outside Duke's rundown hovel. Coincidentally, it was within sight of my back entryway. An abandoned set of railroad tracks from the old Boston line runs through the center of town, bisecting the land between the back of the funeral home and Duke's house at the end of High Street.

House is a generous term for the slovenly construction that houses Duke. High Street is a lovely neighborhood of 200-year-old homes overlooking the town. At its end it runs downhill and intersects the old tracks. There, it has created the kind of deserted spot that seems to collect discarded trash and wind-blown leaves. It has also collected Duke, a big man with stooped shoulders and an awkward gait. His perennially unshaven face has an uneven growth, his bushy eyebrows are always cast down, and his yellowed teeth are the telltale sign of far too many cigarettes. Did I mention the man is as lazy as a drugged coon cat? Am I being too judgmental? Me? Really, sometimes you just have to call a spade a spade.

I ran across the railroad bed, and arrived in time to see Duke being carried out on a stretcher and put into the back of the ambulance. Uncle Henry was nowhere to be seen so I walked to the open front door and leaned in. "Uncle Henry! What's going on? What happened to Duke?"

"You can come in, but don't touch anything, dear," Uncle Henry cautioned. "Not only might you catch some dread disease from the look of things around here, but we have some very interesting evidence. Come back here, and have a look. Seems Duke really tied one on last night. He's going to need some time at the Portland hospital to recover."

I walked through a room that held a stained old maroon velour sofa. The floor around it was littered with a variety of makeshift ashtrays, each full to overflowing with butts. A lamp with a naked bulb stood on a wobbly end table, and two Barcaloungers that had seen better days flanked each side. Two piles of bricks and a plank held an old TV set with a jury-rigged hanger acting as an antenna. What passed as a kitchen was in the back and to the left. I presumed a sink was in the center of the counter, but the latter was so piled with dishes, glasses, and pots and pans that it was impossible to know what lay underneath. I could hear a little old refrigerator trying hard to run. A large metal garbage can in the other corner belched beer cans, old bread crust, eggshells, and greasy tuna fish cans. The smell defied description.

Uncle Henry was in the back room on the right. A mattress covered a portion of the floor and stacked orange crates served as a dresser. This room was actually fairly neat. The bed had a comforter placed neatly on top, and a pillow centered at the end. A few toiletries were lined up on the top crate, and scanty bikini underwear, shorts, tee-shirts, and a grey hoodie filled the crate beneath.

At the very bottom—a pair of flip-flops and tennis shoes. The faint scent of patchouli hung in the air.

A small round table and two mismatched chairs occupied one corner and several mugs and a chipped little dish held the remnants of what appeared to be tea and pastry crumbs.

Next to the bed stood a canvas backpack. It was identical to the one my Charlie carried to school.

I felt a rush of emotions go through me as I looked at those few, paltry possessions, and the familiar backpack. An innocent girl had carried her belongings in that backpack, and had arranged them in an orderly fashion in this room. These things were obviously important to her. She should be here right now putting them into that canvas bag, and going back to wherever she came from to continue on with her life. The similarities to my dear Charlie began to overwhelm me. This was all hitting much too close to home. I desperately wanted to know what had happened here.

It seemed too dastardly even for Duke. Dirty, yes. Lazy and dishonest—maybe. But a murderer? Maybe my overly judgmental self was cutting him too much slack, but this just didn't reverberate in my gut.

"Lizzie, give me a hand here," Uncle Henry called, and for the second time in three hours I found myself helping him cordon off a crime scene with yellow tape. Suddenly Uncle Henry started sputtering and muttering under his breath. Listening, I realized he was calling the state police to come back to look at this new site.

"That fool, Daniels. This is his case so I'll have to call him back. Two times in one day. I'm not paid enough for this."

Following a brief conversation, actually more like a series of grunts, Uncle Henry relayed to me that the detective was not too far down the road, and would return promptly.

The two of us started looking more closely at our surroundings. At Uncle Henry's direction I touched nothing. It wasn't easy.

49

It is more difficult than you might think not to touch anything when you have been told not to do so. I crossed my arms, and held my hands under my armpits.

It was also difficult to look at the mess. I tried mightily to keep my judgment in check, but even Uncle Henry was giving out a few harrumphs looking around the kitchen.

Suddenly the door swung open and the air was suddenly sucked out of the room. I kept my hands firmly in place, and stood stock-still. I noticed Uncle Henry standing ramrod straight as well.

Detective Daniels asked the obvious. "Has either of you touched anything?"

I raised my hands over my head in an attempt to show my innocence but I probably looked more like a baby bird trying to fly. Uncle Henry said, "No, of course not! I am aware of police protocol, detective!" He spat 'detective' out of his mouth like a rotten peanut.

"Well, let me just have a look around," said Daniels. He grabbed some evidence bags, and started filling them with a variety of objects. How he ascertained what held significance and what did not was beyond me. But he performed his investigation with the assurance of a grill chef flipping pancakes. Then he went into the bedroom, where he continued gathering seemingly random items. He gave the mugs and the dish on the table extra attention.

"These mugs and the crumbs could be particularly important, and may contain evidence. I think we should keep this detail to ourselves. Think you can do that?" he asked. Uncle Henry gave him a scathing look, but I nodded my head fervently and promised to do so. I reined in my temptation to salute.

"So where is this fellow, Duke? Have you spoken to him?" inquired the detective.

"Spoken to yes, communicated no," said Uncle Henry. "He was in a heap on the couch, looking like a bag of dirty laundry. He won't dry out sufficiently or be in a position to talk for hours.

Haven't seen him this marinated in awhile. Had to send him off to the hospital in Portland." He shook his head. "That poor little girl. How could she have gotten tangled up with him and his mess of a life?"

Even Daniels softened when faced with this hypothetical question. We collectively shook our heads, and shared a respectful moment of silence.

Still trying my best to see the glass half-full, I said, "You know, there may be a nicer side to Duke that none of us ever sees. When he's not stealing lobsters from someone else's traps. Or drinking, and spitting, and stumbling around town. Or when he's not carrying on about the price of gas and beer."

Daniels let out a puff of air and Uncle Henry merely raised one eyebrow. This non-judgmental stuff was getting tiring.

We retreated outside; I think we were all relieved at that point to go our separate ways.

The town was abuzz with this latest piece of news. It almost seemed like a bad joke that these two characters were intertwined. I couldn't help thinking that it was a bit much to picture Duke as an actual murderer. And why in the world would he dispose of his victim on my embalming table? What could that seemingly sweet little creature have done to provoke such a thing? To my way of thinking, Duke was incapable of that much passion. No, Duke just didn't fill the bill for me. I couldn't wrap my brain around it.

I knew I had to find out more about this girl. *Someone* must know *something* about her. As a last resort, unappealing as it seemed, I realized I might have to talk with Duke.

CHAPTER THIRTEEN

I headed back to work, but my daily duties took a backseat to my preoccupation with the day's events. Mr. Stanley was waiting with a cup of hot tea and a giant M&M cookie directly from the oven of The Bean, our favorite coffee shop. As I sipped and munched, I filled him in on the events at Duke's house.

"I just don't think, Miss G," Mr. Stanley said, "that all is as it seems. It's always nice to wrap things up into neat little boxes, but life doesn't really work that way. Every time I try to simplify a person, making them black or white, they go grey on me. Annoying, really. Duke might be the obvious choice as the villain in this case, but it doesn't seem to be entirely in his makeup. Wouldn't it be nice to just be done with this unpleasantness, and also be done with Duke once and for all? It would be killing two birds with one stone, as it were."

I suppressed a smile at this unfortunate choice of words, and nodded my agreement. "This whole day has been bizarre. Could be the all-time chart topper for Bainbridge Funeral Home, don't you think, Mr. Stanley?"

"Of course, comparing bizarre incidents should not be a contest, but I must admit we have had some whoppers around here. Right before your grandfather left we had a situation involving two clients with identical caskets. Your grandfather was wonderful, but he lacked organization and focus. I was new then, and was hesitant to speak up, but I've never been entirely certain who ended up in which grave. Oh, my! I shouldn't have mentioned that. But your reference to a bizarre day took my mind there."

Mr. Stanley, blessedly, appeared finished with his reminiscences and left me alone. I suddenly felt a need to hear my father's voice and thoughts on the morning's events.

Two rings later his voice greeted me with, "Why, hello, Lizzie Ann!" Just hearing that voice and my ridiculous childhood name made everything seem much better.

"Hi, Dad. You're not going to believe this one." I launched into a recap of what had transpired, ending with how it now appeared to be a full-fledged murder. He was a good audience for all the details I laid out, but seemed to have a hard time getting beyond the unexpected body on the embalming table. That part of the story had occurred in his dominion and he fully comprehended the incongruity of it.

"Well, young lady, that is quite some story. Poor Duke. That fellow is predictably at the heart of this mess. But, really, the poor girl! And how hard for you to be the one to discover her. I am so sorry. Keep us abreast as things develop. Quite something it is, quite something. Your mother is chomping at the bit here to speak with you."

"Honey, what's going on up there? From what I heard on your father's end it sounds terrible! Do you think Charlie is safe? We could certainly have her visit us here until things quiet down," offered my mother, sliding right into her role as grandmother.

"Mom, it's all fine. It's not like we have a serial killer roaming town and hanging out at The Driftwood. Charlie is fine; I won't even mention your offer to her. She would be down there basking in your sunshine quick as a bunny! How is everything at Ding Darling?" I asked then, trying to move on to another topic.

Ding Darling is a wildlife refuge on Sanibel, an island adjoining Captiva. Its 5,200 acres dominate one entire end of the island, and it has a remarkable collection of birds and wildlife. My parents volunteer there as 'rovers,' showing off its treasures to the thousands of tourists who visit every year. With Mom's gift of gab and Dad's remarkable memory, they're great assets. As for Charlie and me, we've voted the pink spoonbills and the alligators Ding Darling's best in show.

"We're having the best time," she told me. "I met two couples this week who had come all the way from Australia to see our birds! It's so exciting! And there is a lecture tonight on the reddish egret, my all-time favorite bird in this area."

"Great. I'll keep you up-to-date on our happenings here. In the meantime, have a good time with your reddish egrets." We said our good-byes and I had that somewhat empty feeling I get when I end a phone conversation that puts my folks far away from me again.

I finished my sugar-laden tea and half-heartedly went about the task of comparing current casket prices. But my mind kept going over the crazy events of the day. Not only had all this transpired in our sweet Woodford Harbor, but I was also smack dab in the middle of it.

CHAPTER FOURTEEN

With the day nearly behind me I hopped in my car and headed to Brown's Market for dinner supplies. Hopefully, a bit of comfort food would quell my nerves and settle my stomach. Brown's is a great little spot with just enough food choices. Too many aisles and I can't think. For Woodford Harbor, Brown's is to the evening what The Driftwood is to the morning.

I walked in, picked up my little plastic basket, and ran right into Trudy. She was none the worse for wear after an entire day of work. I was a bit rumpled, and the dutiful mascara I had applied this morning was long gone. Trudy, on the other hand, looked fresh as a daisy, with nary a wrinkle in her tasteful red suit. How anyone manages to wear a straight skirt, pantyhose, a tailored jacket, and heels all day is mind-boggling to me. And does she spray paint that makeup on, and finish it off with a layer of shellac? I pushed these thoughts from my mind, smiled, and inquired as to her dinner menu.

"Grilled salmon, steamed asparagus, and some duchess potatoes," she responded. "With a kiwi sorbet to finish it off. Divine, don't you think, dear?" She pursed her lips, and threw a kiss upward. "And you?"

"Hamburger stroganoff," I said. "With Parker House rolls."

Trudy doesn't always get to spend a lot of time with the doctor. He seems to make an inordinate number of house calls quite late at night—most of them, apparently unbeknownst to her—to homes occupied by single ladies. Recently the rumor mill had him 'settled down' with just one woman. I wondered if that was better or worse for Trudy.

It seems impossible that she's not in the loop. If she were, though, why would she continue on, apparently looking the other way? I certainly didn't know. But then, we all make choices and then must live with them. To my mind there really is no accounting for the intricate workings of a marriage. Each and every one has its own idiosyncrasies, known only to each couple and accepted by both. God bless, I say, to all who can accomplish it successfully. Trudy seemed to truly care for the doctor, and was certainly doing her best to please him in the culinary department.

I chose my hamburger, mushrooms, mushroom soup, and sour cream with care. I found a box of lovely, wide egg noodles, picked up some frozen Parker House rolls, and I was done. Ah! Since it was a dinner party I went back and grabbed an onion to sauté with the hamburger. I was quick to forsake the sorbet items, and went straight for Ben & Jerry's Cherry Garcia. No cookies—too fattening with this menu.

I stood with Trudy by the little conveyor belt at the lone cash register as we checked out. I was looking forward to being with Charlie and Bode and Archie, knowing their company would be even more comforting than the heavy meal I was preparing. What would Trudy's evening be like? Would the doctor really be with her as they shared the evening time and meal? Would he be envisioning his next interaction with another woman? I felt a rush of sympathy, and turned back to Trudy. "You really are putting together a lovely meal for an ordinary Thursday night. How nice for the doctor."

She turned to me and said, "Why, thank you, Lizzie. I do try to make each day special." As Mr. Stanley says, you just can't put people in a box and expect them to behave consistently. Life is never simply black or white.

My mind wandered then to the mother of the poor girl I had discovered this morning. What was she doing and thinking to-night? Was she calling the police, wondering why she hadn't heard from her daughter? Or was she comfortably making an evening meal, believing everything was fine? I sighed, paid, hoisted my bag, and walked out to the Jeep.

It felt good to walk into my own little house, and fall into its familiarity. It exuded the slight odor of toast and coffee from earlier in the day, the countertops were clean and organized in preparation for the next meal, and Charlie's shoes were thrown haphazardly next to the back door. I said a quick prayer of thanks when I saw them there. The twangy chords of country music floated down from upstairs. I should say the *inevitable* twangy chords of country music. Charlie is a devotee of the genre. She has eclectic tastes, but I fear this particular one was influenced by Bode. Although each listens to his or her own variety, it all pretty much sounds the same to me so I keep my thoughts to myself. But I *do* have thoughts!

"Hi, honey!" I called up. "What's going on?"

"Hi, Mom! I'm just getting started on my homework. Lacrosse was crazy and I almost scored, but missed by inches! Also, I need to get a dress for the prom! I'm not sure my phone is getting all my emails—and I'm starving!" she answered in a whoosh.

Ah, to have those be my biggest concerns. "Dinner will be ready around 7, and Bode and Archie are coming over," I assured her.

I unpacked the groceries and set them out on the counter. Washing the mushrooms, I sorted through the predictable assortment of mail: discount coupons, gas bill, political drivel, and catalogs promising to provide me with a better, happier, and more colorful life.

I actually love my little house just as it is. It was built in the early 1600s. The kitchen is painted a bright periwinkle, and has white counters and shiny white trim around windows that overlook the garden out back. The little room off the kitchen is comfy with a fireplace and overstuffed chairs with ottomans. Its walls are white, with natural wood trim, and its floor is made of centuries-old wide, planked wood. Splashes of coral and periwinkle in the fabric brighten up the furniture and a profusion of green plants add yet more life and color.

A striped cotton rug pulls it all together, while some nautical-type lamps reflect my personal style. An old copy of *Blueberries for Sal* still sits on an end table by the fireplace—a nod to a time when Charlie loved to snuggle into my lap and have me read to her. Bob Dylan cautioned us to, "Take care of all your memories. For you cannot relive them." I've taken great care to treasure these memories.

The living room on the other side of the house holds a ping-pong table, although the room is barely big enough to contain it. The table fills the entire room and we love it. There is something about owning your own home; it means you can do absolutely anything you want. Our ping-pong games are competitive and—I like to think—good-natured. Bode's calm, methodical paddle is predictable, until he throws in a subtle, but deadly curve. My style is more aggressive and I try to put that little ball in the far corners of the table. Charlie is just wild. She whacks and smacks at the ball with a fierceness that only a sixteen-year-old girl can bring to the table.

A small dining room completes that side of the house and a winding, vertical staircase stands in the center. It is so steep we had to install a grab line similar to the ones used on boats so we won't fall going up and down. The second floor is mine. It has two bedrooms with a study between them, and a full bath. One more flight up—via a narrow staircase more akin to a ladder—and you'll find Charlie's kingdom. It's just a bedroom with a tiny little bathroom, but being way up top gives her lots of privacy and a perceived independence. The house suits us to a T.

I hung up my black pants, and folded my shirt. Slipping on my well-worn jeans and a comfy cotton T-shirt, I felt myself returning to life. Barefoot, I happily began my evening.

I climbed up to Charlie's room to deliver a face-to-face welcome. She was on her bed surrounded by heaven knows what: clothes, books, papers, stuffed animals, and a hairbrush or two. Brad Paisley was singing from her little iPhone. I am still amazed at the sounds that come out of such tiny devices. And the world of information! My brain, unfortunately, cannot function under these circumstances, but somehow Charlie makes sense of it all and comes through with a clear head. Her curly brown hair outlines a face that makes my heart skip whenever I look at it. Large, beautiful, piercing blue eyes, smooth rosy cheeks, and a smile that puts mine to shame. We locked eyes for just a moment, and smiled our hellos.

"Do you have much homework tonight, honey?"

"I need to study for a quiz in calculus, and review some vocabulary words for Spanish. My paper on Lincoln is basically done, but it's not due until next Friday. What an amazing man! Wouldn't you love to have had dinner with him? I mean, think about all he did, and from nowhere in Kentucky! I wonder what kind of music he would like if he were alive today!"

"Kentucky isn't 'nowhere'," I replied. "It's just far away from here and different, but it's still a very real place." Charlie's mind always surprises and impresses me. When she studies a topic it comes alive to her.

"Oh! Everyone was talking about you at school! Was there really a dead body on your embalming table? That's just creepy! Bad enough you deal with dead bodies all the time, but a strange one just turning up? What was she doing there?"

"I'm not sure. Uncle Henry is investigating and I'm sure he will identify her soon, and sort it out."

I gave her a quick kiss on the top of her head, loving the familiar feel and smell of her. My universe was on course and I turned to go downstairs to get started on my culinary endeavor.

CHAPTER FIFTEEN

I heard Bode's truck pull up just as the pasta water hit a rolling boil. I quickly added sliced mushrooms to the browned hamburger and onion concoction. Bode opened the kitchen's screen door and entered, filling the air with a waft of his shampoo and a healthy dose of masculine energy. Archie followed somewhat tentatively behind. I gave him a loving smile and he came over for a hug. Bode gave an affectionate whisper of his lips to my forehead, and the inevitable whack to my bottom. There was a loud scratching on the screen door and the forgotten Bob was let in. His head was at the height of the counter, but that big old animal would no more take food off a counter than a pig could pilot a 747. He weighs in at over one hundred pounds and is strong as an ox, but he's also extraordinarily gentle. He almost seems to smile when he lifts his head for a pat.

"Evening, Bob," I said as I reached for the canister of dog cookies on the counter. He obediently plopped his furry bottom down on the floor, raised his right paw, and gently took the little morsel from my outstretched hand. A moment like this with a dog makes up for a lot of annoyance throughout the day with humans.

"Beer? Wine? What's it to be, Z? Cranberry juice for you, Archman?" asked Bode, reaching in the refrigerator for his beer. Archie, Bode's Archman, reveled in the warmth of his nickname.

"Red wine for me, please. There's an open box in the corner cupboard." A box of wine is far superior to bottles in so many ways. The vineyard that boxed this one was the same one that bottled one of my favorite reds. Three bottles fit in one box, which greatly reduces the number of bottles to be recycled, a positive for so many reasons. Additionally, because the wine is vacuum packed it never goes bad. And the final notch in its belt? How indiscriminate the amount of wine consumed becomes. A half-bottle? More? Who knows? It's all so indeterminate.

Bode handed Archie an ice-filled glass with cranberry juice, and me a glass of wine. We all clinked and I noticed Archie edging up against Bode, leaning into him.

"How 'ya doing, buddy? Heard you're doing great work down at The Driftwood. Place wouldn't run half so smoothly without you! What time are the Red Sox on?" asked Bode. Archie didn't reply, but kind of snuggled in closer.

"You're my really good friend, Bode," said Archie then, looking up at him.

"Well, sure, buddy, always."

"Really, Bode," repeated Archie. "You are my really good friend."

"Wanna hit some ping-pong balls, Archman?"

Again, not much of a response. Archie just sidled in closer to Bode.

"Hey, I think I hear Don Orsillo in the living room. Must be time for the first pitch! Nava is probably leading off, don't you think?"

"I want to stay with you, Bode," said Archie, almost clinging to him now.

"Well, sure, let's sit over on these stools," said Bode. Bode gave me a quizzical look, but we cut Archie a lot of slack and pretty much go with the flow and let him dictate how things move along.

"So how's your mom, Bode?"

"She seems content, and is enjoying the warmer weather. She was outside for awhile this afternoon, and loved it."

Just then Charlie came blasting into the room, legs flapping and arms flailing.

"Hi, guys!" she offered as a composite greeting. "Hey, Bode! I have the new Blake Shelton album downloaded! It is so awesome! Do you want to hear it?"

"Nice, Lil' Chuck, maybe later. How does he rank next to George Strait?" Bode is an old-time country music devotee and Charlie's tastes gravitate more toward the new artists. Bode claims they don't even really perform country music, but rather a new form of rock. However, the joking is always good-natured and Bode shows respect for her taste. It's more for her enthusiasm, I think, than for the music itself. There is also an unwritten rule that when they compare their favorite tunes it is best to leave me out of it. There are a few Alan Jackson songs that I truly enjoy, but the rest leaves me cold. And I am not terribly subtle in this regard.

"When do we eat? Smells so good! What's this?" Charlie held up a book on the end table by the couch, A *One-step Guide for Overall Improvement.*

"Oh, that's my new self-help book," I told her. "I figured if it was only one step maybe I could actually master it. It claims that if you are nicer to people—or less judgmental of them—your world will brighten, people will like you better, and you, in turn, will feel better. Overall improvement!"

There was a simultaneous chuckle around the room. I looked wide-eyed at them all. "What?" I blurted out incredulously.

"Mom, does this mean you will no longer be giving out fashion citations for wardrobe violations? Or wearing your snarky face whenever a perky little tourist in white shorts waltzes into The Driftwood for breakfast?" Charlie laughed.

"Do you think you'll stop making obscene gestures every time a big, fancy car cuts you off? Or someone pronounces realtor 'relator'?" added Bode.

They were in convulsions now, and working themselves into a frenzy.

"Now you wait, you two," I stammered. "I'm a new person already! I even mentally cut Trudy a little slack today."

"Maybe in terms of chit chat, but truly, deeply in your soul of souls? Talk about a tiger that can't change its stripes!" Bode practically howled.

"Do you guys want dinner or not?" I snapped. "Watch it or I'll crack you both upside the head!"

I handed everyone a tray, and then heaped fat, steaming noodles topped with a giant spoonful of hamburger delight on the plates. We all grabbed rolls and butter, and found our familiar spots in front of the TV. Archie slid close to Bode on the couch, and remained uncharacteristically quiet. But when Big Papi smashed his first pitch over the Green Monster he had a big grin, and we settled in to convivially munch our 4,000-calorie meals.

CHAPTER SIXTEEN

We watched the Red Sox get two more runs, and the Orioles remain scoreless. Charlie went into the kitchen and washed the dishes while Archie stood by her side, drying pots and pans. It is important for Archie to have set duties and reasonable expectations. He feels best when routines are in place. Predictably, Charlie then went upstairs to ostensibly do homework. She is a good student and her teachers assure me she is working hard, so I leave her schoolwork to her. I am not one to hover over every little thing she does. Not for lack of affection, but because I think we all have roles in this life and she should learn to assume hers while she still has me to pick her up if there's a bump.

Archie usually walks home when Charlie goes upstairs. He lives in a big old Victorian house with six other mentally-challenged young adults. A wonderful couple, the Duncans, look after them. The household is funded by a trust set up by Doctor Wilson and Trudy from monies left by Archie's parents. I have never been quite sure whether this was an act of generosity on the doctor's part, or because Trudy didn't want to be burdened with Archie. The young people pay as they are able, and work with the goal of living independently one day. A certain amount of personal freedom and responsibility are encouraged. Archie had long ago shown that he was capable of walking the half-mile from my house to the home with no problem. I usually call the Duncans to let them know that he's on his way so they can keep a lookout for him. The trust, loyalty, and respect shown by the entire household toward each other is remarkable, due in large part to Ben and Karen Duncan.

This evening, however, Archie came back into the living room and again snuggled up against Bode, declaring what a good friend he was over and over. Bode reassured him repeatedly until it became apparent that Archie was exhausted and needed his bed.

"What do you say, buddy, can I walk you home?" inquired Bode.

"Oh, yes, I would like that very much, Bode," Archie answered. "Thanks for everything, Miss G. I love you!"

I gave him a hug, and responded in kind.

Bode came over to me, and murmured his thanks for dinner. I leaned in and asked him to come back.

"Sure" he replied, grinning. "Ping-pong?"

"Et cetera," I replied.

Men. They can be 16, 24, or 45, as Bode is, and they all flash that same ridiculous smile when an overture is made.

Bode was back before the sixth inning. The Red Sox were smacking the ball all over the park, and could do no wrong on the field. When they are good they are so, so good. But my, when they are not, it is so painful. I think it's important to enjoy the good times, and skim over the bad as quickly as possible.

When Bode came back, I asked him about his chat with Glenda earlier in the day.

"I asked her about Archie," he told me. "There are times I'm uncomfortable with her, you know. I just wanted to talk about Archie's pay, but she was very defensive, backpedaling whenever I pushed a point. I know she wanted to say something about his mental state, but she knew better than to try that with me. He is a real hard-working kid. Has his limits, but he certainly has improved over the past year and I think he should be rewarded accordingly. She grudgingly said she would review his salary."

"She's a pill," I said. "Archie is really lucky to have you at his back. The Duncans are amazing, but they can't cover every base. You're a good one, my dear Bode.

"Oh! Did you hear that the dead girl's things were found at Duke's house?" I asked him.

"I did hear that. Amazing! I also heard that Duke is over at Portland General drying out. What a sorry tale he is. It does surprise me, though, that he would do something like this. But I guess if you steal another man's lobsters and cut his lines for spite, you must be capable of just about anything!" Bode almost growled.

"That might be going a bit far, Bode," I said. "And, bad as he is, he's not stupid. Why on earth would he pass out on his own couch, and with no alibi? And what would possibly possess him to carry a body over to my embalming table? It's an easy and slippery slope to point the finger at Duke, but I find it a tough story to swallow." "Well, you don't always have to look for logic when there may well be none. What's the rationale, for instance, for Duke grabbing my lines, cutting…"

"Please, don't start down that oh-so-familiar road," I countered. "Let's think about something other than dead girls, lobster lines, and horrible men. What do you think?"

Bode flashed me a grin that was the visual equivalent of the mating call of every single animal since time immemorial. His male mind had suddenly forgotten everything but the immediate situation. And that was fine with me. I was with him all the way.

I don't know how Bob knows, but he gathered himself up off the floor, and plodded directly upstairs to my bedroom.

CHAPTER SEVENTEEN

A pleasant ribbon of sunshine crossed my long-shut eyes about 6:30 the next morning. For a millisecond nothing existed but the sun's warmth, and the soft sheets and pillow under my head. I am so blessed that even when faced with reality I find myself at peace and ready for another day. I try not to take this for granted, and to remember to be thankful for my good fortune.

Bode is always up and out before sunrise to go lobstering. He and Bob have their own routine, which requires no direction from me. I am content to be in charge of my own life, and happy that Bode does well with his. We had made plans to go to The Old Port for dinner tonight, so all was well in my little world.

I stretched, yawned, and threw back the covers. I went through my routine for the new day by checking the tide clock, and slipping into my ratty old black bathing suit. Relieved to hear Charlie up and moving, I threw a cozy towel around me, and padded down the spiral stairs to the front door. The spring air still had a nip to it, but it had the feel of a day that would warm up nicely under the sun. My flip-flops slapped down the crooked stone path to the street. I crossed, and made my way down the boat ramp next to the lobster pound.

"Hey, Lizzie! Good morning!" called Joey, one of the lobster-men who keeps his boat in the little harbor there. "Water's still in the '50s—you're a brave one!"

"Ha! I love it! Have a good day on the water," I said.

I discarded my footwear and towel and waded in. The water was a bit chilly, but it had passed the bone-chilling stage and I found it tolerable. Admittedly, the first plunge was breath shattering, but I could tell in the first few strokes that I would adapt. If my arms ache during these initial strokes I know the temperature is too cold for me. The alternative to swimming in the chlorinated water at the Y, though, was a great incentive to bear the cold temperatures. I set my waterproof watch timer to 20 minutes, and took off. The best part of an ocean swim is the salty smell and taste of the water. Its curative powers feel almost palpable to me. The top of my head relishes the cold water and all my cobwebs are washed away.

I contemplated the day before me. Whatever would we find out about our poor Jane Doe? I couldn't clear the symmetry between her and Charlie from my mind—and the similarity with my own young life as well. Her circumstance was seemingly a bit on the wild side, but certainly nothing worthy of this horrible outcome. Why was she here? What was she doing with Duke? How could that young soul have angered anyone sufficiently to murder her?

My mind then wandered to the details of the upcoming day. Charlie was off to a lacrosse tournament in Kittery, and I needed to double-check her packing, remember to give her money, and remind her to take the charger so her cell phone would remain intact if she needed me.

Then I pondered my day at the funeral home. Mr. Stanley need-ed to clean out the storeroom, recheck expiration dates on the chemicals, and restock instruments. I thought of his discomfort when he realized he'd forgotten to lock the back door the other night. He is such a sweet fixture in my life that I was unhappier about his distress over not securing the door than I was about the unlocked door itself. I would think of some way to make him feel special—and needed—today. It being a potentially beautiful spring day, I might even begin cleaning up outside the home. My father always emphasizes the importance of appearance, from the hedges outside to the spotless restrooms inside. He is a nitpicker and the apple hasn't fallen far from the tree.

I heard my watch beeping, telling me that 20 minutes had elapsed. Having lost myself in the rhythm of my strokes, I found myself all the way out by Redmond's Island, a lovely little piece of land about 100 yards offshore. Grudgingly, I headed back to the ramp to accomplish all the tasks I had contemplated in the water.

I hopped into the outdoor shower on the side of the house, where I enjoyed a soapy rinse and the delights of a sweet-smelling shampoo. The warm water felt good. I wrapped my towel around me and headed in.

"Charlie!" I called up the stairs. "How are you doing?"

"Fine, fine," came a somewhat cloudy reply. Charlie gets herself up and does whatever needs to be done, but it not always with a cheery demeanor.

"I'll make you some scrambled eggs if you have time," I said.

"No. No, I just want an English muffin with peanut butter," she answered. I could identify with that. I don't think there's a food group on earth that surpasses extra-crunchy peanut butter melting into a warm English muffin.

I looked longingly at my gardening jeans and the long-sleeved T-shirt with the Lazy Flamingo logo. That's my favorite bar near my parent's house on Captiva. Just wearing the logo makes me happy. And hey—if it makes you happy why not? But for now it was a stay press pair of black pants and a wrinkle-free white shirt. I try not to wear the same black slacks two days in a row, but a friend had once enquired if I really thought people would notice? Since then, I often wear the same pair of black pants for several days. I dried my hair, pulled it back into a ponytail, applied a dab of mascara on the stubs over both my eyes, and grabbed black flats to put on downstairs. Charlie was grunting down the stairs with her Blues duffel bag filled to the gills.

"What have you got in there?" I asked, helping her down the steep staircase.

"I don't know, stuff," she replied in her cloudy haze.

"Here's some orange juice; the muffin will be done in a sec. Do you have your charger? Do you need money?"

"I've got the charger, but could use maybe twenty dollars. We might go out for pizza Saturday night," she answered. I doubted that the girls were going to have the run of Kittery on Saturday night, but I handed her the money. Twenty-dollar bills don't seem to count for as much as they did when I was sixteen. Things change. I grabbed the edges of the English muffins out of the toaster, singeing two fingers on each one. Slathering them with peanut butter, I slid my finger across both sides of the knife and popped the remainder in my mouth.

We managed to get the bulky duffel into the back of the Jeep, along with her books and the lacrosse stick. Down the driveway we went. Taking a left onto Beacon Street, we were off to the high school. We drove the mile in silence. Traffic was backed up, but we finally edged up to the curb and Charlie began the arduous task of hauling the books, lacrosse stick, and duffel out of the car. A lanky, blond kid gave her a playful shove, and asked if he could help. She smiled her assent and I had a momentary impulse to offer my help as well. "No," I cautioned myself. "Remember, things change. It's probably time to let a young man help her."

We smiled our goodbyes, and went our separate ways.

CHAPTER EIGHTEEN

Charlie would be gone for two days. Let it rip! Well, maybe that's a bit of an overreaction. I doubt Bode and I will get drunk and dance naked in the living room, but there is a better chance we would now than on other weekends. Yeah, about as likely as the sun rising early in the west! With my new sense of wild abandon I decided to forego checking in at work, and headed straight to The Driftwood. I parked at the funeral home and walked down State Street. The daffodils were out now alongside the crocuses. The tulips hadn't quite popped, but they were certainly ready. I am not much of a bulb planter, but I do enjoy the efforts of others.

I smelled the bacon before I arrived at The Driftwood's front door. The familiar sound of the door as I opened it and the chatter of cheerful conversations greeted me. I seemed to enjoy a new-found status as 'Discoverer of Jane Doe,' as folks assumed I had all the dirt.

"Lizzie, what's up? Talk to us about that body that took the express lane to your embalming table!" roared Tommy, the cook.

"You guys, I know from nothing. I might be less appalled by a dead body than you, but I am not accustomed to finding one where it doesn't belong!" I threw back congenially.

Tommy was hanging over Trudy's table with a rapt look. I often thought Tommy must be Trudy's second biggest fan after the doctor—although at times I wasn't entirely sure about the latter.

Years ago, when Tommy's eldest daughter was about three years old, she popped a large gumball in her mouth, and proceeded to choke on it. Trudy was there at the time, and expertly whacked her back and dislodged the candy. Tommy has always felt he can never adequately repay her—and likely never will. His loyalty and devotion to her are a puzzle to me, but there is one person who finds his attention infuriating.

Glenda, you see, is one of Doc Wilson's secret nocturnal visitors. Watching her brother fawning daily over her nemesis, the doctor's wife, is sometimes more than she can take. Trudy, on the other hand, has never met a man whose attentions she didn't like and Tommy fits the mold. He is forever presenting her with cakes and breads and cookies. The days when he presents Trudy with one of Glenda's Big Blues, though, are priceless. He is totally oblivious to the situation he is creating between Trudy and Glenda when he hands the latter's most prized creations over to the woman who stands in the way of Glenda's happiness. And—as fate so often decrees—Glenda always seems to be in the room when it happens, staring daggers at poor Tommy.

No one really knows the truth, but those intimately involved. It does seem almost certain, though, that the good doctor and Glenda are an item of some sort. His car is parked outside her house far too often and when they speak they exhibit an energy that is uniquely theirs. Intellectually, they're also quite similar. Glenda is far more likely to be reading *The New Yorker* than *People*, which is Trudy's magazine of choice. It's a shame Glenda and the doctor can't limit their relationship to just an intellectual one.

As Tommy handed Trudy a bag of delicacies, they traded air kisses. I noticed that she was, as always, dressed to the nines. She sported a beautifully tailored pair of black slacks and a stunning turquoise shirt accessorized with a heavy silver necklace. And heels! How on earth, and why on earth, would she choose to endure high heels around Woodford Harbor? We traded good mornings and she and the doctor were off. But the next moment Trudy reappeared to grab his eyeglasses and cell phone. "I am his keeper," she chirped.

I plopped down at Pepper's table and Jenny set a glass of iced tea in front of me. I squeezed the sliver of lemon carefully, wondering why I bothered as it always afforded only the tiniest squirt of juice, hardly enough to flavor a pint-sized glass of tea. Opening a yellow packet of Splenda, and saving myself sixteen calories of sugar, I sat back to enjoy it. Iced tea in the morning and red wine at night, I always say.

Jenny brought sugar-free syrup in anticipation of my French toast. I'm beginning to fear how structured I will be as an old lady if I am so predictable already.

"So, what's the deal?" asked Pepper. "Has Henry spoken with Duke yet?"

"I haven't spoken with Uncle Henry since yesterday. He was waiting for Duke to dry out and sober up before he talked to him. It is so over the top that that poor young girl was involved with Duke at all. I don't know if it's predictable or pathetic. I just find it so, so sad."

Everyone around the table murmured their agreement as my blueberry French toast arrived. The pats of butter melted nicely on the warm toast as I poured the syrup over their spreading puddles.

Archie stepped behind my table to clear dishes from the one by the window, and hit my elbow. He gasped and jumped back, apologizing profusely. "Oh, I'm so sorry! I didn't mean to hurt you. Are you okay? I'm so sorry!"

"Hey, Arch, I'm fine, honey. No big deal. Everything okay? Happy with the Red Sox win?"

"Oh, yes, Miss G," he said, collecting himself. "Big Papi did it again last night! We travel to Chicago tonight, which makes me a little nervous. But Buchholtz is pitching, so that's good. I'm going to watch it at home with my friends. Tonight is pizza night and I'm pretty excited! I wish Bode would come and watch with me, though. Do you think I'll I see him today? He's such a good friend!"

"Well, if I see him when he gets in I'll tell him to drop by and say 'hi'. He knows what a good friend you are, Archie. Even when he doesn't see you he thinks of you, and he's glad when you're happy. We might be going out to dinner tonight, but we'll think of you having a great time with all your friends."

I saw a little cloud pass over his endearing features, but he finished wiping up and moved on. I looked longingly at the fourth slice of French toast, but pushed my plate away. My weight is good, I cautioned myself; don't mess with success.

"So, what's up for the clambake tomorrow night?" asked Pepper. "Is Bode involved?"

Woodford Harbor sponsors a spring clambake every May. Donations of $32 a head bring in quite a sum, which is later donated to our local YMCA.

"Up to his ears," I said. "He really gets into it. All the lobstermen have been down at the beach digging a giant hole for the event and they've been accumulating lobsters and clams for weeks now. They're such good guys. The potato drive has collected massive amounts in the bin up by the bank, and Brown's is donating corn again. I'm bringing blueberry bread. What are you bringing, your famous cheesecake?" My blueberry bread comes right out of a Betty Crocker box, but no one needs to know. I add the eggs and oil, bake it, transfer it to an aluminum foil pan, and voila—homemade blueberry bread!

"Yes," she chortled. "I'd better get home and get started if I want to get it finished in time. Oh, my! I do love this clambake! Who will make my account of the event in my column this year?" She conveyed an air of anticipated drama that I chose to ignore.

The dessert table at this extravaganza is a diabetic's hell. There is more sugar per square inch on that table than there is salt in the Great Salt Lake.

"Anyway, let me know when you see Henry, okay? I'd love to know what's going on," said Pepper. What a surprise! And Mary Poppins carries an umbrella!

I dropped my obligatory six dollars on the table, and added two additional singles. It wasn't Jenny's fault I had inexpensive taste.

CHAPTER NINETEEN

I walked back to the funeral home, enjoying the first bit of warmth as the sun rose on a cloudless sky. It was quiet when I opened the door, but it was 8:15 so I had no doubt Mr. Stanley had arrived.

"Morning!" I heard the inevitable greeting. "A lovely morning, wouldn't you say?" sang Mr. Stanley in his soft, lilting voice.

"It is," I said. There is comfort in gentle, predictable daily events. It was then I heard a soft, persistent sound emanating from Mr. Stanley's pocket. It ascended in scale like the notes on a xylophone. I looked at this old gentleman, and was speechless.

"Why, Mr. Stanley!" I said. "What do you have in your pocket?"

Mr. Stanley colored slightly, and pulled out a little black iPhone—not just any cell phone mind you, but an iPhone.

"Well, I thought it was time to be current. I purchased this little device last week, and have been working with it ever since. Remarkable little machine, I think."

You could have pushed me over with a feather. I guess I have come to see the dear man as something of a robot—a character with completely predictable behavior. He had thrown me for a loop! And I marveled that someone had actually called him. My judgments and preconceptions were falling like flies. What next? I hesitated before asking if I might have his cell phone number.

"Why, of course, my dear." He rattled off ten numbers in succession and it was a done deal.

"Would you like mine?"

"Oh, I already have it," he replied with some satisfaction.

The bell at the front door rang and we both turned to greet Mrs. Arthur's three daughters.

The air they carried in held a dour edge and I felt yesterday's reconciliation evaporating before my eyes. Each stood in her own space, looking everywhere but at the others. I couldn't imagine what could have caused this. Sigh, round two.

"Good morning, ladies! Coffee?" I offered in my best 'Isn't-this-fun' tone of voice.

"Thank you, no." This from Meg.

"I think not." This from Josie.

"No," squeaked Miranda.

"Well, come in and sit down. Do you have something for Mr. Stanley, Josie?"

"Here," she said, shoving a piece of paper into his hands.

"Does anyone have anything to add?" I asked. No movement of any kind.

"Divine then, I'll get on with it," said Mr. Stanley, whereupon the fortunate man took his cue and left me with The Three Musketeers.

"Yesterday you gave me Mother's jewelry and the other personal effects that were at the hospital," said Meg, looking directly at me with a combative look. "It does not appear everything is here."

"The hospital gave me everything she was wearing at the time of her death. I didn't even look at it; it was in a sealed envelope."

"Well, there's something missing," said Josie.

"Whatever..." I began, but was interrupted by Meg's voice rising in anger.

"A ring! There is a ring missing! It has been the subject of much speculation for our entire lives, and now it has gone missing!"

I stumbled for words. "When a person dies in the hospital," I explained, "his or her personal effects are immediately put in an envelope, which is sealed, signed by a nurse, and witnessed by a second party. The signatures were all intact yesterday and I didn't take any notice of it. Do you know the value of the ring? I suppose there could be petty thievery over at the hospital, but I have certainly never been witness to it."

"The ring has sentimental value," Meg said.

"Mother always made quite a to-do about the ring," said Josie. "Since we were little she would use that ring to get the three of us all stirred up. We would compete in little challenges she'd come up with and the winner would get to wear the ring for an hour or so. In retrospect, it was probably a somewhat unkind game, as she was always making jokes and speculating about which of us would eventually get the ring. It has gone on for so many years that it has taken on a life of it's own. I think we all feel entitled to the ring for our own reasons. It may be just a small pearl ring, but that's not what defines its worth."

"Well, I am the eldest and obviously the one who should inherit the ring," huffed Meg.

"I have taken personal care of Mother for years and I should think she would want me to have it out of sheer gratitude," said Josie in a wavering voice.

"Well, I have three adorable little girls and they certainly should carry on the tradition of the ring! Therefore, I should have it," said Miranda with uncharacteristic bravado.

"Josie, you were with her constantly leading up to her death. Why should we believe you don't already have it?" asked Meg.

"Please!" said Josie.

Oh, dear. From an objective point of view it was not difficult to see what was going on. Old Mrs. Arthur needed attention and her three daughters were the only ones who could adequately supply it. She had used the ring as an instrument to guarantee their devotion to the end—and she had done it with surprising success. I realized that it was up to me to play Solomon and I knew I had to think both quickly and creatively. This had not been covered in any of my course work in mortuary science.

"I would suggest," I said, "that we all think as objectively as possible about this dilemma over the weekend. The memorial service isn't until the middle of next week so we have plenty of time to figure it out. Let's try to resolve this without tearing your sisterly bonds to shreds. You're all each other has for family now and that shouldn't be taken lightly. Certainly your parents would want you to remain close." I spewed all this out, believing only about half of it but wanting them out of my office.

"I'll contact the hospital, but I doubt anything will come of it."

None of the three was backing down. I wasn't entirely certain that time would help dissolve this animosity, but I *was* certain that nothing good was going to come of the three of them standing here with me in my office any longer.

"As I say, I will call the hospital to verify what happened. Even if you think you have looked everywhere, take another look. Try to be as objective as possible, and be kind to one another. This is a difficult time for all of you. Practice patience and understanding." I was starting to feel like Billy Graham.

CHAPTER TWENTY

I saw them to the door, and was relieved to hear my phone ring as it hastened their exodus. Any diversion at this point was welcome. I had a momentary flash, thinking it might be Mr. Stanley, but my caller ID identified Uncle Henry.

"Hello, dear," I heard that familiar voice intone. "Free for lunch in an hour or so?"

"Oh, yes!" I answered, perhaps a bit too quickly. "I'll do pie. At the bench. 12:30. Can you do drinks?"

"Yes, dear."

Translated, that means I will meet Uncle Henry on our favorite bench at Darling Park, which overlooks the harbor, with four slices of pizza, and he will bring water for me and a Coca-Cola for himself. The Woodford Harbor House of Pizza is the best. Pepperoni and mushroom for Uncle Henry, and plain cheese for me, I tell the friendly Greek owner when I call. I like my pizza the way I like my French toast. Simple.

I looked forward to catching up with Uncle Henry. I wasn't sure what was up at his end, but I certainly wanted to pick his brain about the missing ring fiasco.

I spent the next hour looking over options for next year's Bainbridge Funeral Home calendar. Funeral homes and calendars are like ice scrapers in rental cars. You might never use them, but you always expect them to be there. I immediately put aside the one that claimed, 'We Put the FUN in Funerals.'

I also put in a call to Portland Memorial Hospital, where I learned that Mrs. Arthur had actually been fairly lucid until the time of her death, and that she had passed on alone, with no one at her side. I guess her shouts for attention had dimmed by then, poor thing. The nurse on the line was clear that not only had all her personal effects been included in the large bag, but that the nurse on duty, Maggie Burns, had been with the hospital for almost forty years and had an impeccable reputation. Just to be thorough, I asked when she would be on duty next so that I might speak with her. The answer was tomorrow from 7 am to 3 pm. This problem was getting as annoying as a mosquito in the middle of the night—I just couldn't get rid of it.

A light knock was followed by Mr. Stanley's entrance. "I finished Mrs. Arthur's obituary. It is complete, I believe, but not terribly interesting."

"Well, you know what I always say," I said. "If you want to have an interesting obituary you had better live an interesting life. The more I hear her daughters describe Mrs. Arthur's life, the less impressed I am. I guess some people just can't get out of their own way. I'm sure she loved her girls, but her neediness was as disruptive during her lifetime as it is now at her death."

"I'm sorry to hear that. I never knew her very well. As a Congregationalist I am not always acquainted with those from the Episcopal part of town," said Mr. Stanley.

"I am off to meet Uncle Henry for lunch so you are on your own. The girls brought Mrs. Arthur's outfit. Can you give her a once-over and dress her so we can take her over to the crematorium later this afternoon?"

"Sure, Miss G. I'll treat her well."

It felt good to put at least part of Mrs. Arthur's final drama into someone else's hands. Not to speak ill of the dead, but I'm pretty sure she would have annoyed the hell out of me in real life.

CHAPTER TWENTY-ONE

The Woodford House of Pizza is just three blocks up Pleasant Street and the park only four blocks back to the harbor, but I grabbed my Jeep and drove the distance. I am not a big fan of walking. If I had my choice I think I would rather swim a mile than walk it. Why walk when you can drive? That's my motto.

I pulled into a space right in front, and made short work of grabbing the pizzas. I was over the hill and headed for the bench by 12:27, but of course Uncle Henry was already there. A wonderful salty breeze was blowing gently from the west. The cold, early spring water temperatures gave it a slight chill, but when combined with the newly warm sun it was perfect.

Darling Park is on a rocky promenade overlooking the middle of the harbor. An early morning walk up there is almost reason enough to live in Woodford Harbor. It has a single swing next to a delightful gazebo that the local Rotary clubs built last year. The dock at the base of the steps to the water wasn't in yet. However, in a couple months time it will be full of kids laughing and screaming and jumping off it into the water.

The waterside perimeter of the park almost seems like a giant English muffin full of interesting nooks and crannies. At various levels one can find benches and flat spaces just large enough to hold a blanket for sitting. It's always fun to see the townsfolk there and its contours allow for plenty of privacy. Looking at some of the spots now I could almost feel my face blush with memories.

Uncle Henry looked quite satisfied on his perch, but I knew his need for lunch was probably gnawing at him. Sure enough, he gave me a beaming smile of welcome, and reached for the flat boxes.

"Here's your water. Did you remember napkins?"

"With these greasy things it would be a crime to forget them," I said. We indulged ourselves in silence as we launched into the cheesy messes. Munching in companionable silence we enjoyed our lunch with sufficient relish to momentarily forget the caloric intake. After my two slices I came up for air, took a swig of water, and began to explain the Mrs. Arthur saga. Uncle Henry kept his eyes on the harbor and focused on his pizza, but I knew he was listening. He didn't respond until his pizza was gone. His remark was somewhat disappointing. 'People certainly are strange' was his only comment.

"Well, what do you suggest I do?" I asked somewhat testily.

"Dear, there really is not a lot you can do. You have checked with the hospital, and attempted to quell the storm. Now these three adult women need to sort this out among themselves. Much as you would like to solve every problem in the world, you just can't. Of course, I love you for this little idiosyncrasy. I believe your mother has the same problem. But I fear your job is done."

This did not sit well with me. I do like to solve problems, particularly when they occur around a death. In my position I need to feel I have done everything possible for the grieving people left behind during tough times such as this. Maybe that's why Uncle Henry is the sheriff in the family, and I'm not.

"But I do have some news for you, dear. I was finally able to speak with Duke. He is quite something—and much more agreeable sober. Too bad he so seldom finds himself in that condition. He has built himself a reputation, however, and folks do judge people on their past performances. I'm afraid he has an upward battle."

"What did he have to say for himself?" I asked eagerly, prejudging him just as Uncle Henry had predicted I would.

"Maybe it was because he had shaved and had on clean clothes, but I think it is important not to put Duke—or anyone for that matter—into a box. They will inevitably behave outside it."

Again? Mr. Stanley and Uncle Henry? Sharing the same metaphor? I began to think that maybe the answer to a better life lay in the 'box' philosophy rather than in *A One-step Guide for Overall Improvement*.

"Duke claims he had no inkling that anything was out of the ordinary that night. He met the girl—who, by the way, is named April—at the laundromat. Apparently she arrived in town just recently, and found herself a job there. Unbeknownst to the owner, she was also staying there at night, sleeping in piles of towels and cleaning up in the ladies' room.

"Duke relayed a story from his past that sheds some light on his own unfortunate circumstances. He was one of eight children, and was born outside Bangor. His father was not of much consequence to the family, and when his mother suddenly died the department of family services put the children in foster homes—each in a different one. Duke was especially fond of his littlest sister, but sadly lost touch with her. I'm afraid the entire situation did him in and he has certainly not attached himself to anyone emotionally since.

"When he ran into April, he felt sorry for her, and offered to let her stay with him. He said she was very clean and orderly, and that it was not a hardship for him to relinquish his bedroom to her as he most often fell asleep on the couch. He told me she's been there about ten days, and has caused him no trouble at all. I think he actually felt good about helping her out, but that was about as far as it went.

"He wasn't ready to get involved with her in any personal way, and that extended to not even wanting to know why she was here or what she was doing. The fact that she was killed, though, seems to have had a genuine impact on him. Of course he's upset because everyone in town will immediately point the finger at him, but also because he—in point of fact—cared about her."

"Wow! It's a real challenge to think that far outside his box. Who would have thought that Duke was ever a child, but I guess everyone is at one time or another," I mused. I was having an exceedingly difficult time digesting all this. It took my quick knee-jerk judgments to a whole new level. Everyone knew that Duke was a bum. Big breath, I told myself. Rethink.

"Of course I have nothing with which to charge him," continued Uncle Henry. "He just seems to have a penchant for being in the wrong place at the wrong time—and that alone is no crime."

"Sometimes when you are in the wrong place at the wrong time too often it does say something!" I snapped.

Uncle Henry gave me a close look, and raised an eyebrow. I felt judged, condemned, and humiliated. I gave Uncle Henry a quick goodbye, and hurried back to my car.

CHAPTER TWENTY-TWO

It was one of those early spring days you can't quite believe is real, especially after a difficult winter. I drove the long way back to the funeral home, this time with the Jeep's top down. I went up Darling Street and around the town hall, past the House of Pizza, and back down Pleasant Street. Lovely as this was, it did not quite quell my unease with either Mrs. Arthur or Duke. In my world Mrs. Arthur had manipulated her daughters relentlessly and Duke was just too horrible not to be involved with that poor girl's death. Is that being judgmental or realistic?

Back at work, Mr. Stanley announced that Mrs. Arthur was ready for transport to the crematorium. It was a 45-minute drive north and I took a bit of pleasure telling Mr. Stanley he could drive her up on Monday, and was free to leave early. Ha! She might have made everyone miserable around her for years, but she was going to have to play second fiddle to Mr. Stanley this afternoon.

"Why, that's so kind of you, Miss G! Perhaps I'll start the spring cleanup in my vegetable garden. I need to get it ready to plant. Have a nice weekend!"

"You as well, Mr. Stanley," I called after him.

It was quiet and a bit lonely with the departure of the dear man. Friday afternoons can be a pensive time for me. I still marvel that I am sitting at my grandfather and father's desk, doing what they did so long and so well. It makes me wonder what my father thinks when he sees his "little one" sitting at this desk. How would I feel if Charlie was sitting here? Charlie. I hoped she was having a good time at her lacrosse tournament. She just loves twisting and tilting that bagged stick around. As for me, I find every game in which her million-dollar orthodontia remains intact a victory.

The warm spring air drifted through the window and I roused myself, transferred my calls the to the answering service, and headed for my own garden. I needed some personal time; Bainbridge Funeral Home would just have to wait.

Once home I headed straight to the closet for a reunion with the jeans and T-shirt I had passed over this morning, then made a beeline to my beloved garden. The Montauk daisies and sedum reappear every year and I welcome them back like the miracles they are. Before their arrival, though, I have to clean up all the debris the winter has deposited on the beds, and decide on the annuals to plant for a splash of color. Usually I stick with variations of pink for the impatiens, then intersperse blue salvia for contrast. A few nice white New Guinea impatiens and I'm done. It's colorful and simple, and provides enough contrast to keep it interesting. Actually, the garden is pretty much a reflection of my life.

I thought of Mr. Stanley laying down strings to ensure rigidly straight lines for his vegetables. His garden, unlike mine, speaks to his need for structure and is reflective of his pragmatic nature. His provides more than aesthetic pleasure; he'll also have vegetables. It occurred to me then that Trudy was probably busy planting her formal rose gardens. Structured in form, they were nonetheless highly artistic.

Suddenly I had a very painful thought. That poor girl, April, would never get to create a garden for herself. So many things are missed when one experiences such an early death. And, taking Mrs. Arthur out of the 'box' I had put her in, I realized she couldn't have been all bad if she loved her garden. I planned on driving down to Portland first thing in the morning to chat with her nurse. Uncle Henry might feel the Arthur girls are not my concern, but a clear conscience is a good pillow; for me to sleep soundly, I needed to do all I could to help them solve this problem.

I yanked weeds, swept them up, and gathered all the garden's flotsam and jetsam. Shoving the lot into a barrel, I readied for a trip to the dump. Taking off my gardening gloves, I wiped my butt with a vengeance to remove all the dirt that had stuck to it and heaved the barrel into the back of the Jeep. The Woodford Harbor dump is another social center in town. It's actually just a transfer station, with a giant hopper for the trash and recycling bins for cardboard, metal, paper, cans, and bottles. We take our trash sorting seriously here, and tossing a recyclable piece of cardboard or a tin can in the hopper is akin to blasphemy.

I went to the back of the lot to dispose of my yard clippings, and ran into Pepper. She was laden with an enormous load of bittersweet for the pile.

"Oh, brother, I hate this stuff!" she growled. "Every year, every goddamn year it comes back like crazy! I swear I get the roots, but it outsmarts me every time! Now that it's gone I'm going to plant some nice lupine and a few blueberry bushes along the fence next to my walkway. I might also put some hostas out back. I've decided against the veggie garden this year. I'm getting too long in the tooth for that. Vegetables I can buy at Brown's." And she was off in a cloud of dust.

I drove back to the house, swept the mess I had made off the sidewalks, and rinsed my gardening tools. I saw Martha Stewart do this once. I find her existence tolerable if for no other reason than her having encouraged me to adopt this habit. I examined my handiwork, and was anxious to start planting, although I knew I had to wait a few weeks still.

I felt an emptiness as I walked into the kitchen. Even the house seems to know that Charlie is not going to come bursting through the door in an hour. Throwing my dirty clothes in the hamper I wrapped a towel around myself, and headed outside to wash up. I consider it a sure sign of spring when the outdoor shower is turned on and I love the feeling of the open air around me as I stand under a warm spray of water. I worked shampoo into my scalp, as much to get the dirt out from under my fingernails as to wash my hair, then dried off, wrapped the towel around me, and scampered back upstairs to get dressed.

I considered pouring myself a small glass of red wine to celebrate my cleanliness, but thought better of it when I remembered the size of the drinks at The Old Port. The place is legendary for serving cocktails in enormous glasses, and has for years been included among the top ten sailing bars in the world. Wine is served in more traditional glasses, but the bartenders fill them to the very tippy top. Never does a waitress spill a drop, which is really a small miracle.

My cellphone suddenly played "Hey, Good Lookin'" and I happily greeted Bode at the other end.

"Hi! Just back from seeing Mom. I'll get cleaned up, and come for you in about an hour."

"Great! Perfect! See you then!" I said. I sat down on the porch swing, only to get right up again. I deserved that wine! I poured myself a small glass of red, and sat back down again, happy as a clam.

CHAPTER TWENTY-THREE

B ode and I walked up the rickety outdoor stairs, and opened the door into the craziness that is The Old Port on Friday night. I felt as comfortable as an old shoe—perhaps because I knew two glasses of wine awaited me, as well as a chicken parmesan sandwich and a third glass if I decided to be wild and crazy. The cast of characters there is a who's who of Woodford Harbor. The mayor was pontificating in one corner and a group of young professionals was crowded into the corner at the other end of the bar. Actually, they were all in their late twenties—how old am I getting to be if that seems young? Three middle-aged, buxom women looked to be out trolling for the night, and two really old couples, in their sixties, were conversing animatedly as they were led to their table.

We fought our way in, me following in Bode's wake. His next question would be his biggest of the night. "Do you want Malbec or merlot?"

"The merlot!" I replied, getting that out of the way.

"Hey, Lizzie!" called out the good doctor. He had obviously been there for awhile as his usual reserve was worn away. But even this late in the day his aftershave permeated the air around him. Sometimes I wondered if his cologne was a case of 'the best defense is a good offense.' Thankfully, our thoughts are silent so the doctor hadn't a clue what slightly malicious thought had just passed through my brain.

Trudy was right behind him, teetering on her four-inch heels.

"Are you going to the clambake tomorrow night?" the doctor asked.

"Absolutely!" I said in response. "What's the weather supposed to be?"

"Let me check my phone. Darn! Trudy, can you see what the weather forecast is for tomorrow night? I just can't quite get the hang of using this thing."

Trudy took the phone, but by the time she had brought up the app and was reading the information the doctor had already been distracted by a tall brunette pushing through the crowd. Trudy seemed not to notice and we exchanged pleasant remarks on the good weather expected to come our way—low 70s during the day, and just ten degrees cooler with no wind that night.

Then Trudy asked, rather abruptly, "Do you have any more information about the murdered girl? I heard she was staying at Duke's. What do they know?"

"Actually I do. Uncle Henry finally spoke to Duke, and learned that she had been working at the laundromat. When Duke noticed she was sleeping there as well he offered her a room. He said her name was April, but he didn't seem to know much beyond that."

Trudy began searching for her mate, as I did for mine. I had the distinct feeling that my search was less frantic than hers. Another twinge of sympathy ran through me as I watched her scan the bar. I would hate to even think that Bode was not totally with me. The institution of marriage, I mused, certainly doesn't define the real bond between two people.

Next, I ran into Tommy, from The Driftwood, making his rounds. A big smile spread across his face and we pumped fists like two teenagers.

"What's up?" I asked.

"The Patriots just drafted a kid from Eastern Illinois as a back-up quarterback, Jimmy Garoppolo. He could be really good, but I'm sure Brady will be with us for at least four or five more years. Man, I can't wait! Gotta go, though, the wife is home with the kids and I promised I wouldn't be here long."

Tommy's enthusiasm was contagious. I hoped Jimmy Whomever would be good. If he was good enough for Tommy he was good enough for me.

I found Bode over in the corner, chatting with the Duncans. "Hey," I greeted them. "Nice to see you two out for the night. Archie was just saying how pleased he was that it's pizza night. You two do such a great job over there."

"Thanks, Lizzie. We love those kids. They all work really hard and it's so rewarding when you see them achieve success with their personal life skills," replied Ben Duncan.

I took a big breath, and asked a question with which I wasn't sure I was comfortable. "I know I am not Archie's legal guardian, but I care so much for him and see a lot of him, especially with Bode. Would it be appropriate for me to ask you about his recent behavior? He seems a bit agitated, a little jumpy, maybe somewhat on edge. He's usually such an easygoing kid. I'm just wondering."

"Oh, Lizzie, we know you're asking for all the right reasons and I don't think we're overstepping any boundaries by discussing the hard time he seems to be having," said Karen Duncan. "He isn't himself. For the past couple of nights he's been quite restless. Usually at lights out, around nine or ten, he slips into his room and emerges bright-eyed in the morning. Last night, though, I found him outside sitting under a tree. He keeps asking odd questions, which is not like him at all, like how people die. He's also being overly sensitive about his personal space. He takes a wide berth in the hallway when someone is approaching him, and was terribly apologetic when he hit my arm inadvertently the other day."

"Yes, he acted the same way when his arm bumped mine this morning at The Driftwood. Poor kid. He's such a sweetheart it's hard to see him unhappy. We're thinking of taking him out for a picnic on the *Lizzie G* on Sunday. Maybe we can figure out what's up."

"I'm coming over tomorrow about noon to pick up all the boys to help with the clambake, right?" asked Bode. "We can use all that young muscle to gather seaweed, stones, and driftwood for the pit."

"Sure thing," said Ben. "Tire them out all you can. We'll bring them back over before the clambake starts so they can see all the food going in the hole. Does five o'clock sound good?"

"Sounds good to me," said Bode. "These things are really fun. See you there."

Just then, out of the corner of my eye, I spied Glenda sitting at the end of the bar. I felt a stab of sympathy for her as the stereotype of a woman alone at a bar ran through me. Of course, women have every right to sit at a bar on their own, but my knee jerk response was to make her feel comfortable. I started to move in that direction, and was about to speak to her when I noticed that her eyes were a bit glassy, and were fixed on Hank Duvall, a former Woodford Harbor football star. Glenda and Trudy are a few years older than I am, and had been in the same class in high school. I remember hearing that Hank had hooked up with Trudy as his steady; a foregone conclusion in those days. Glenda was a few months older, though, and had a fake ID, so she could buy beer.

She would buy beer for Hank, but would then be left behind when the party began. Trudy would be the one holding on to

Hank's arm. Fast forward twenty years and it seemed as if she was still being left behind. I decided to steer clear, spotted Bode in the restaurant area, and retreated over there.

We had just been seated when Pepper plopped down next to me. "Hey, kids, how's it going?" she asked. A whiff of bourbon sailed across the space between us. She did love her Old Crow.

"What's the news? Henry locked up Duke yet? I sure wish he would. Whole town does. Guy is a menace, and now he's really done it. Too bad tar and feathering has gone out of fashion, I say."

"Hey easy..." I started to interject.

"Anyway, here's a good one! Phil, down to the gas station, told me this morning that he'd gotten an emergency phone call last night to fix a flat tire. Down off Peach Highlands. At 2 am. Guess who it was? Trudy, all by herself! Obviously following the doctor around on his 'rounds,' I'd say! Two blocks from Glenda's house!"

There is always talk that Trudy has been seen following the doctor around town when he is out. Somehow the proof of it didn't amuse me much. Having seen and felt their disconnect so recently gave the story a reality that made me feel sorry. Sorry for everyone.

"Well, I'm off. Got to get some good shut-eye before the big clambake! Working on those cheesecakes has worn me right out!" Pepper ambled off in her happy little haze. Blessedly, she lived just two doors away so she would not pose a threat on the roads.

"You stopped by to see your mom before you picked me up?" I asked Bode.

"Yeah. She seemed in relatively good spirits. It's hard when she talks about the house. I'm not sure if she knows she's not going back. She wanted to know if I had had a plumber look at that tricky disposal and she wondered if the living room rug might need a cleaning with Bob in the house.

"She also asked if you had started cleaning up the garden. You seem to be relegated to the outside of her house," he laughed, "while I am the caretaker indoors."

"I think there might be a message there, my friend. I am allowed outside the house, in fact she really welcomes me in the garden. But the real heart and soul of the house—the indoors—is off limits to me. I am not a true relative and I think folks of her generation have a hard time with the whole marriage business. Fact is, I'm not her daughter-in-law. I know *we're* both good with this, but we still have to understand that there are fine lines. Anyway, I sure do love her son!"

"And I don't mind not raking, and digging, and grubbing around in the yard, so it's not all bad," said Bode.

Our waitress came and we ordered. Bode's second rum and Coke arrived along with my next wine. We smiled across the table and Bode cocked his head, inviting me sit next to him on his side. I happily scrambled over. We could see the TV in the bar from there, and snuggled in to watch the Red Sox being trounced by the White Sox. I was having a better night than Clay Buchholtz.

CHAPTER TWENTY-FOUR

The chilly water was a challenge the next morning, but I had succumbed to that third glass of wine and I needed to get myself going. The first few minutes made me wonder whether this was indeed what my body needed, and not just one more insult. But after five minutes I was in a rhythm and my brain, if not thanking me, was at least functioning.

No one was around the lobster pound as I passed it. I guessed they were all down at the beach preparing the feast for the evening.

Creating an authentic New England clambake is a real art form. First, an enormous hole is dug in the sand, usually about three-feet deep. It was going to be a big hole for this crowd, probably about six-feet in diameter. Next, the hole is lined with large, smooth stones. Then the beach is combed for driftwood, which is piled high over the stones. The fire is lit, and burns for about four hours. More wood is added during this time to keep it good and hot. Then the wood, ash, and embers are raked out and down between the stones and one is left with a bed of sizzling hot rocks.

Piles of wet seaweed are then strewn over them, covering them completely. Rockweed is the seaweed of choice because it has little pockets of water bubbles that release moisture evenly. It's essential at this point to engage many hands in the seaweed gathering, as it should be fresh and moist when it's tossed in. The collective hands of Archie and his friends would be crucial. Cheesecloth bags filled with clams and potatoes are laid atop the seaweed, then corn and finally the lobsters. The lobstermen then soak giant tarps with water, and throw them over the whole mess, securing them with more rocks around the sides to keep the steam in. A couple of hours later you have the biggest, messiest feast ever!

I hopped in the outdoor shower, dressed in black pants and a fresh white shirt, and chose flip-flops rather than flats as a nod to Saturday. I was anxious to get on the road to Portland to see Mrs. Arthur's nurse, so I toasted an English muffin at home, slathered it with extra-crunchy peanut butter, and was soon in the Jeep and off.

I pulled out of my long driveway next to the boatyard, and waved at the folks who had come to clean up their boats after several months of winter storage. The atmosphere was upbeat and convivial, as everyone anticipated a good summer season on the water. Even minor problems like a dead battery or rusted cleats were happily resolved; it seems money becomes irrelevant when it comes to boats. In fact, we turn BOAT into an acronym around here—Break Out Another Thousand.

I turned right onto Beacon Street, and made my way to 295 South toward Portland. Approaching Freeport, I decided to make my obligatory stop at LL Bean earlier rather than later as the crowds would be less. A retail giant like Bean, which is open 24 hours a day, 365 days a year, is—if you can believe it—always busy, but a visit early on Saturday morning finds it a bit less so. The weekend warriors tend not to arrive until later in the afternoon.

I smiled as I passed the giant LL Bean boot outside the store, and heard the familiar sounds of water splashing in the fishpond. My parents had charmed me with that pond as a child and I had done the same with Charlie. Maybe if Charlie has a little one someday I can share the magic again.

Making my way through the guns, kayaks, and tents, I headed straight to the ladies' shoe department. It was spring, and time for my annual purchase of a new pair of boat shoes. That's a bit of a misnomer, I suppose, as I actually sport boat shoes everywhere a flip-flop can't take me in summer. On my feet they're certainly not exclusive to boats. I own many pair, and delegate them for different purposes: the worst for gardening, the next worst for lobstering on the *Lizzie G,* my new ones for fancy, and the next best for biking and day trips on the *Lizzie G.* While there, I poked around the polo shirts. I have a rule that I cannot buy a new one until I dispose of an old one and I just couldn't think of any I wanted to part with, so no sale today! Old friends, I find, are the best friends.

As I leaned over to pick up a Topsider box marked size 7, I caught a glimpse of a man sitting on the bench outside the women's changing room. The familiar mop of white hair caught my attention and I recognized Doctor Wilson. I started to smile and raise my hand when I suddenly realized that the doctor was outside a ladies' changing room. He was waiting for a woman. But which woman would it be? It only took a nanosecond to realize I did not want to know. I grabbed the box, hoping my feet hadn't had any growth spurts, and hightailed it to the checkout counter. Soon I was rolling out of the parking lot, relieved to be anonymous once again on Route 295.

I exited the highway in Portland, followed the square blue 'H' signs to the hospital, and pulled into a relatively empty visitors' parking lot. Inside, a volunteer cheerfully pointed me to Maggie Burns' station. It's often said that hospitals are depressing, but the helpful, happy volunteers at Portland General make this hospital anything but cheerless.

I found Mrs. Arthur's former nurse leaning against a wall next to the coffee machine; she appeared tired. Her physical persona fit her voice perfectly. Short and round, she kept her grey hair away from her face by fashioning it into a bun. Although her light blue uniform did not set her apart, there was something about her hands as they held a mug of coffee that did. They were scrubbed pink and the flesh around her fingers was ample. These were clearly hands that could comfort with a simple touch to the forehead. I approached her, feeling guilty about interrupting her quiet moment. She smiled graciously at the sound of her name, and suggested we walk to the end of the hall and chat in a small seating area.

"Would you like some coffee?" she inquired in a soft, lilting Irish brogue. How many dying patients, I thought, had heard her soothing voice as their last sound on earth? They must have thought they were already in heaven.

"Thank you, no," I answered. "I don't want to bother you, or take up too much of your time. You and your colleagues work so hard you shouldn't be asked to expend additional energy on other things. My name is Lizzie George, and I called yesterday to enquire about one of your patients, Abigail Arthur. I'm a funeral director and I'm working right now with her three surviving daughters. There seems to be a question about a pearl ring that Mrs. Arthur always wore. It was not with the other possessions that were sent from the hospital to the funeral home. I understand you were on duty with her at the end and I wonder if you remember it. It has no monetary value, but great sentimental meaning."

"Yes," Maggie said. "When she was agitated she would twist that ring around and around. Her daughters had been here on and off for weeks—old Mrs. Arthur was one of those people who seemed quite set on staying with us here on earth. I don't know if she was afraid, or just too ornery to go. Oh my, please don't think me disrespectful! It's just that I've seen so many people pass I find myself categorizing them. No, Mrs. Arthur wanted the attention of those girls—and attention they gave! But at some point it's just over. Life is over, and to refuse to go is not in anyone's best interest.

"The more she moaned the more she twisted that ring. It went on and on and on. I'm afraid that when her time finally came, though, I was not in the room with her, nor was anyone else. Frankly, I had had enough of her. Although I always feel a holy presence in the room when a person dies, the energy that remained in Mrs. Arthur's room was somewhat rattled. In retrospect, I don't recall taking that ring off her finger when I prepared her. She was obsessed with which daughter was to have it.

"So it's gone. The rooms are cleaned thoroughly from top to bottom and the bed linens are meticulously laundered so if it had been here it would have been found. From the short time I knew Mrs. Arthur, my dear, I would believe almost anything. She could very well have swallowed that ring just to keep it to herself."

"Oh, my!" It is not often that I am at a loss for words, but this was most assuredly the case right now. "Oh, my," I repeated again, beginning to feel like a tongue-tied adolescent. "I just don't know…"

"It's just a hunch dear, but after more than 35 years attending to these situations one develops a bit of a sixth sense. So, for whatever reason, that would be my guess. God bless you now, and blessings to the dear departed's daughters." She crossed herself, and got up. My legs were not responding so I remained seated for a moment. I could hardly wait to get back to Bainbridge, and put an end to this dilemma.

I drove back to Woodford Harbor as fast as my Jeep and the Maine state police would allow. Once there, I put on my lab coat and quickly reversed the nice job Mr. Stanley had done dressing Mrs. Arthur. It didn't take much poking to validate Maggie Burns' suspicions. I made short work of the ring's removal, and did a final patch job on Mrs. Arthur. I was losing patience with the dear departed woman at this point. I put her on my list of things to worry about later, and moved on.

CHAPTER TWENTY-FIVE

It was close to noon so I grabbed a piece of bread, heaped a bit of Brown's egg salad on it, rolled it up, and crossed off my second meal of the day.

As Bode was busy at the beach preparing for the clambake, I had offered to drop in on his mother, Thistle, after lunch. I drove to Bode's house, and found some flowers to bring from the garden. The yard was a bit the worse for wear after being ignored all winter. Thistle had rescued an old millstone from up north many years ago, and turned it into a table that had, over the years, hosted its share of wine bottles. Its simplicity and mass created a work of art. I brushed some fallen twigs away and, looking around, found tall spikes of purple loosestrife growing around the damp, back corner of the yard. Grabbing a bunch, I left for the nursing home.

Thistle had met life head-on when James, her husband of forty years, passed away. She realized she needed change, and opened a flower shop called Pamela's Thistle. She had a real eye for flowers, and created beautiful arrangements for every anniversary and event in town. Her real passion, though, was wildflowers.

Saturday mornings before a wedding would often find her combing the fields around town in search of Queen Anne's lace or pink clover. She would then combine exotic flowers with these wild ones in such unique ways that the end result almost seemed more beautiful than nature itself. Although known as Pammy her entire life, she spent so much time puttering around at the shop that she and the shop became one, and everyone started calling her Thistle.

I have always found her response to James' death inspirational. One chapter of her life had closed and she created another. She kept moving. Flowers were what she knew, so she used that as her base. By her bedside now she has a framed copy of the first few stanzas of Linda Ellis's poem, "The Dash;" for years it had sat on her kitchen windowsill.

> I read of a man who stood to speak
> at the funeral of a friend.
> He referred to the dates on her tombstone
> from the beginning...to the end.
>
> He noted that first came the date of birth
> and spoke of the following date with tears,
> but he said what mattered most of all
> was the dash between those years.
>
> For that dash represents all the time
> that they spent alive on earth.
> And now only those who loved them
> know what that little line is worth.

For it matters not, how much we own,
the cars...the house...the cash.
What matters most is how we live and love
And how we spend our dash.

Thistle spent the next six years ensconced in that little shop, and doing a bang-up business. Some might wonder how often men came in solely to purchase flowers; some simply enjoyed spending time with the charming proprietor. She has never lost the engaging sparkle that draws people to her.

One sad day Thistle took a step too quickly. The broken hip that resulted has put her in the local nursing home, where she seems destined to remain. Fortunately, she has plenty of friends there, including one gentleman in particular. Mr. Augustus Beethoven was at one time the town's wisest of counselors, but now resides at the Woodford Harbor Home. He has always been known as Gus, but Thistle refers to him as Augustus, in almost a whisper. It sounds somewhat salacious, even between octogenarians.

Bode faithfully visits her most every day and I am frequent company for her, too. She holds out hope that someday she will return to the family home. Bode does not disallow this dream, and keeps the house at the ready for her. Unfortunately, it doesn't seem very likely.

Thistle was out in the garden, wrapped in a blanket in her wheelchair. Her body sat straight, and with a certain grace. Her face was devoid of makeup, but her round, cherry cheeks and sparkling blue eyes radiated a warmth Revlon could never replicate.

I approached her with my bouquet, and was rewarded with her lovely smile. It brought me right back to the feeling I had had as a child when she greeted me.

"Dearie, hello! How are you? And don't you look splendid! Loosestrife! I know right where that came from! I don't care if it has been deemed invasive; I love it! But I must get home, and clear that back corner. It collects so many leaves and debris over the winter. Oh, my, come sit down next to me so I can get a better look at you."

"Well, hello to you too, dear Thistle! Isn't it lovely to be out-doors in the garden again? You're right! These little beauties were in the back corner of your garden. I just did a cleanup at my house, and plan to spend some time Sunday tidying up your garden. It already looks beautiful. The way you plant things looks so natural that even the leaves from the winter can't ruin it."

"If I'm not home in time, I hope you will plant some annuals to spruce it up a bit. Only white, of course."

"Certainly, Thistle." Her garden had so many shades of green and varieties of textures that color was unnecessary. White just showed off her genius.

"Now tell me, dear, what's going on around town? The girls are coming to see me tomorrow, but not everyone is here this time of year and I do so worry that they don't give me every morsel of information out there!" The 'girls' had an average age of eighty.

"Well, let's see. The Courdaroys are due back soon from their month-long visit to Italy, so you should be seeing her soon. Their granddaughter, Emily, has become engaged to that nice Robinson boy! It's crazy to think that your friends' grandchildren are now getting married, isn't it?"

"Oh, how lovely. It's so nice when two people can commit to each other that way. Marriage is a wonderful institution."

I felt my dander go up. Realizing that this was a segue into 'the subject,' I took control of the conversation. "Yes, I couldn't agree more. Marriage is ideal for two young people just starting their joint lives. It's an opportunity to grow together and experience so many firsts as a pair.

"But, as time goes by and years define circumstances in peoples' lives, it gets a bit more tricky. Marriage can define a couple's rela-tionship only so far—and it certainly doesn't guarantee happiness.

And neither do I think it measures the love between two people. There are many marriages devoid of love. Then again, a couple can have a relationship overflowing with love, but not be in a position to marry." I stopped abruptly, hoping I hadn't sounded too strident.

"Well, yes, quite so, I imagine. Aren't you something, dear Lizzie George? And how are your parents? Chasing turtles down on Captiva?"

"Yes, you have that right. The nesting season has just begun for the turtles, and they're quite involved at Ding Darling—and loving every minute of it! Oh, Thistle, I almost forgot my other gift!"

"Oh, how I do love your visits!"

I opened my bag, and pulled out a six-ounce bottle of Chardonnay. Thistle was allowed to have all the wine she wanted starting at five o'clock, but she enjoyed a bit at noontime on special occasions. Like this one.

"Here's your little plastic cup. Now try to finish this while we are chatting so I can take the bottle."

"I'll certainly try," she said, smiling.

We continued chatting for a bit. When the last drop of wine disappeared we exchanged a warm hug. Blessedly, I spied Augustus coming through the French doors and into the garden. It's so much easier to say goodbye when another warm body is moving in.

I had promised Bode I would pick up Bob, and walk him over to the beach to view the clambake preparations. Although Bode insists time and again that dogs have no sense of time—one of his many random dog factoids—I still like to break up Bob's day if he is left behind. I fired up the Jeep, and drove back to Bode's. Bob had his nose scrunched up against the screen, and was happily sleeping the day away. He lifted his head when he heard my footsteps on the stones, and wagged his tail in joyful recognition. His fish breath abated on the weekends, which was nice.

As I opened the screen door, Bob bounded out and proceeded to do a little dance and slurp my ankle. He jumped into the Jeep without hesitation and we were off. Bob is an excellent co-pilot. He has lots of enthusiasm for the drive, with very little advice on how to operate the vehicle or how best to reach the destination. We pulled into the beach parking lot to the buzz of activity.

The fire was blazing. People were hauling all sorts of scrap wood to throw on it to keep up the intensity. Archie and his friends were combing the beach for all the seaweed they could carry. The pit was near the water's edge so they could keep the piles of seaweed moist. The clerks from Brown's were lined up at the picnic tables, removing silk from the corn, then twisting the husks back on. They had huge buckets to soak them in once they were prepared. A local rental company was madly assembling chairs and tables in the parking lot for dinner seating.

Bob and I parked, and started off to find Bode. Not surprisingly, Bob found him before I did. While humans can differentiate far more colors than dogs, and have a higher clarity of vision, dogs have a much better ability to identify motion. Because Bode was moving, Bob picked him up before I did. I followed his wagging tail to the right, through the crowd and over to the edge of the fire pit. The lobstermen were having a gay old time laughing and joking and feeling, fairly enough, quite important. I spotted Bode before he saw me. I love watching him interact with other people. His whole demeanor is so open and friendly. And he's all man. He walks like a man, talks like a man, and—for better or worse—behaves like a man.

Bob bounded up to him, and got his pat on the head just before I received my whack on the butt.

"Looks like you guys have been busy! Everything on schedule?" I asked the group.

"Sure thing, Lizzie, we've got this under control. You should have your man under this much control," chortled one of the older guys.

"Yup! Fire is insanely hot! Those stones would melt if it was any hotter! Won't be long before we tone it down a notch, spread it all out, and line those suckers with seaweed. Then we'll have us a *clam-bake!*" hollered a younger lobsterman. The preparations seemed to be well-steeped in beer. Hopefully, there were others who would be in charge of unwrapping this feast in six hours.

Bode led Bob and me over to the ocean's edge, toward Archie and the other boys. "These kids are working like crazy collecting the seaweed. They have been down the beach almost a mile, then carried it all back. What a great day! Isn't it amazing what a group of diverse people can do? Talk about many hands..."

Bode's eyes reflected the intensity of his feelings. The power of good radiating from a group working toward a common goal can be huge. The trick is to know it, and enjoy it.

"Lizzie! Lizzie! Have some seaweed!" shouted Archie, coming at me with a handful. He laughed and threw it down. It was wonderful to see him having such a good, carefree time. I loved hugging him, and tousling his hair.

I chatted with different groups on the beach, and eventually found Bob again. Another wave to Archie, the predictable whack on the butt, and we were off. I dropped a happy Bob at Bode's, and drove home to see to my blueberry bread. Half-cup water, quarter-cup oil, one egg, and I am done!

CHAPTER TWENTY-SIX

It was a special day, so I graced it with a second shower. It just feels festive to spiff up a bit at the end of the day. I squeezed into my dress jeans, noting that they were ever so slightly snug. Would I cut back on the wine or the French toast? Maybe add five minutes to the swim. Whatever. I reached for the new sweater I had planned to bring out for the occasion, but then thought better of it. I more often than not spill butter as I navigate lobster to my mouth. Instead, I selected an old Woodford Harbor YMCA sweatshirt in keeping with the theme. It was the Saturday night of the big clambake and I fairly tingled with anticipation. Of course it's the same old people you see every day, but the atmosphere always seems charged the way it was when, as a kid, you went back to school after dark for an event. A bit magical.

I packed up a box of wine and a few red Solo cups, and wrapped my blueberry bread in four layers of tinfoil. Not so good for the environment, I suppose, but the presentation was vastly improved by the stiff corners I made. I heard Bode's truck pull up before I saw it, and flipped on the outdoor light.

"Are you ready, little lady?" teased Bode.

"Yee haw!" I gave back.

We piled in and I considered sharing the story of the swallowed ring, but decided it was too lighthearted a moment to dampen it with that. We drove back around the corner of the harbor to get to Archie's house on Crowninshield Road. The Duncans were corralling the boys into their minivan, but we grabbed Archie and he jumped in the back of the truck. It was cramped, and smelled a bit like the seawater left by the traps that usually occupied the back. A New England version of a cattle truck, I thought.

We drove the two miles back to the beach. The sun was still fairly high in the sky, so it was easy to see and get situated. I carried my blueberry bread masterpiece over to several combined tables that acted as a serving area. There were no exclamations of praise as I laid it on the table, but I knew plenty of folks would find it comforting in the deep recesses of their stomachs after the rich lobster and butter. I found Bode and Archie setting our things down at a table at the far end, closest to the beach. Bode opened his cooler of beer, and popped the top, poured me a cup of wine from the box's spigot, and walked to the drinks table with Archie to find him something as well. I met them over there. We raised our various beverages, clinked them together, looked in one another's eyes, and smiled. Cheers!

Three girls a bit younger than Charlie walked by and I felt a tug of disappointment at her absence. But then I realized that she was with the entire lacrosse team, which was made up of almost all her closest friends. Although it was too bad she wasn't here, she was in another good place. Actually, I was pleased, for events after dark on the beach, with all the drinking, create fertile ground for sixteen-year-olds to get in trouble. Maybe it was all for the best that she was away.

People were arriving en masse. I waved to Uncle Henry, who sported his dress khaki shorts and a clean white Oxford shirt.

This was quite a statement for the likes of him. He eyed the table where Pepper and the local town employees had gathered, then came across the parking lot to sit with us. I smiled. Ben and Karen Duncan were setting up at the table just inside ours with all the boys, so Archie would have a good group with which to pal around. Trudy and the doctor were already seated with the local lawyer and the librarian from Woodford Harbor Public Library. She's nice, but such a stereotypical librarian. Trudy waved and I saw that her white silk pants were topped with a creamy full top sporting a red lobster in sequins. I took a quick peak at her feet. Her sandals had an outrageous assortment of faux jewels on them, but no heels.

Tommy and his sisters, Carly and Glenda, were settling at a table adjacent to the doctor's. Each of Tommy's three kids wore little Patriots Jerseys. Tommy led the pack with a big number 12 shirt with BRADY emblazoned on the back. He and Louise had their little guys under control, while Carly tried hard to control her herd of four. Glenda squeezed in at the end of the table, looking a bit confused amid all the commotion. Perhaps more out of place than distracted, I thought. She didn't really seem to belong there, but then again there was no other table where she *would* fit.

I overheard a conversation Doc Wilson and the librarian were having about the Atul Gawande book, *Being Mortal*. As the doctor explained the theme, the librarian commented that it was quite a damning book on doctors.

"No, not necessarily," he explained. "It's a book meant to educate doctors and patients alike on the issues that surround death."

"I don't want to even discuss death," said Trudy.

Glenda swiveled on her bench to enter the discussion. "Really," she said, "it's such a complex issue. That doctors see patients as nothing more than a challenge, a body to be kept alive, is disconcerting at best. A person's end involves much more than just the length of his breathing days."

"Exactly, Glenda," agreed the doctor. "I found it reassuring that Gawande was able to articulate all the many factors involved at the end of life. Death is inevitable for everyone, but it is so seldom discussed in the United States."

"I found it particularly interesting to examine the realities that are oftentimes swept aside as unacceptable topics," said Glenda.

"Well, I suggest we enjoy this clambake, and give death a rest!" harrumphed Trudy, abruptly ending the conversation. It was a conversation that obviously made her feel uncomfortable; it was also perhaps a bit above her intellect. Glenda and the doctor exchanged a meaningful glance as Glenda twisted back to her original position at the table.

People began to congregate around the giant, steaming pit, which was by now covered with the enormous tarp. It had an ominous look to it. Steam escaped from the sides with a slight sizzle, and almost seemed alive. There was shouting among the lobstermen and everyone was asked to step aside as the cover was removed. Two flannel-shirted lobstermen flanked the tarp on each side, and peeled it back, exposing red-hot stones and charred shapes. The explosion of steam was near volcanic in its ferocity. And then, as quickly as it had erupted it dissipated, exposing piles of steamers, corn, and lobster. The smell created a veritable olfactory paradise. The crowd impulsively cheered and the mood around the pit crested to new heights.

Just as the sun dipped below the horizon, everyone scrambled for plates and bibs and silverware. A band of at least twelve little girls in Brownie uniforms appeared with trays and trays of little cups of melted butter. It looked like a parade of characters from Whoville in Dr. Seuss' *The Grinch Who Stole Christmas*. How they managed hundreds of little butter-filled cups was beyond me; organizing a bunch of little girls in brown uniforms would be even more difficult, I think. A line spontaneously formed along the pavilion that bordered the beach. Bode led our little group, which included Archie, Uncle Henry, and me. And this is where the Great Clambake of 2014 ended for all of us.

From the shadows of the beach, Duke stumbled over the rim of the pavilion, bumping into Bode. Except for the surprise factor, it seemed an innocuous incident. That is, until Archie suddenly shot forward like a ball out of a cannon, and started pummeling Duke with a vengeance. He might be slow in some ways, but Archie is a big, strong, sixteen-year-old young man and he was currently fueled by adrenaline and exponential anger.

Duke was ill-prepared, and fell backward. Archie fell forward onto him. Sitting astride his downed victim, Archie's clenched fists hammered Duke's chest and face viciously. I instinctively stepped back from the violence just as Bode stepped swiftly into it. He pulled Archie off Duke. Uncle Henry stepped over them both, and dragged Duke onto the beach. Bode held a shivering Archie in his arms and I stepped forward to encircle them both. The Duncans had drawn tight around the other boys.

Everyone else seemed frozen in place. It seemed like minutes before the next unlikely moment unfolded, but I am sure it was immediate. Duke broke away from Uncle Henry, shouting, "Get that big retard out of here!"

Bode threw himself across the concrete into Duke's gut and I was left holding Archie by myself. I shoved Archie away from the fracas and all we could hear from a distance was sound. It seemed like the smacks and slaps and grunts and thumps went on forever. It finally ended in an enormous scuffle; one that involved many of the lobstermen. Separating the two hadn't proved easy. Suddenly Ben Duncan was embracing Archie and me, and quietly reassuring us. The doctor came over, and gave Archie a quick examination.

"Why don't you get Archie home, and quieted down?" he suggested. "Call me if he can't get settled, and I can give him something for sleep. He looks fine physically," said the doctor.

People began to move about again as the boys were shepherded into their van; sadly, the evening had ended for them. I slowly approached Bode, who was standing off to the side in the shadows of the pavilion. His left eye looked swollen and his lip trailed blood. He was holding his right hand gingerly. Uncle Henry escorted Duke to the parking lot. The crowd began to once again form the line to the pit, this time in a hushed, slow procession. I hoped I wouldn't see a satisfied look on Pepper's face; ever the gossip columnist, she revels in debacles like this.

I followed Bode across the parking lot to his truck. The evening had suddenly become an unpleasant memory.

CHAPTER TWENTY-SEVEN

T he next morning evolved slowly. Bode lay on the other side of the bed making unfamiliar snizzling sounds. His body seemed different somehow. The gentle soul that resided in that 200 pounds of flesh had exhibited a side I had not known existed last night. He was violent—not cruel or vicious, but perhaps a bit brutal. Men are a different breed of cat. As Brad Paisley points out in "I'm Still a Guy":

> When you see a deer you see Bambi
> And I see antlers up on the wall
> When you see a lake you think picnic
> And I see a large mouth up under that log
> You're probably thinking that you're going to change me
> In some ways well maybe you might
> Scrub me down, dress me up, oh but no matter what
> Remember I'm still a guy

I've always thought of Bode as my sweet little big man, but last night fractured that myth. It was an honorable incident that triggered the fiasco, to be certain, and Duke's comment had hit a chord in Bode.

His right hand was above the covers, still covered in the Ace bandage I had put on it last night. His eye had mostly recovered and the scab on his lip had a healthy, healing look to it. The wounds to his body would heal soon, but something else had changed forever. Did I love and admire him more because of his defense of Archie? Yes, I did. On further reflection, in fact, I began to appreciate the necessity of violence in some situations. It was unfamiliar territory for me, though, and I needed time to work through it.

A final snort through his nose, and my Bode was back, smiling across the covers at me.

"Come here, little lady," he said, reaching toward me.

"Bode, be careful—"

But apparently the old Bode was back with no major harm done.

We showered later and fed Bob, and then the three of us made our way to The Driftwood. Bob sank down in the shade of the flower boxes outside and we went in. The buzzing from within the old wooden structure sounded like a beehive. When we opened the door Bode was met with the looks Neil Armstrong must have gotten upon his return from the moon. This business of being the center of attention was beginning to lose its luster fast, as far as I was concerned.

"Hey, take it easy, you guys!" said Bode. "It was a shame the whole thing happened, but everyone is all right, so let's just let it go."

He edged me over to an empty table just inside the door. Jenny came over, quickly took our order, and skittered away. She looked uncertain, as if Bode might deal her a quick blow. Oh, dear.

The doctor was the first to pull a chair up to our table.

"You look like you weathered the storm relatively well," he said, looking Bode over. "If that hand is still swollen in a couple of days let's take an x-ray. Have you spoken with the Duncans today?"

"No," Bode answered. "We're on our way there after breakfast to pick up Archie. We're going to take him out on the *Lizzie G* for a bit. I'll give you a call later, and let you know how he seems."

"He was quite volatile last night," noted the doctor. "It wasn't at all like his usual temperament. Something seems bottled up in that young man. One thing's for certain: He was not going to allow anything whatsoever to hurt you. Duke's quick bump was sudden, but in no way threatening. Archie overreacted dramatically. I wonder what that is all about?"

"Do you think I overreacted?" asked Bode.

"I'm afraid, Bode, that every one of us harbors some negative energy toward Duke. Your reaction was appropriate after what he said, but I must admit," he confessed with a wink, "I think the throttling you gave him provided many of us a bit of satisfaction."

I guess the doctor is a man after all.

He walked back to join Trudy just as Tommy was leaning over her adoringly with a bag of some goody. Some things never change.

Soon Pepper found her way to our table.

"Wasn't that quite something last night? We don't get much violent drama here in Woodford Harbor. Such a shame *The Woodford Reserve* is a family paper. Man, I would love to write that up on the front page!"

Maybe women can be good audiences for violence as well. It had never attracted me. Perhaps I had watched *The Sound of Music* one too many times.

"Here's another thing I would love to write about. After all the uproar, and after you had left, I was behind Glenda and Trudy in line. Glenda, who was holding a couple of those little butter cups, wormed her way in behind Trudy, and poured one right down her ivory silk pants! They were billowing in the wind so Trudy didn't notice, but I guarantee you those pure silk babies will never make another appearance!"

Here it was again, violence in yet another form.

We finally escaped, grabbed Bob, and started our walk to the Duncans' to see how they all were doing. Archie didn't work on Sundays, so was fortunately spared the foolishness we had just encountered.

Karen had a commercial-grade waffle iron going, and was turning out waffles as fast as the boys could eat them. They all seemed nonplussed about the previous night's activities, and were laughing, joking, and eating happily. Archie was a bit subdued, though, and seemed very glad to see Bode. I let them sit together, and chat quietly.

After all twelve voracious appetites were satisfied, I helped Karen clean up while Ben and Bode and the boys went outside to throw a Frisbee.

"That was so unnerving last night," said Karen.

"I know," I replied. "I don't do well with conflict of any sort, and that seemed particularly awful."

"The boys seemed to take it pretty much in stride," Karen noted. "I don't know if it's because they see so much of it on TV, or if..."

"I know—or if that's just a male thing. Don't ask me!" I was relieved to have at least one person validate my perception of brutality and excessive force.

"How was Archie after you got home?"

"He was really upset. Ben sat out in the backyard with him for over an hour, waiting until he felt better. We can't figure out what provoked him so. You guys are going out on the *Lizzie G* this afternoon, aren't you?"

"Yes," I answered. "I find that being at sea is especially conducive to conversation."

"Let me know if there is anything we can do. I love that boy so," said Karen.

I marveled again at the goodness that surrounds us.

CHAPTER TWENTY-EIGHT

I walked out to watch the Frisbee action, and noticed Archie standing alone in the shade of an old oak at the side of the yard. I caught Bode's eye and we both joined him.

"Ready to go, Archman?" Bode smiled at the forlorn figure.

"Sure," he said, but his response was muted. We walked back to Bode's, and hopped in his big truck. Bob sat in the back, although he doesn't particularly like it. Bode claims dogs understand up to 250 words, and can be as smart as a two-year-old. I'm not sure what Bode believes Bob's vocabulary is, but he assures me that Bob isn't hurt when Archie and I trump him and grab the front. I hope he's right.

I had already packed sandwiches, drinks, and cookies, so we went right to the boat. Bode pulled his dinghy, *The Little G,* in on its hauling line, while Archie grabbed the oars in the back of the truck, and hopped in the bow. Bob stepped in adeptly, and positioned himself at Archie's feet. Bode pushed the boat out and I climbed into the stern as he stepped gracefully onto the middle seat and rowed us out. I remember being mesmerized watching oars dip in the water as a little girl. And I still marvel at the graceful half moons made by each dip.

The *Lizzie G* is moored in Record Cove, a little harbor that hosts two beautiful islands. Redmond's Island is officially maintained by a private land trust, but its five acres also receive a lot of attention from locals who go out and clean it up every year. It's always seemed like a microcosm of New England with its small, sandy beach, a meadow, a small growth of trees, and a rocky cliff on one side. Years ago someone rigged an old lobster buoy to two ropes off a low-hanging branch at one end; it's provided countless hours of entertainment for little ones.. The entire island looks as if it's just waiting to be sketched in watercolor.

The smaller Grace Island lies beyond. It is privately-owned, and was populated with cottages decades ago. It changes hands periodically, but no owner has built anything out there—and hopefully never will.

There are about a half dozen lobster boats clustered in the cove. Their names hold a great deal of significance. Traditionally, these boats are given female names to honor mothers, wives, daughters, and girlfriends. But others tell different stories. Among them are *Independence*, *Luna Sea*, and—one of my favorites—*A Loan Again*. Boats like these can easily cost more than a home up here in Maine.

We stepped over the bright red topsides, and into the cockpit. There was a memory of baitfish in the air, but it was more comforting than offensive. Bob looked at the bait buckets, waiting for Bode to load them up and begin their routine, but Bode explained it was Sunday and this was a pleasure cruise. Bob wagged his tail and relaxed. Bode cranked the engine and Archie cast us off, settling himself on the bow for the ride out of the harbor.

It was a day so beautiful it was nearly impossible to decide what to do with it. Reminded of those final days in the fall when you're sure it will be the last warmth you'll feel for months, I feel almost frantic to absorb every bit of nice weather when it comes. I took my place in the seat next to Bode at the helm and we motored out.

"What a tableau. Looks like a Norman Rockwell painting, " I commented.

Bode smiled and out we putted. We took a quick ride around Redmond's Island, then headed back in for a leisurely cruise through Woodford Harbor itself. It's relatively large, and home to about three-hundred boats. These include million-dollar yachts, sturdy lobster boats, One-Design sailboats, prams, and seemingly anything with an engine on its back that will float. Lots of folks were on their boats this morning, either heading out to open water, or sitting lazily at their moorings. It was almost as festive as the dump on Saturday.

Bode called Archie back from his bow seat and we, too, took off across the open ocean. We hoped to find a leeward-facing inlet on one of the small, outer islands that would shelter us from the breeze that was just now picking up.

We found an empty cove, and quickly claimed it for our own. Archie went forward, and dropped the anchor at Bode's direction. Soon we were bobbing quietly among pines and sea gulls, watching the water lap onto the island's rocky beach. Bode grabbed a drop line, and handed it to Archie. "See what you can catch with that, buddy," he said.

The line plunked in and all was very peaceful. Still, there was something unsettling in the air that belied this idyllic feel. We had all just shared in an incident that was way outside our normal boundaries.

Suddenly, Archie jumped up and started pulling his line in. He hauled it in hand over hand until there was a sudden jerk and the line abruptly went slack.

"Damn it!" swore Archie. "It got away!"

Bode gently took the line from his hands, and coiled it on the floor. "Come here, buddy," invited Bode gently. "Let's figure this all out."

With that, Archie started to cry. It was soft at first, but he just kept crying and crying and crying. It was heart-wrenching to watch. Bode engulfed him in his broad reach, and let it run its course. My chest ached for everyone.

Finally, Archie had wrung himself out, and sat back on the bench seat, still huddled next to Bode.

"Oh, honey," I said, unable to contain myself any longer. "What is it that's troubling you, Archie? Bode and I love you; we three are like family. We'll do anything to make this better for you, if we can, but you have to tell us what it is so we can help. We don't know everything, but we're older and sometimes that helps."

Archie gave Bode a long, dismal look. Bode smiled, and quietly drew him closer.

"You are my friend," sputtered Archie at last. His eyes began to well up again and it took him a moment to compose himself. But it was obvious that he was ready to say what was on his mind. "Bode, I love you and you are my friend—my best friend. You do everything for me and I want to be your friend back."

"I know that, buddy. I totally know that."

"Well, you know how Duke is always doing bad things to people? And he seems to do more bad things to you than anyone else. I hate it. I hate that he does bad things to you. And I want to make it right for you. I want him to have something bad happen to him."

"Well, that's not always the right way to see things. Why did you start hitting him so hard when he bumped into me?" asked Bode softly.

"He bumped into you! He bumped into you! And..." And then the real sobbing began. Archie sank further into Bode's arms, sobbing and wailing, seemingly inconsolable. Bode allowed this to continue, but I could tell he feared it would escalate without some intervention. He eventually sat Archie up, and held him at eye level until the latter made eye contact. At last he began to calm down.

"Archie, I want you to tell me what is going on. I want to know. I want to help you. What is it? " said Bode, somewhat harshly.

"I killed that girl! I did it! I went to see Duke; I wanted to get him. I was so upset when I got there that I just kind of shoved my way into the house. This girl was standing there and I pushed her. I don't even know why! I just wanted to get Duke so badly! I was so mad! And then she fell and it was so quiet. So quiet. I figured Duke wasn't there, so I just turned and ran. I was so scared! I didn't mean for anything like that to happen! I'm so sorry!" He collapsed completely then and Bode had to pick him up to get him back on the seat.

He caught his breath, and then continued. "And so I didn't know what to do! I felt so bad about running away like that so after a couple of hours I went back and there she was! Still lying on the floor! I didn't know what to do! I didn't know what to do! I wanted to help her, and make it right. The only thing I could think of was to take her to the funeral home, because that's where dead people go. I picked her up and carried her across the tracks, and put her on Lizzie's table. But it didn't help much! She's dead and I made it happen! Help me, Bode!" he whimpered.

I looked into the distraught eyes of Bode, and felt as though the earth had moved. It was a different place now. And I feared it would never be right again.

CHAPTER TWENTY-NINE

I called Uncle Henry on my cell phone and he was waiting for us on the dock when we came back in. Archie had stopped crying, and was ramrod rigid. His eyes didn't move and his movements were rather spasmodic, as if he didn't have complete control of them. The police car was there with a deputy sheriff driving. Uncle Henry escorted Archie and Bode into the back of the car, and off they went without a word. No siren, just a car full of some of my favorite people on earth going on a very painful ride.

I put Bob in the truck, and drove listlessly back to Bode's. Bob sat up front next to me, looking confused. "What," the poor creature seemed to be thinking, "could possibly have happened in the past two hours that has led to this horrific atmosphere?"

I walked the mile back to my own house in a daze. I was sick with worry for Archie, and felt dreadful for Bode. I knew that somehow this whole thing would have an ending. But what it would be was beyond my imagination.

I put the picnic makings away, and tidied up the kitchen. At moments like this I never know what to do. Time still exists and something has to fill it. But everything I could think of seemed so trivial.

I decided to stick with my plan of cleaning up Thistle's yard, so drove back to Bode's. I put my nervous energy to good use, and started raking up the winter debris. Then I started pulling weeds. If one can pull weeds violently, then I guess that's what I was doing. My bushel basket filled up over and over again with the evil plants until I finally heard "Hey, Good Lookin" on my cell phone. I picked it up, and heard Bode say, "Where are you? I'm on my way home."

"Cleaning up Thistle's garden."

"Be right there."

All the sweat and anxiety made me a less-than-pretty picture when Bode arrived. I didn't want to add to his troubles by being part of the problem, but it took everything I had not to fall into his arms for comfort.

"It's as good as it can be under the circumstances," he told me straight off. "Henry was predictably kind, and is warding off Daniels in whatever ways he can. Rather than have the state police come here, sirens wailing, Henry took Archie to Portland Memorial Hospital for evaluation. Other than being frightened at his unfamiliar surroundings, Archie is being taken care of very well. The Duncans are going to visit, and bring him dinner later.

"According to Henry, the coroner's report hasn't been completed yet, so no charges are being filed. They expect to have the report by late tomorrow and that will determine the next step. If that detective doesn't back off, though, I'm afraid we'll have an assault charge against Henry on our hands." Bode gave me a half smile that comforted me more than any drug could. His wisdom and clear-headed thinking were the best antidotes for what ailed me right now.

In retrospect, Archie's recent behavior started to make some sense. He was so horrified at his unrestrained act of aggression against that poor girl that any human contact imitating it brought the horror back—and frightened him. I now understood his unease at bumping into Karen Duncan and me. His need to prove to Bode what a good friend he was was even more heartbreaking. He had such a big heart, and was being so misunderstood.

We went back to my house and half-heartedly ate the salvaged sandwiches as we talked about vegetable gardens. I happen to agree with Pepper that Brown's Market has an ample assortment of fruits and vegetables, but Bode has always wanted me to plant the latter in my garden. For some reason, I wasn't as annoyed today when he started talking about it for the hundredth time. Finally, he talked himself out.

As Bode drove off after lunch I realized that life was still going on and I had a part to play. Charlie would be home soon and I needed to pick her up and have dinner ready. I pulled into the parking lot at Brown's, and went through the door at the same time as Glenda.

"So, I heard all the news. What next?" she exclaimed. "What a horrible experience for that poor kid. Who am I going to get to bus tables if he's in the slammer?"

I could think of no reasonable response, so said nothing. I wandered the aisles for a bit, finding it hard to focus on dinner. Finally I picked up some chicken and salsa; it was something I could easily throw in the oven with a few Tater Tots.

I rounded the corner to check out just as Trudy came in.

"What a mess," was her commentary on Archie's troubles. "Whatever would my dear sister say?" I had the unnerving feeling that she was actually trying to distance herself from 'the mess.'

Again, I had no reasonable response, so said nothing. My blood pressure, however, was rising by leaps and bounds. How good it would feel to smack the two of them, Glenda *and* Trudy!

Having accomplished my shopping I waited for Charlie outside the high school. She and I had long ago worked out a plan to avoid being smack dab in the center of all the traffic surrounding a mass pickup. It involved me idling a bit outside the immediate zone of greatest activity.

Soon enough, I saw her curls bouncing toward me. A big grin showed on her adorable face. I hated what I had to tell her, and found my eyes filling up as she jumped in the car. She didn't notice as she began her personal news report.

"So we came in second in the whole tournament. We played Saturday, and were undefeated! Undefeated! Then Saturday night we got to go out and have pizza and then frozen yogurt at this awesome place called Orange Leaf! And then we were actually so tired we fell asleep! And then today we played in the semi-finals and lost, but to the really best team in the whole tournament, and then we played the consolation final and won! I played defense the whole time, and just wiggled my stick in every girl's face like crazy! So what's going on here?"

By the time she had concluded her monologue we were home and I had composed myself. I suggested she go upstairs, throw her dirty clothes in the hamper, and shower. We could chat before dinner.

A somewhat winded Charlie finally sat down on the porch swing. She looked at me expectantly. I started the story by relaying the information that the poor deceased girl had been staying at Duke's. It occurred to me she had missed quite a lot during the lacrosse tournament.

"Her name is April, and she was apparently staying with Duke temporarily while she worked at the laundromat," I started.

"The laundromat? No way! I know her! I met her there! She's not much older than me! She's way nice! She's looking for her father or something. She came from some little town in the western part of Massachusetts, near Tanglewood, she said, and…

"Oh no! It can't be her. That's just awful." She stopped and looked at me like a fearful deer frozen in someone's headlights, unable to digest all this information at once. Her mouth remained open, but nothing came out. I sensed I should be hugging her, but her body language spoke otherwise. After a few moments she tried to continue. "But that just can't be right. She can't be dead. She's not that old! And I just saw her! And she was really nice! Please, no…"

I held her, but it wasn't tears that came, just silence. For Charlie, this is indeed rare. "I feel like I should be crying, Mom, but I can't. It's so creepy! I just don't get it. How could that have happened? It's all just not real. Her name is April?" she asked me.

I nodded, and put my hand on her knee. Charlie went on. "She came to find her father. She had always lived with her mother, she said, and they traveled all around the country. She seemed different from anyone I had ever met, and said she felt at home working at the laundromat. She told me she was sleeping there, too, although Mr. Nelson didn't know it. That seemed really scary to me, but she appeared okay with it. She said her mother had died of cancer right after Christmas and she had been staying with her Aunt Martha since then. They lived near Tanglewood—you know, where we went last summer for those concerts—and I told her I knew where it was.

"She wanted to find her father, and was sure he was here in Woodford Harbor. Oh ick, this is so gross. I feel so badly. I feel sick. But I don't feel like crying! What's wrong with me?"

"Honey, you're fine. You didn't really know the girl and it seems unnatural to you to have someone so close to your own age die. It's very different when it's someone's grandparents or an elderly aunt. Just try to take some big breaths, and slow down. We'll figure this out," I assured her, feeling totally unequipped to do so.

"Tell me again what you know," I encouraged. She repeated the information in a different sequence, but with identical facts. I left her to straighten it all out in her mind as best she could, and went inside to call Uncle Henry.

When he answered I began, "Uncle Henry, Charlie just got home and told me she knew this girl April from the laundromat." I repeated what Charlie had shared, and was surprised to hear a sigh from the other end of the phone.

"So you want me to call Daniels, and tell him that Charlie says the deceased came from somewhere in western Massachusetts, has an Aunt Martha, and thinks her biological father lives in Woodford Harbor?" he snorted. "Lizzie dear, he would laugh me out of the state. We need more than that to go on."

I was indignant. "What are you talking about? Don't you want to find out about this poor girl, and what happened to her? This took place in our own town and it feels almost dirty to me! It's terrible! We owe it to this poor young thing to find a proper family to inform. She needs people to care about her, and give her short life some meaning. Someone needs to step up to the plate and at least give her a dignified end. I might just drive out there myself! I'm disappointed in you," I fumed.

"Lizzie, this is a Jane Doe who happened to end up here in Woodford Harbor. I can't get emotionally involved in every case that crosses my desk. You are free to do any investigating you like, but I am not going to offer this piecemeal bit of information to Daniels."

I hung up feeling about as self-righteous as a single, white, 39-year-old female can. Somehow, the added information that the girl's name was April, and that my Charlie had made her acquaintance, personalized this for me. A very real part of who I am is dedicated to making the endings of peoples' lives dignified. If April's life had ended in Woodford Harbor, she became my responsibility and I wanted to do right by her.

CHAPTER THIRTY

It wasn't until I was helping myself to a second helping of Tater Tots that it hit me. "Charlie," I began, "what were you doing at the laundromat?"

A stricken look crossed her face. It was the second time that day that I felt the earth move. This was a quiver compared to the last quake, but it was movement nonetheless. "Oh, yeah. Yeah. Yeah, that's right. I guess I was there washing some clothes."

I did no more than raise an eyebrow.

"So I had been at this place that was really smoky and smelly and I didn't think you would want those clothes in our washing machine."

"Charlie, where would you be that is smoky and smelly?"

"Well," she chirped, "well…"

"Charlie—"

"Well, me and Susie and Judy all wanted to hear the new country band that was playing down at Indian Flats—the Horse Whips. We really, really wanted to hear them so we went in and didn't even drink beer! We just really wanted to hear them!"

"You know you don't belong in a place like that! The beer drinking isn't the only problem in that kind of place! Who knows who might follow you out? What could happen to the three of you? Charlie, that is a big lack of good judgment on your part. I'm surprised at Susie, but I imagine it was Judy who put you up to it."

Charlie's face blushed crimson and I had my answer to that question as well.

"Well, that's it for the three of you going out by yourselves. Big mistake, young lady. I want you to think about this for the next two weeks while you are going nowhere."

I had just finished delivering this proclamation when Bode stepped into the room, probably looking for dessert. "What goes on here?"

I explained Charlie's infraction, and was not pleased with the expression on his face. Rather than stern disapproval I thought I saw a shadow of a smile.

"The Horse Whips! They're a real up-and-coming band," he said to Charlie.

"That is not the point!" I interjected. "Sneaking off with two little girlfriends to a place like that, then going over to the laundromat and secretly washing clothes—I don't like any of this. Charlie, go on upstairs. I'll do the dishes."

She scrambled upstairs like a trapped squirrel suddenly released from a cage. Bode's face still had a suspect expression.

"You just don't know what it's like to be a parent," I began.

"No, but I was sixteen, and that sounds pretty normal to me." I scooped him a bowl of ice cream, and scrubbed dishes until I felt I could go in and watch the Red Sox and be civil. There wasn't much chitchat. What had begun as a joyful homecoming had suddenly turned unpleasant.

"Do you seriously not understand why I am so worried?" I shot at Bode in the middle of the sixth inning.

"No, seriously, I can't. Get off your high horse, and think about where you were when you were sixteen. What were you up to that was so terribly wholesome and perfect? She went to a bar, and didn't even drink! And she washed her clothes at a laundromat to get away with it? You are seriously overreacting to a dumb little incident. Do you want Charlie to tell you each and every little thing she does? Get over it! She's a great kid with some spirit! You'd better start giving her some space or it will not go well when she hits eighteen, and wants more than just Woodford Harbor in her life! It won't be so bad for her, but you had better be careful."

I opened my mouth to speak but Bode was up and saying good night. "I'm going into Portland tomorrow morning to spend the day with Archie. When that coroner's report comes out we need to be ready." And he was gone.

The earth moved yet again. It wasn't the harsh delivery of Bode's words that hurt, it was their validity. It all left me reeling. When I was sixteen— well, actually seventeen, but close enough—I was selling fake IDs. I had perfected the doctoring of Maine drivers' licenses, and could alter the year of birth so well I ought to have been on the FBI's most-wanted list. Of course I knew Charlie was growing up. But did that mean she had to lie and deceive me?

Perhaps I'm being a little harsh, but the bond between the two of us is almost magical to me. I can't imagine any other mother and daughter having this kind of connection. Okay, maybe that's a bit foolish, but in my world it feels that way. It needs to be controlled, monitored, and treated with the utmost care, but on the other hand I suppose I must do my part to let her go—and trust that she will return for a lifetime of memories. It's easier said than done; frankly, I was done with this day, and just wanted to go to sleep. Red Sox and Tampa tied in the eighth? Sorry, they'd have to slug out the last inning without me. Good night.

CHAPTER THIRTY-ONE

The next day began very early. I was on my way to Bode's house before the sun peeked up over the horizon. He heard the squeak of the gate, and was ready with the covers drawn back before I made it to the second floor. We made up in the universal fashion. By the time I slipped into the water for my seven o'clock swim I had already had a superlative day.

The sky was quickly becoming overcast, though, and it gave me an ominous feeling. I was scheduled to meet with the Arthur girls, and was anxious about delivering my news. If a carnivore eats meat, I thought, and a vegetarian eats veggies, then what does one call a creature that ingests metal? A metaletarian? I don't know, but the bad joke brought a smile to my lips. Following the meeting I was going to meet with Mr. Stanley, then head out to western Massachusetts. To do what, I wasn't entirely certain, but I had to do something.

I hopped in the outdoor shower, rinsed myself, and dried off, then pulled on rather nice black pants and a shirt fresh from the dry cleaner's. This was dressy for me. I wasn't completely certain where I would go, and with whom I would meet today, but I figured it was best to err on the side of looking professional.

A subdued Charlie came down for breakfast. We were both a bit uncomfortable. I gave her an almost imperceptible nod and she moved to sit down beside me on the couch. I put my hand on her knee.

"Honey, I'm sorry I was so upset last night. I will say that I don't like the idea of you three girls going to Indian Flats by yourselves and I will also say that I find it worrisome when you hide things from me. That being said, I think a combination of things upset me more than usual. The whole April thing has me a bit unhinged. I was the one who discovered her, and now I find out you had met her. I'm really glad you told me about meeting her. I want to find out as much as I can about her—and her life before she came here.

"I'm going to drive out to western Massachusetts today to find out all I can, using the information you gave me. It's a three-hour drive and I think I may well end up staying overnight. Would it be all right if I call Pepper to see if you two can have dinner together? And you would spend the night with her. I realize I said you were grounded last night, but I guess that's lifted when it interferes with my life." We both smiled.

"I thought of one more thing last night, Mom. April told me she had found her real father, but said she wasn't sure how much it really mattered. She seemed pleased that she had found him, but also kind of sad and disappointed that it didn't include the new family she had hoped for. She also said that some woman in town had befriended her, and came in to chat sometimes. I just feel so sad."

"Well, Peanut, we'll do our best to care for her now," I reassured her. I slathered butter on a toasted English muffin, handed it to her, and we were off to school.

I put a call in to Pepper to explain what I was doing. She seemed pleased to have Charlie for the night. It seemed everyone wanted to do something to help. I decided some breakfast might settle the rumbling in my stomach, and headed for The Driftwood.

The first thing that caught my eye as I approached was a beautiful bow of thick white ribbon hanging on the front door. Entering, I noticed the usual buzz had been replaced with low murmurings and hushed voices. Even Pepper was quiet. I sat down at her table, and waited for Jenny to come over.

"What's that beautiful white bow for?" I inquired.

"We put it on there for Archie. We're all so worried about him, and can't believe what's happening. It's so hard. We all want to do something, but there really is nothing we can do right now. Putting up the ribbon in his honor makes us all feel better," explained Carly. "Our dear Archie. I think something like this brings home the fact that we are all one big extended family of sorts," she went on. "Tommy and Glenda and I, Jenny, Archie, everyone who comes in here every day. I remember reading one time that family isn't who you share blood with, but who you care about. Archie's a very important part of our world."

"That's all true and it certainly comes to the fore at a time like this," I agreed. "This whole, terrible incident happened in *our* town, our very own town. It affects all of us in different ways, but I think it's changed the complexion of Woodford Harbor. A young girl came here, found shelter and a job, and was murdered. Although we're not all responsible for this atrocity, we're still a part of it. I think it's time to start thinking about this young girl, April. We need to take care of her as well.

"I'm trying to find out where she came from so I can inform anyone who needs to know. If no one steps forward to offer a final celebration of her short life, I think we all owe her that. Shouldn't we include April in our thoughts as well as we look at that white bow? Maybe we should hang these white bows around town as a sign of support for Archie and respect for April."

"I know!" said Carly. "We can put white bows on our front bumpers, too! It would be so meaningful to see every car with a big white bow on the front."

"Well, I'm afraid it might be lost on my white Mercedes," remarked Trudy. A collective sigh went through the room.

Overall, though, I felt our great little town was rising in unison to do an honorable thing.

"Bode has driven down to Portland to be with Archie today. The Duncans went down last night to see him."

"Yes," piped Trudy from the corner table. "They called when they got home, and said he was in relatively good spirits, considering." Again there was a silence in the room that spoke volumes. Trudy was Archie's mother's sister. Why wasn't she going down to be with him? To take care of him when he needed family most? Carly's definition of family hung in the air. This seemed to be a judgmental moment shared by everyone in The Driftwood.

"I'll go down to the crafts store, and buy all the white ribbon they have," offered Carly. "I can also order more online. I'll drop some off here, and you can come by my house to pick up the rest. The word should travel fast."

And so the great White Bow Show began in Woodford Harbor. Even Bob was sporting one before the end of the day!

CHAPTER THIRTY-TWO

I walked to the funeral home with a feeling of resignation, knowing I had to get through the meeting with Mrs. Arthur's daughters before I could begin the day's bigger adventure. Sure enough, they were all seated in the small living room off the front door. In silence, I noticed. I smiled, and invited them into my office.

Mr. Stanley arrived, and offered coffee. More as a distraction than from thirst, I gratefully accepted. Each daughter sat on the edge of her seat. Meg began.

"We have each started on our part of Mother's memorial service. I'm not sure how we will work it all into a cohesive program, though."

I interrupted before she could expand. "If you each give me what you have I can pull it all together," I told them. "But there is something else we need to discuss first. I went down to Portland, and spoke with the nurse on duty the night your mother passed away. She was very kind, and told me she was with your mother at the end, and that she had had a peaceful passing." I don't know why I was so comfortable with this blatant lie, but I didn't see any benefit to report otherwise, and there is seldom any quarrel from the deceased.

"However," I continued, "there was a rather extraordinary circumstance surrounding the pearl ring. The nurse had noticed your mother frequently twisting the ring on her finger, but did not recall seeing it when she packed your mother's possessions. She shared a hunch with me when I informed her it was missing and I came back here and followed up. Her instinct was correct. I removed the ring from your mother's stomach unharmed. She apparently swallowed it moments before her passing."

You could have cut the air with a knife at that moment. I waited for Miranda to start crying, or for Meg to let loose an angry one-liner. Instead, Josie was speechless, as were her sisters. Then I heard what sounded like a small chortle from Josie. She put her face down, but couldn't seem to contain herself. I suddenly found myself attempting to choke back a laugh, though not entirely successfully. Then I looked up and saw a small smile spreading across Meg's face. It wasn't long before Miranda looked around, and fell into the mood enveloping the room.

The giggles expanded to a collection of chuckles, which soon became uproarious laughter. I knew that much of it was probably compounded by nervous energy, but laugh we did. No one seemed capable of—nor wanted to—stop. Although it was the very last thing I had expected, it was preferable to what I had anticipated. The absurdity of old Mrs. Arthur's final act was just ludicrous and it felt good to acknowledge it.

A somewhat shocked Mr. Stanley entered the room with a pot of coffee and a tray with cups, sugar, and cream. He laid it on the coffee table, and scurried out. After catching our collective breaths, we served ourselves, and sat back with a fresh attitude.

"I am sure I can work with what you ladies have put together," I said. "Each of you has a different perspective, of course, and that's as it should be, as you are grown women who experienced your mother in a variety of ways. The memorial service details have been included in her obituary, so by Wednesday everyone should know the place and time. I'll lead the service, and let each of you know when it's your turn to present your portion. May I see what you've put together for the program?"

Josie handed me the program outline I had given her, filled in neatly with all her mother's information. There was a recent, dignified photo of Mrs. Arthur on the cover, with the gardening quotation I had suggested earlier.

Miranda spoke up. "I contacted members of Mom's garden club. They were so pleased with the idea of having the service in her garden, and offered to go over and spruce it up on Wednesday morning. Two of the ladies offered to place gardening sayings on stakes throughout the garden to inspire people. And Gloria, Mom's very best friend, asked if she could do a short eulogy. Of course I thanked her, and agreed. I have chosen two hymns, if that's all right. It might seem a cliché, but I think everyone is familiar with *Amazing Grace*; we could sing it at the end."

"Miranda, just because "Amazing Grace" is sung so often at funerals does not mean it's trite," I said. "Quite the opposite, it is timeless and lovely. What else are you thinking?"

"Well, I love "In the Garden.""

"How does it go?" asked Josie.

Miranda hummed a few bars and sang the refrain:

And he walks with me
And he talks with me
And He tells me I am His own
And the joy we share
As we tarry there
None other has ever known

Miranda choked up at this point. I was pleased to see Josie put a comforting hand on her arm.

"I'm still trying to find a nice piece of poetry, but I haven't found just the right one yet," said Meg.

"I had a thought that might be nice if we could do it," offered Josie. "I'm not sure how it's done, but I think you can take a small clipping from a plant, and then put it in water or dirt to replicate the original. Do you think we could do that with some of Mom's plants? We could give the cuttings to people as they leave. It would certainly keep her garden alive."

"Josie, that's so nice!" exclaimed Miranda. "Let me talk to the ladies in the garden club. I bet they'll love it! Oh, that's so nice!" Her eyes gleamed and Josie looked pleased as punch.

"One more thing that might personalize the service and include your Mother's spirit," I suggested, "would be to attach photos of her during all stages of her life to a large board. There could be photos from her early days, and others that include her with your father and you girls as you were growing up. It would evoke memories from many facets of her life, and give them the significance they deserve."

"Oh, what fun that would be," Meg said. "Let's meet at Mom's this afternoon, and go through all her old photos. They're in the big drawer next to the candle drawer in the dining room."

I left the three of them with their heads together, quite satisfied. I felt as happy as a seagull with a French fry. Families don't always pull together at a time like this, but if the base is strong enough it can be very rewarding and a memorable experience for everyone. The garden seemed to be working its magic on those ladies.

I stopped downstairs and Mr. Stanley and I finalized the details of Mrs. Arthur's journey to the crematorium. I told him of my plans to head out to western Massachusetts, and he was, of course, both kind and supportive of my mission.

"That's a lovely thing to do, Miss G. I wish you all the luck and I'm sure you will have news upon your return. You do so often defy the odds," he said.

I left feeling energized and positive. I stopped at the house, and grabbed a toothbrush, underwear, a fresh white shirt, and a brush, then poured a jug of ice tea, and grabbed an unopened bag of Pepperidge Farm Geneva cookies. At the last minute I threw in a bottle of red wine, and a corkscrew. Now I was ready for anything. My last stop was at Pepper's to drop off some things for Charlie.

"I just can't decide what to serve that sweet girl tonight," said Pepper. "I know girls her age are munching salads all the time like little rabbits, but that just doesn't qualify as dinner to me. I see her so seldom that I want it to be a big event that she'll remember. Oh my, this godmother thing is exhausting! I'll try to serve something wholesome."

"Pepper, what are those words coming out of your mouth? Put your brain back in gear, and do something fun. *That*'s who you are, and I'm afraid that's exactly what Charlie loves best about you!"

Pepper seemed both pleased and reassured. "Yes," she said. "Right you are."

I wondered what would be in store for Charlie tonight.

CHAPTER THIRTY-THREE

It was an overcast day that seemed in keeping with the tiresome three-hour drive ahead of me. Southern Maine and Massachusetts are pretty enough country, but you don't see much of it driving seventy-five miles per hour on highways.

I picked up the Mass Pike in Boston, and headed west to Stockbridge. I cannot look at a sign pointing to Stockbridge without replaying James Taylor's line from "Sweet Baby James—'from Stockbridge to Boston...' It thrills me to be traveling the same iconic route.

I worried about dear Archie for a good forty miles, then included Charlie, poor April, what Bode's catch was like today, what Pepper might be having for dinner, and what shoes Trudy was sporting today. These weren't so much the problems of the world, but the personal issues surrounding *my* world. Before I knew it, I was close to Beckett and the highest elevation on the turnpike. Knowing it was a full 1,724 feet above sea level had always excited me as a child and I'm glad to report it still does. After that it was an easy cruise to Exit 2 in Lee.

I had mapped out the funeral homes closest to Tanglewood, and arranged them geographically. I had to start somewhere. I assumed April's mother had had a funeral, and hoped to find the home where it was held. It was how my mind worked.

Once in Lee, I found a McDonald's and treated myself to a diet Coke and a small cheeseburger. My stomach was so full of cookies at this point that I just needed something on top to calm it down. The burger was just the trick. I freshened up in the ladies room, and then there was nothing to do but start my search.

I quickly found the funeral home in Lee. A woman invited me inside when I rang the outside bell. She was comfort personified— short and buxom, with a belted floral dress hugging her spacious hips, and glasses dangling from a ribbon. I wondered momentarily if I could hire her away; I always worried that my own appearance wasn't quite right for my position. Hers was perfect. Then again, if I ate many more cookies, I would have her girth in a month.

I introduced myself, adding that I, too, ran a funeral home. I hoped it would give me some credibility, but that all but disappeared when I explained that my deceased had been living in a laundromat. The look on the poor woman's face was telling, but it didn't stop me. Continuing my story, I ended with my final *Jeopardy* question: "Has this funeral home hosted any funerals around Christmas with an Aunt Martha involved?"

She smiled slightly, shook her head no, and got up to see me out. I realized then that perhaps a Cliff Notes version of my story would give me a better outcome.

I drove a short way up the road to Lenox, and drove by the Tanglewood grounds. The Boston Symphony Orchestra summers in this lovely spot, giving concerts from a large wooden shed surrounded by acres of beautiful green lawn. To experience Tanglewood properly, I—like many others—have found that a picnic on the lawn, stretched out on a blanket, and listening to the concert is topnotch. Some folks bring chairs, tables, and candelabra for their picnics. It looks quite grand, but cold chicken and wine from a box works well for me. There were cars scattered across the parking lot and I could almost hear the violins tuning up. It seemed a shame to have come all this way and not hear a concert. I sighed, made a U-turn, and headed back to Lenox.

A large, beautiful Victorian housed the next funeral home. A barrel-chested, white-haired gentleman ushered me in. He was perfectly nice, but had either no wife to tell him when he'd overdone the aftershave, or no olfactory senses to notice on his own. I abbreviated my story—but struck out again.

I drove up Route 7 to Pittsfield, and called on four more funeral homes, all to no avail. Heading south, I arrived in Great Barrington around 4:30 that afternoon, giving me enough time to check in with one of the five funeral homes there. The news was no more helpful so I dragged myself to what I hoped was a quaint motel, and checked in.

If your definition of 'quaint' is brown shag carpeting, shiny, slippery bed spreads, a paper shower mat, and a plastic drinking cup wrapped in Saran Wrap, then this would be your kind of place. After a cursory inspection I knew this was not a spot where I would enjoy drinking my red wine. I'm not terribly fussy about where I imbibe, but I do have scruples about where I sleep.

Down the road a bit, I found a small restaurant that, from the Leaning Tower of Pisa on its sign, appeared to be Italian. Numerous cars filled the parking area, which I found reassuring. It seemed reasonable to expect a menu of multiple pasta shapes and a good wine selection. I turned in, and shut off the car.

As I pulled my phone from my bag to check in with Charlie, it indicated I had a call. I felt a rush of happiness that had been lacking the entire day. "Bode, how's everything?" I smiled into the phone.

"Oh, Z, best news ever! The coroner finally released his report a few minutes ago and the cause of death for our poor girl had nothing to do with the bump on her head. She had ingested some kind of poison. I didn't think the bump did it, but it doesn't hurt to have a hunch verified. Archie is being released from the hospital right now and I'm taking him home. He's taken a beating from this whole debacle, but I think he'll be fine when he's back on his own turf and around all the people who love him. He's a strong little guy. I sure wish you were here to hug!"

"I am, Bode. I'm giving you a giant hug this very minute. Pass one along to Archie, too. After a long day of dead ends this is awesome news. I think I may have bitten off more than I can chew in this venture, but I feel good knowing I'm doing everything I can."

"What's been going on?" asked Bode.

I gave him a recap of the day's drive, along with its disappointments.

"Keep going, kiddo. You've eliminated quite a few prospects, but the funeral had to happen somewhere. Keep on truckin'!" urged my dear Bode.

"I stopped by to see Mom," he added. "She was in good spirits, and had a grand old time with 'the girls' yesterday. They're all agog about one of their granddaughters getting married. I tell you, those ladies overflow with romance!

"It's funny, but at one point Mom started reminiscing about how long you and I have known each other. She recounted the day she was so angry at me for throwing a stone at you, and hitting you over the eye."

"Ha! And I still have the scar to prove it, my friend! She was plenty mad at you that day, but you were only a little boy doing boyish things—like taunting girls. It might well be the most angry I have ever seen her."

"I'm sure I've done worse things, but she either doesn't know about them, or holds you in pretty high esteem. Anyway, I'll let you go. Hope you can at least salvage a pleasant evening out of this trip."

"Thanks. I'll try. I'm about to have some Italian food, and a gallon or two of red wine. Thanks so much for calling. Really, do give my love to the Archman!"

"Will do. Sleep well, Z."

"Thanks," I answered, hating to disconnect the line.

A few minutes later, I called Charlie.

"Hey, Mom!" She picked up on the first ring of her little cell phone. "I'm at Pepper's. She was making this eggplant thing when I got here, but I think she maybe saw that I wasn't too into it so now we're going across the street to The Old Port. It's just so cool that she lives right here in the middle of everything! Pepper just heard about Archie, by the way. Isn't that just the best! It's so nice he'll be home and everyone will start leaving him alone. Whew!"

"Good, honey," I offered in response to her latest monologue. "I should be back before you get out of school tomorrow. Take care, and sleep well!"

"Nighty night, Mommy." Ah, she did remember to whom she was talking.

CHAPTER THIRTY-FOUR

With all the cars in the parking lot of The Leaning Tower, I hoped it was a sign the food would be pretty good. As it turned out, it was.

I pulled out a stool at the end of the bar, and slid in. The TV was on and the five other patrons at the bar made my own entrance less noticeable. They looked like they had all known each other for a collective 175 years. When feeling insecure about entering a new group, I always think, 'There's nothing wrong with me. There's nothing wrong with me,' until I am proven otherwise by some horrific breach of etiquette. Usually, though, I hold my own pretty well.

The bartender ambled toward me, wiping the bar in circular motions in the ancient tradition of bartenders. He looked as though he might have been wiping that bar with the same movements—and the same towel—since Richard Nixon resigned. I made eye contact with him and, with my most winning smile, asked, "What's your best red wine by the glass?"

"We only have one," was the reply.

"Well then, by definition that must be the best! I'll have a glass," I chirped. I didn't think we were hitting it off as well as I had hoped. But then, with one swing of the bat, the great equalizer descended on the group as Big Papi smacked a resounding single, scoring Dustin Pedroia. We all cheered. "I think that's his fourteenth single of the year," I observed somewhat loudly. "He must be hitting over .300 now!"

This astute observation immediately raised my status, and made me one of the guys.

We all looked on as Napoli advanced Papi to third base with a double to right, then Brock Holt did it again by smashing a three-run homer. The four runs had everyone laughing and drinking like there was not another event going on in the world. I loved it. Three consecutive fly balls ended the inning, but the elation still hung in the air.

Three of the five fellows at the bar were together, having just come from their lawn maintenance jobs judging from their T-shirts and grass stains. The oldest one seemed to be the leader of the pack, and was already tanned by the sun even though it was only early spring. The two younger men had clearly just been hired; their bodies wore the scorched look of those who hadn't yet spent much time in the sun. They seemed to be having a great time and I almost envied them their upcoming summer together. Mowing lawns, trimming hedges, and pulling weeds in the beautiful outdoors—followed by a few beers and the Red Sox at night—sounded idyllic.

The man to my immediate right introduced himself as Alex, an assistant minister at the local Congregational church. A guy at the far end of the bar cheered along with us, but his closest companion seemed to be his beer.

Alex and I traded facts and statistics about the Red Sox until we were each satisfied that the other was worthy of further conversation. Alex had lived in Great Barrington for about five years, and was engaged to a local teacher. They were as happy as could be, he said; his only nagging worry was that he might be transferred to another church. I often wonder how people live satisfying lives when they're beholden to someone or something else's whims or needs. I wouldn't do well if someone had the power to make me move from a place I wanted to be. How do people work for other people? Give them that power? I stopped before my inner monologue became an hour-long tirade. This man's quandary was not my hill to die on. He's the one who had signed on with the church so he knew the possibility of being moved around. Different strokes for different folks, I say.

I turned my attention back to the Red Sox, and my dinner order. Fettuccini alfredo? Lasagna? Spaghetti and meatballs? What would it be? I smiled at the bartender, and ordered the chicken parmigiana. With it I ordered a second house red, then turned my attention to Alex. He enquired what I was doing in Great Barrington, and it occurred to me suddenly that he might be helpful. I retold the shortened version of my story, and ended with my quest to find the funeral home that had dealt with the burial of a single mother with a sister named Martha.

"Those are rather sketchy details," smiled Alex. "It doesn't ring a bell with me. Who have you seen so far?" I listed the funeral homes in Lee and Lenox, and then the one I had visited in Great Barrington. I told him the others I hoped to visit tomorrow.

He shook his head, and agreed I was covering all the bases. "There is one other avenue you might pursue," he suggested. "Just outside Great Barrington there's a group promoting green cemeteries, and educating the public about them. Bodies there are not embalmed, or buried in caskets with liners. They are instead placed in an environmentally-friendly casket or wrapped in a fine linen, and left in the earth to decompose naturally, giving nutrients back to nature.

"As no monuments are erected, and only natural vegetation is allowed," he continued, "these cemeteries actually become conservation land. A GPS system allows relatives and others to locate exact burial plots, but the open space is left to be enjoyed by all. This group also officiates at burials, so they might know something."

"I've heard of that idea," I said. "There are some good points in their favor, but it's a hard sell. So few people in our country think in advance about dying that death—when it comes—is often a great shock. I try to encourage people to at least consider what they might want when they pass on, but it's an uphill battle.

"Because I'm a funeral director it's especially difficult for me to encourage individuals to think ahead. When I do they think I'm greedy; the consummate salesperson looking to make a personal killing—oops, sorry about the pun!—off someone's death. I pride myself on being as helpful as possible when people are grieving, but it's so hard to watch them struggle with all the details when a simple letter from the deceased might have eliminated all the difficulties. And if I were to suggest putting their loved one in the ground in a bag of linen? You can imagine the reaction I'd get to that, can't you? No, a lot more needs to be done before this idea catches on."

Our conversation was interrupted by the arrival of my enormous platter of chicken parm. We each ordered another glass of wine, and half-heartedly looked up at the TV screen. Just as I was finishing Alex handed me a napkin with writing on it.

"This is the name and address of a woman who belongs to our church; she's active in the green movement. If the person you're seeking was a rolling stone living on the edge, this might have been her cup of tea. I wish you luck. Let me know if I can be of any additional help."

I leaned across the stool separating us, and spontaneously gave him a hug. Our eyes met and I knew I had connected with an honorable man who seemed to be in just the right business.

CHAPTER THIRTY-FIVE

I drove back to the motel carefully, well aware that I had consumed three glasses of wine. Three *small* glasses, but three
glasses nonetheless. I was grateful for my full stomach and the
aforementioned wine; they made me tired enough to fall right to
sleep without having to contemplate the hideous bed linens. At
the first peek of light I was up and out of that bed, showering in
the tinny little shower stall with foamless soap, drying off with a
towel that spread the water rather than absorbed it, and cursing
the hair dryer that didn't work. I checked out feeling damp and a
bit slimy.

Breakfast improved my mood: I was lucky to find a great diner
serving good hash browns with over-easy eggs done to perfection.
The iced tea was marginal; as a connoisseur of the beverage, I am
quite discriminating. Actually, I might well be more persnickety
about my iced tea than my red wine. To my mind, though, no one
can top The Driftwood in that category.

I sat in the parking lot, and checked in by phone with Charlie
and Bode. Both seemed to have survived my absence, but I was

almost sure I heard something in their voices that implied they were looking forward to my return.

I backed out of the diner parking lot, and set my GPS to the next funeral home. That little purple line on the tiny cell phone screen gave excellent directions and before long I had arrived at my destination. This one was of English Tudor design, and was surrounded by perfectly manicured shrubs, a sculpted stone walkway, and matching light fixtures at the front door. The latter looked as though they had come directly from an English castle. I rang the bell, and was quickly welcomed by a gentlemen dressed more like a caricature of a funeral director than the real thing. I was quick to judge that we most likely had very little in common.

I gave a more abbreviated version of the already abridged account of my story, and was soon on my way. With just two more funeral homes on my list, I was getting discouraged and feeling rather foolish. The next home was a low concrete block building with dying brown shrubs around its perimeter. The bell was answered in a few minutes by a somewhat disheveled man. He appeared to be in his fifties, but might well have had a hard life and be only in his forties. The entryway was tiled with beige linoleum squares similar in design to those that had been in our church Sunday school classes many years ago. My host invited me to have a seat on a plastic chair and I once again launched into my story. His blank look made me wonder if he had fully absorbed the information. Certainly a single mother with a sister named Martha should ring a bell if this funeral home was the big winner.

Starting to feel like Goldilocks, I followed the little purple line to the final address, where I was met with a Mama Bear version of the three businesses. Again, no luck.

It was now almost noon. I remembered the napkin with the name and phone number Alex had given me. Should I venture into that world of green and sustainable death, or just grab a Whopper for my troubles and head home? I had read extensively about the green movement in the industry, and decided finally that this might be a good opportunity to investigate it a bit. The name on the napkin was Joyce Dingle. I punched the 10-digit number into my phone. A breathy voice answered, "Martha's Vitamin Books."

"Vitamin Books?" was all that came out of my mouth.

"Yes, dear, we sell books and vitamins—all the essentials for a successful life on this planet. Can I help you?"

"Two things," I said. "Are you Joyce Dingle and is Martha there?"

"Yes, I am, and Martha should be in shortly. Would you like to drop by? It would be lovely to meet you," she gushed.

"And where might you be?" I enquired.

"17 East Street," came the reply.

"Thank you," I said. "I'll be there shortly." It's lucky that the name Martha had popped up because I had momentarily had one foot on the accelerator and had set the GPS for home.

East Street was a short dead end off what served as the main street in Great Barrington. The shop was hidden in shadows, but I could discern a faded green awning and window boxes full of coleus plants. A small wooden sign identified the establishment. I went in.

I identified Miss Air Breath, aka Joyce Dingle, immediately. Emerging from the shadows, she had thinning, long, grey hair, a face mottled with mysterious discolorations, and lips painted mauve. A flowered linen dress hung loosely over her shapeless body. She was, of course, drinking tea and holding a well-worn book that could either have been moss green or—more likely—a bit moldy. The interior smelled of old books. Dusty old books.

Her face brightened and she welcomed me enthusiastically. My hard heart wondered when a stranger had last wandered into these quarters. Books on leaning shelves lined the right side of the room while plastic shelves at the back held rows and rows of Vitamin jars. I was underwhelmed, but stepped forward nonetheless and introduced myself, referencing Alex and her involvement with green funerals.

She was off in a heartbeat, describing and endorsing the latter as the only humane way to treat death. It seems the more marginal an idea, the more adamant its believers are. Finally I was able to interject that I was, myself, a funeral director. She looked at me as though I was promoting E-books in a bookstore, and caught her breath. She did not, however, stop talking.

Blessedly, the front door opened and another woman entered. I hoped it was Martha. Sure enough, she introduced herself as Martha Campbell, and suggested we all have a seat on a small sofa and chair near the front window. Martha appeared to be a cleaned-up, articulate version of Joyce. She had the same long grey hair, but it was pulled back neatly in a bun and her long, trim body suggested a life of exercise supplemented with Vitamins rather than dependent on them. She also wore flowered linen, but it was worn as a long skirt with a pretty white peasant blouse on top. She wore half glasses of a beautiful periwinkle color that accentuated her striking blue eyes and rosy cheeks. Martha poured each of us a mug of tea, offered brown sugar and milk, then sat back and relaxed.

Joyce took the lead, still assuming I had come to learn about green funerals. I listened to the familiar introduction about its environmental merits and the evil of conventional burials. After a bit, however, I interrupted and explained the real reason for my visit.

"I'm from Woodford Harbor, Maine," I began, "and I'm looking for a person in the area who might know a young girl named—"

"April," interrupted Martha. "How is April? I have been so concerned, but really had no way of contacting her. I'm afraid I'm somewhat technically challenged. Dear April."

I'm afraid the look on my face delivered the initial blow to this poor woman. I explained the story as far as I knew it, hating every minute of my soliloquy. Martha was stone grey by the time I finished, and crumbled into a heap in her own lap, sobbing. I wished then that I had stayed in Woodford Harbor. I would be picking Charlie up from school just about now.

CHAPTER THIRTY-SIX

Intellectually, I realized I was having a Sherlock Holmes 'Aha!' moment. I had tracked down the mysterious Aunt Martha, but was not at all pleased with myself for having to deliver such heartbreaking news. Joyce Dingle immediately began cooing and hovering over poor Martha. I wanted to swat her away, but held back. After a time Martha quieted down, and over a cup of some other kind of unusual tea I explained all I knew about April. As I related the story, I sensed that Martha had been unsettled about April's quest from the beginning.

"April's mother, Sarah, was my younger sister," she began. "We were born and raised here in Great Barrington, but she always wanted to see what else was out in the world. Jason and Georgia—we called our parents by their first names—passed away in a freak accident while hunting for rare mushrooms and smoking marijuana in the woods. Sarah and I were still in our late teens.

Our parents, you see, were hippies who had settled here as farmers. They wanted to work the land. Sarah and I were largely left to take care of ourselves; we both survived in our separate ways.

It was just the two of us and, though we stayed in touch, I wouldn't describe our relationship as terribly close. Sarah got her degree in nursing, which enabled her to move whenever she pleased and secure a job to support herself. I was content to stay here while she took off."

I considered calling my parents Ken and Mildred, but it didn't feel at all right. I felt both appalled by and sympathetic toward these two women.

"Sarah got her degree in Portland, at the Maine Medical Center. She worked hard, but I think she played equally hard. In the early nineties she moved out to the West Coast; she never even stopped here on her way. One day I received a surprising letter, one that included a photo of her 10-month-old daughter, April. She claimed all was well and that was it. I usually spoke with her at Christmas, and she always called on my birthday. It seemed to suit both our needs and life went on."

Joyce rose to assist a pregnant woman looking for Vitamins to reduce her morning sickness. I mentally wished her well, but speculated that Kate Middleton was probably getting better advice with *her* pregnancy.

Martha sighed, and went on. "Last summer, Sarah called. She explained that she had cancer, and wondered if she could come home. I agreed—not without some hesitation, mind you—but when she arrived the bond that sisters have was still there. I was grateful she had come. April, of course, came with her. The two of us shared the responsibilities of taking care of Sarah and we grew quite close. She is…was…a very sweet soul. She was also a bit ungrounded, I'm afraid; something that no doubt came from her somewhat nomadic lifestyle."

Joyce returned, and took up where Martha had left off. "We had a lovely service for Sarah and she is now in the Barrington Green Cemetery. It was…"

"Not now, Joyce dear," said Martha. "Her death made some logical sense, sad as it was. But April…"

Martha began to get weepy again. She looked at me through teary eyes and stammered, "I really have no family at all now. My sister, my niece…"

I looked her in the eye, and inquired hesitantly, "Would you like something other than tea right now? If you'd like a little glass of wine I would be more than happy to join you."

Her look was so appreciative I wondered if perhaps I was the first to understand the poor woman and her needs.

"I would just love to get out of here for a little something stronger than tea," she responded gratefully.

"Well, if you don't think it too bizarre, I have an unopened bottle of red wine in my car that might hit the spot."

"Let's go," said Martha, with a hint of a smile. She grabbed two glasses and we moved outside.

We walked to a bench at the side of the shop and I did the honors. Soon we were huddled together sipping wine like conspiratorial teenagers. The fresh air, combined with the wine, seemed to bring everything into a more objective focus.

"Poor dear," she continued. "I wasn't sure what to do after Sarah passed, but it was clear that Great Barrington was not where April intended to settle. The finality of Sarah's death hit each of us in different ways. While I was pleased to have April remain in my life I saw that she needed more. After some time had elapsed, April told me that in order to begin her new life she first needed to find her biological father.

"It surprised me at first, but then I understood. I told her not to get her hopes up, not to expect too much. She reassured me that she wasn't overly hopeful, but I sensed that it meant a great deal to her. Like her mother, she wanted to get her nursing degree. If her father was, by some remote chance, a physician, perhaps he could be of some help. To myself I thought, 'That all depends on how he'll feel about the sudden appearance of a long-forgotten daughter.' I worried, but she was not to be discouraged.

"I told her all I knew about him. Sarah had been working at the Maine Medical Center when she became pregnant; this would have been in the early nineties. I do believe she mentioned that her boyfriend was either a doctor or worked at the hospital. It wasn't much to go on, but it was all I knew. I gave April $500, and bought her a bus ticket to Portland. She seemed so fragile, and yet was so determined in her own gentle way. What a terrible, terrible ending for her! I can't imagine anyone acting violently toward such a girl. Good heavens!"

I didn't have much to say to console her, so said nothing. We sat in silence, sharing the peace of the moment.

"I wonder if it might shed some fresh light on this if we were to find April's father," I suggested. "He might have been the last person with whom she was in touch."

Martha nodded her agreement. "The only keepsake Sarah had from this man was a ring; neither April nor I could make sense of it. April left it here with me. Let me get it, and show it to you," she said, getting up.

A few moments later she handed me a bulky man's ring. I recognized it immediately as a fraternity ring, as I had seen similar ones at the University of Michigan. The Greek letters Sigma Alpha Epsilon circled a central stone in raised relief. I asked if I might keep the ring for awhile and Martha immediately agreed. I hoped it might lead me to our mysterious man.

As I was gathering my things to leave, I told Martha about the white bows hanging about town to honor April. "We all feel somehow responsible for such a terrible thing happening in our town. It would be my privilege to put together a service for her in Woodland Harbor if you are comfortable with it. We can do it whenever you are ready."

Her astonished face was reward enough for my spontaneous offer.

"Oh, Lizzie, it means so much to me that April somehow mattered to someone. She was a lost soul who didn't deserve any of this. It would be remarkable if you would do that. Let's be in touch. Thank you so much."

We parted after sharing contact information. I gave Martha the name and phone number of the coroner's office in Portland, and my number and email as well. As I drove off I felt like Dorothy in *The Wizard of Oz*. There really is 'no place like home' and that's exactly where I wanted to be right now.

CHAPTER THIRTY-SEVEN

Before I pulled onto the Mass. Pike, I stopped at a little sandwich shop and grabbed a ham-and-cheese sub. I hoped it would soak up the wine that lingered in my stomach. The bottle of water would also help. As luck would have it, this little shop made an absolutely fabulous sandwich. The honey ham, baby Swiss, fresh lettuce, tasty tomatoes, and honey mustard spread packed quite a wallop on the foot-long loaf of Italian bread. Predictably, I dribbled some of the golden spread down my white shirt, but the next stop was Woodford Harbor, so I didn't give it a thought.

The straight road home left me plenty of time for contemplation. I was pleased with myself for offering to conduct a service for April. It was a win/win for the town, and for Martha as well.

My thoughts then strayed to the man for whom April had been looking. It seemed logical that if her search had ended in Woodford Harbor, that was where her father might be. I couldn't imagine how she had expected to solve this puzzle without understanding the evidence the ring held. To me, the ring seemed like the logical place to start.

My only experience with Greek letters was in connection with the fraternities and sororities at Michigan, where I knew there had been a Sigma Alpha Epsilon chapter. If Sarah had taken her nursing courses in Portland, there was a good chance the ring originally belonged to a fellow studying at a campus nearby. The search intrigued me intellectually, but the personal aspect of the mission was even more important.

Martha had made April a reality—a living, breathing person with hopes, dreams, and a trail of tragedies. Although April and Charlie's lives and experiences were different, they had enough similarities—and I found that disturbing.

I also had to wrap my brain around the fact that April had likely discovered her biological father and he was living in Woodford Harbor. Could it be possible that he was somehow involved with her murder? Woodford Harbor? My sweet, little town? It all seemed rather overwhelming, and a bit sinister at the moment.

The next fifty miles were consumed by thoughts of Archie. He's such a sweet and simple person that it hurt to think of his having additional problems and issues. I felt certain that his stay at the hospital had been traumatic regardless of how kind everyone was, and was relieved that Bode was there to pick him up. How would Archie deal with all of it when he got home? His routines are important; hopefully, they would be restored soon.

Charlie and her obsession with country music—and what it had led to—was next on my list. The initial anger I had felt over the laundromat incident had quelled, but I still found it a bit unsettling. It had become clear to me that the element of the incident I found most disturbing was her not telling me the truth about where she had been. Deceit is not beneficial in any relationship and I wanted to establish a more secure footing with her. The break we had had last night was a good thing. I knew we had some tricky times ahead and I wanted us to be on the same page as much as possible.

I suddenly had a need to connect with my roots, and called my parents in Captiva. The Bluetooth in my Jeep had opened up a new world of conversation for me on the road.

"Hey, Mom! It's me! What are you guys up to?"

"Oh, honey, it's so nice to hear from you! We just got in, and have decided to head down to the Mucky Duck to watch the sunset. It's a beautiful night down here and it looks like a green flash sighting might be in store!" Captiva is one of the prime spots on earth to see this unique optical phenomenon. It occurs at sunset, and occasionally at sunrise, when a green spot suddenly becomes visible above the upper rim of the sun's disk. There is debate about what causes it, but I'm content just to enjoy it when it happens.

I don't know if I was more jealous of the potential for a green flash, or of sitting on the beach with a glass of wine outside the Mucky Duck to view it. Mom didn't help when she added, "And then we're going down to the Lazy Flamingo for oysters."

"Okay, Mom, I'm within inches of turning my Jeep south and joining you! You're making me crazy!"

"Sorry," she said, and I could hear the smile in her voice. "What are you doing up there?"

I gave her a detailed account of my trip in search of April's aunt. She seemed impressed with my success, but her desire to get off the phone to catch the sunset was equally palpable. We signed off with a promise to speak soon.

Before I knew it, I was at the Natick rest area. I pulled off for gas, the ladies' room, and a chocolate chip cookie. The turnpike authority should be commended for having a restaurant supplying fresh cookies at just the spot where I needed it. The treat rejuvenated me and I was excited now to complete the last portion of my journey and return to my wonderful hometown. Wonderful, perhaps, but it did appear that within the confines of its limits there resided a person who had murdered a seemingly innocent twenty-three-year-old girl.

I was amazed at the sea of white bows that welcomed me back into town. There were bows on front doors, on lampposts, on fences, and on the fronts of shops. The spirit was everywhere.

I had called ahead, and learned that Bode and Charlie were listening to country music at my house. Archie was back home with the Duncans. As no one had mentioned putting anything together for dinner, I decided to stop at Brown's. I'll admit I was mildly annoyed, as oftentimes Bode brings dinner over or Charlie comes up with some concoction. I quickly pushed the irritation aside, looking forward instead to the expectation of a warm homecoming. I grabbed my little basket and headed to the produce table. Avocado, tomato, and some nice lettuce would make a good salad. I rounded the corner and almost ran smack-dab into Glenda, who was griping about the size of the pre-packaged hamburger meat.

"It's too big for one person, but not enough for two," she almost snarled in her nasal voice. I smiled, and tried to avoid the conversation by bending over to grab a package. Just then Trudy appeared from the bread aisle and we were all uncomfortably crowded around the refrigerated meat. Try as I might, I was unable to extricate myself from the trio so I just stepped back a pace to leave them to themselves. An uncomfortable look passed between them. I was about to head for the pasta when Glenda looked at me, and began to speak.

"Your man certainly let Duke know who's boss," she commented. "Really whacked him around the block!"

"I found it quite distressing that an incident like that took place at a family event," Trudy intoned in an exaggerated, melodious voice.

"Oh, please, get off your high horse! Men should have at it every now and then! It's good for them!" retorted Glenda.

"What makes you think you know anything about men, my dear?" sniped Trudy.

Glenda took a step toward her, at which point I reassessed my menu and stepped between them to grab a package of chicken. "Really, ladies, it happened, it's over, and it surely will not affect us in the future," I pointed out. My logic made very little sense, but it did interrupt the momentum that had been building. Glenda grabbed a package of hamburger, and marched off in a huff.

"That one does get me going," said Trudy, describing the obvious. I grabbed some barbecue sauce and baked beans, and checked out behind Glenda and before Trudy.

I was a bit ruffled as I got in the Jeep, and headed home. I was sure, though, that things would settle down once I was home. Opening the back door, I tripped over poor Bob, who had planted himself right in front of it. I called out, but was drowned out by a loud chorus.

> We're just hanging around,
> Burnin' it down
> Sippin' on some cold Jack Daniel's,
> Jammin' to some old Alabama with you, baby."

I called again, but still was not heard. Climbing upstairs, I found Bode and Charlie huddled over her iPhone speakers. They finally glanced up and saw me. They waited for the chorus to play one more time, came over for the obligatory kisses, gave me a quick smile, and said, 'Welcome home.' Just as quickly they resumed their argument. Bode contended that George Strait had it all over Jason Aldean; Charlie apparently disagreed. Bode plugged in his iPhone and we were suddenly surrounded by George himself warbling.

> Baby, write this down,
> Take a little note to remind you in case you didn't know,
> Tell yourself I love you and I don't want you to go,
> Write this down.

At this point I turned and went downstairs to change.

In my comfy clothes, I headed straight to the kitchen to start dinner. As I gathered my ingredients, the two finally tumbled down the stairs, laughing, and went into the living room to play one of their outrageously raucous games of Ping-Pong. By turns, each was yelling with glee and then agony. They finally flung down their paddles, and came into the kitchen.

Smiling at them both, I accepted a whack on my butt that suddenly felt sexist. But I cordially accepted a glass of wine from the chauvinist. When we were all settled with our drinks Charlie seemed to finally take real notice of me.

"Mom," she said, "Bode told me he would take me down to Indian Flats on the 17th to hear the new country band, Movin' Along. Would that be all right?"

I took a big breath—a very big breath. I counted backwards from ten. Then I looked at them both. "Hey!" I said. "Let's rewind and start over, what do you say? 'Hi Mom, I'm so glad you're home! I missed you!' would be nice. Or 'Really good to have you back, sweet Z! Are you tired? What did you find out on your trip?' That would also work.

"And then you say, "'Oh! Maybe it's too much for you to make dinner for everyone after all you've been through. How about we all go down to The Old Port for dinner?'

Then I say, "Wow! That's a great idea!"

I smiled. They smiled. And we all trooped out the door laughing.

CHAPTER THIRTY-EIGHT

I opened my eyes to a flash of lightening; it seemed to coincide with a deafening clap of thunder. In my next conscious moment, I took in Bode lying next to me. It was 6:30 am. At my puzzled look, he grunted, "You wouldn't want Bob out in something like this, would you? Or me either, for that matter." I connected the dots relating to lightening, lobster boats, and danger, smiled, and rolled over. We cuddled in.

We had stayed up late last night talking about my trip to western Massachusetts, and Archie. Bode was curious about the fraternity ring. There were Sigma Alpha Epsilon chapters at Maine schools, but not at Bates, Colby, or Bowdoin. This left the University of Maine at Orono as my best bet. I decided to head up there tomorrow.

Bode was impressed with my sleuthing and I must say I was quite pleased with myself as well for tracking down Martha.

Bode told me that his arrest had been very unsettling to Archie, and that it would take some extra effort on everyone's part to build up his self-confidence again. Fortuitously, his birthday was today. I decided to speak with the Duncans about throwing him a little party tonight. It would be a win-win for everyone. I had drifted off thinking about menus and decorations when I suddenly realized it was 7 o'clock, and time to get moving. Bode laid a restraining hand on my elbow, but I pushed myself from the bed and was brushing my teeth within moments.

Bode groaned and started to settle back into the still-warm bedding, but then thought better of it. He lifted his considerable heft out of bed, scratched, and jumped into the shower. This, of course, precluded me from doing the same. The devil is certainly in the details when it comes to cohabitation and sharing a bathroom, I thought. Poking my head up the stairs, I heard Charlie rummaging around, but gave her a quick 'hurry up!' for good measure.

Bode and Bob were long gone before I made it downstairs. Charlie drifted into the kitchen, downed an English muffin that was hardly discernible under the massive mound of peanut butter, and started for the Jeep. I stopped her in her tracks. "Charlie, it's pouring out. Raincoat, please." She grabbed her yellow foul weather jacket, I did the same, and we ran out.

We enjoyed a quiet, companionable ride to the high school where, upon arrival, Charlie jumped out to make the wet trudge up the hill. There are times I feel slightly guilty for delivering to her teachers a half-asleep 16-year-old, but I know she's not the only one. Those poor educators had to deal with a room full of teenagers in the same condition every day. Funeral director or teacher? Give me embalming any day!

The rain was coming down in sheets when I pulled up at The Driftwood, and dashed in for a quick bite. Quick bite, breakfast, it was all the same. I ordered a child's plate of blueberry French toast, thinking that maybe on my birthday I'd splurge and order their 'masterpiece': two poached eggs on English muffin halves, each topped with a slice of ham and melted cheese. It always seemed a bit decadent, but it was perfect for a celebration. I love my birthday, and tend to go hog wild on that day—especially because it's in

February, a particularly glum time of year that needs some lightening up.

Those thoughts suddenly reminded me of Archie's birthday, and the celebration tonight. I didn't see him busing tables, but I did see Glenda at the end of the counter. I caught her eye, and asked about Archie.

"Apparently, he's still too traumatized to work. There are no free lunches here, I can tell you. If he doesn't show up for work he doesn't get paid."

Behind me, I suddenly heard Bode's voice. "No one is asking to be paid when they're not working," he retorted. "It's the wage while he *is* working that we've been talking about, Glenda."

I turned around, and was surprised to see Bode just inside the door, standing in the puddles of his foul weather gear. He was thoroughly drenched.

"What have you been up to?" I asked him. "I thought you weren't going out today."

"Went down to the dock just to check on everything and I found Duke coming in; one of his lines was wrapped around the propeller. Why anyone would be out in this is beyond me, but then again I certainly don't pretend to understand that man. He cut the engine, and threw me a line and I secured it for him. I'm not sure, but I think he might have smiled at me. Well, a positive grunt anyway."

I took Bode's arm and, with a tug, suggested we sit down. It was way too early in the morning for me to deal with unpleasantness. Glenda turned and went into the kitchen, the antithesis of Jenny's cheerfulness.

"Usual?" she smiled at me. I smiled back my assent. Bode ordered two eggs over easy with hash. I frowned, as hash takes longer to prepare than regular meals.

Bode smiled at me. "Are you frowning because I will use up seven extra minutes of your day? Have you been taking Glenda pills?"

I sighed, and relented. "How about Archie's party tonight? I thought we could ask the Duncans and the boys, maybe Uncle Henry, Pepper, and the doctor and Trudy."

"Trudy?" Bode looked at me somewhat quizzically.

"She is his aunt, after all," I replied.

"Hmmph! It seems so unlikely it often slips my mind. Sure," he said, "the more the merrier. By the way, I stopped to see Archie before I came here. He was reading in the kitchen while Mrs. D was cleaning up. He seemed to be almost back to his old self, just a bit tired. After a restful day at home, he should be ready for a little celebration tonight."

"You know, I wish we could bring Mom to the party. She just loves things like this."

"I know," I told him, "but they're showing *An Affair to Remember* at the home tonight. She'll be just as happy there."

Bode smiled his thanks.

"It's supposed to stop raining by mid-afternoon," I continued, "so I thought we could do burgers and hot dogs on the grill, baked beans, and potato chips. Then I thought I would have a photo cake made for dessert. The kids love those." It was one of those magical thing bakeries do now. You give them any old photo and they blow it up so it covers the entire cake—*and* it's edible!

"Are you kidding? I love those!" Bode smiled. "What photo are you going to use?"

"I thought the one I took of all the boys collecting firewood for the clambake. That way, everyone can eat his own face! I thought it might be fun to make Archie masks, too. I'll blow up a cute photo of his face, and make it life-sized. Then I'll print them up, cut out just the face, and glue them to paint sticks. That way, when we sing "Happy Birthday" everyone can hold Archie's face in front of his own. When we sing, Archie will see a sea of his own image!"

"You're a good one, Z," said Bode, with a twinkle in his eye. "Good fun."

I noticed Tommy fawning over Trudy, giving her one of his goodie bags. I spied a big blue inside. I couldn't see Glenda in the kitchen, but I could almost feel her fury through the walls. Tommy is such a good-hearted, trusting guy he's oblivious to the machinations of the women around him.

As they were leaving, I stopped the doctor and Trudy. and invited them to the party that night. I thought of mentioning that it was informal, as Trudy looked ready to shop Fifth Avenue, but knew it would come out sounding a bit snarky. Maybe she would trade in the fitted camisole for sweats knowing the menu was merely hot dogs. Or maybe not.

Pepper ambled over and joined us, so I took the opportunity to invite her as well. Her response was positive and this picked up my spirits. I filled her in on my Aunt Martha information from Great Barrington. She was all ears, and wanted to be kept abreast of the entire story as it unfolded.

"Well, my little friend," she whispered to me then, lowering her head and leaning in close, "you are not the only detective in the pool. I just overheard an interesting piece of information through the ceiling grate." Her eyes moved conspiratorially to the large metal plate in the ceiling; it was situated above the middle section of The Driftwood's counter. The second-floor storeroom is on its other side. If you occupy the right seat at the counter you can overhear everything that's said upstairs.

"Glenda was just on the phone with one of her low-life girlfriends," snitched Pepper. "She was complaining that *her* doctor had been seen with a young girl. She's remarkably presumptuous, that one. You know what they say, 'Never underestimate the impudence of a impudent man'—or woman, as the case may be." I smiled my agreement.

Somehow, in a very convoluted way, I almost felt bad for Glenda if Doc Wilson was cheating on her. "Oh, what a tangled web we weave when first we practice to deceive!" Walter Scott had hit the nail on the head.

When I mentioned the idea of a memorial service to honor April, Pepper perked right up. "Now, *there*'s an idea! Nicely done, Lizzie. I'll help get things organized when you have a date. Yes, very nice," she mused. "Judging from all the white bows around town, it will be well attended."

CHAPTER THIRTY-NINE

I decided to drive straight to Uncle Henry's office to report on my trip. I found him hunched over a pile of papers on his desk, grumbling under his breath. I enjoyed observing him undetected for a moment. Good men are few and far between and Uncle Henry is one of the good guys. It seems right that he is my mother's brother. I can see the two of them tumbling around as kids, Uncle Henry teasing and causing all kinds of trouble. But if you know his character, you know that he always had her back. He would protect his little sister from everything that threatened her. I know, too, that's how he feels about me, and I him.

He sensed my presence then, and whipped off his reading glasses, looking up to greet me. When people reach that certain age when they need reading glasses, it seems to take awhile before they're comfortable with the idea. When caught wearing them, they feel suddenly old. Although Uncle Henry might be a tad self-conscious about his glasses, he has no problem with me hearing his grumbling. His first words, in fact, were an articulated grouse.

"Why, why, why must there be so much paper work! I signed on to keep law and order in this little town, not to write an encyclopedia on its happenings," he growled.

"Well, good morning to you, too," I replied.

"Yes, well, I decided skip The Driftwood, and not eat such big breakfasts every morning, but I think it's taking a toll. I'm miserable! Give me eggs and I can deal with most anything."

"Big mistake, Uncle Henry. Man was not meant to skip meals."

"Then it must be genetic, my dear! I feel the same way! My newfangled idea is dead to me as of now. I will never skip another breakfast. So tell me, how is your investigation going?" Although I sensed a slight mocking tone in his voice, I didn't dignify it with a response, instead giving him all the details of my trip to western Massachusetts. His attention seemed to wander when I described the motel room, but otherwise he was very attentive.

"Lizzie, you are a regular Nancy Drew. I'm delighted you've found Aunt Martha, which is very important. For her, as well as our poor April."

"It's interesting, Uncle Henry. I feel as though April is 'ours' as well. I offered to have a memorial service for her, which will naturally include Martha. I could tell she was quite moved. I gave her the coroner's contact information so she can retrieve April's belongings. We should be hearing from her soon."

An odd silence hung in the air as we contemplated those details. It was Uncle Henry who broke the silence. "Do you think Charlie might ever want to find *her* father?" he asked gently.

The world stopped turning for a moment as I considered this. Honestly, the thought had never entered my mind. I found myself feeling angry, ashamed, and defensive—all in that split second it took Uncle Henry to pose the question. My face must have registered these emotions, for Uncle Henry said no more. Trying to absorb it all, I smiled weakly, nodded, and headed out the door.

I got in my Jeep feeling somewhat paralyzed. Maybe it was a sort of emotional shock, but my mind was completely blank. The top of my head felt numb. Everything was fine, nothing had changed, and yet I was reeling inside. I started the engine, and drove to a small inlet across from Grace Island. As I looked out over the water, nothing looked as I had always known it. There seemed to have been a scene change in the play of my life. The familiar looked somehow different, in the ways that water can change from mid-afternoon to later in the day; in the way that swells change from summer to fall. It was the same, and yet so different.

How strange, I thought, that this question had never occurred to me. I think I've created a wonderful life for Charlie. She is growing up in Woodford Harbor, which I think is one of the most perfect places on earth. She has my parents and Uncle Henry as family to support her. And while Bode isn't her biological father, their relationship is strong and solid. Her achievements in life are many, and have always been acknowledged with much love and support. In my heart of hearts, I have always thought of her father as nothing more than a sperm donor. Could it be that there is more to this than I've admitted? Hearing those words from Uncle Henry hit me hard. This was family.

I sat for a long time, then realized I was just driving myself crazy—and getting nowhere. I wanted to find Bode, and talk to him. I wanted my mother. I wanted my father. And then I realized I needed to process some of this in my own mind before asking for further input. For now, however, I needed to concentrate on the present. The world was still spinning on its axis and there were other things that needed my attention. I started the Jeep, and drove back to my real world—the world of Bainbridge Funeral Home.

I arrived to a hearty, reassuring hello from Mr. Stanley, who handed me a pile of telephone messages. I looked them over, and felt myself coming back to earth. Here, I could control things. It felt good—really good.

My first call was to Martha. She answered immediately, and seemed pleased to hear from me.

"How are you doing?" I asked.

"You know, Lizzie, I think the news about April brought back all the sadness I had when Sarah passed away. Even though we hadn't been in touch, or what people would describe as close, we each knew the other was out there. Family ties are different from other relationships, as I'm sure you well know. When Sarah needed me, I was there. I feel so bad that this terrible thing happened to April. I sent her off with the best intentions, and now her life has ended prematurely and in such an ugly way."

I immediately thought of Charlie, and this new idea of her father. I think I was a bit over-sensitized at this point.

"No, Martha. There was nothing you could have done to change what happened to poor April. You sent her off just as you should have, to find and live her life. That such a thing could have happened, much less in Woodford Harbor, is just inconceivable. She should have been as safe here as anywhere on earth—perhaps more so. She must have somehow walked into an accident, an unforeseen calamity no one could have predicted. You did just the right thing."

"Thank you, Lizzie," she replied, this time with a stronger voice. "Intellectually, I know I did nothing wrong, but when you're in bed thinking about these things in the middle of the night, well, you know…"

"Of course I do," I reassured her.

"Thank you so much. May I also ask your advice about having April cremated before the memorial service? I want to bring her back here, and bury her next to her mother."

"That's so nice, Martha. You're doing all the right things, too. Why don't I contact a local crematorium to schedule it; we can choose a date for the memorial service after that."

"Yes, Lizzie, that would be wonderful. I'll look forward to hearing from you—and thank you again for everything," said Martha, the quaver back in her voice.

We ended our conversation; my heart went out to her.

I was digging through my pile of messages when Mr. Stanley knocked on my door. Just the sound of his voice made me realize I was hungry. Right on cue, he suggested we order out for lunch. "It seems you might need a bit of extra cheer today, Miss G," he announced sweetly. "Shall I order us roast beef sandwiches from Slice of Heaven?"

"Oh, my! What a grand idea! Yes, please, extra sauce on mine!" It is amazing what a little care on one person's part can do to lift the spirits of another.

"I'll give them a call so the order will be ready for you," he said, reaching for the phone book and flipping through its pages.

"Mr. Stanley," I admonished him, laughing as I did so, "You have a cell phone now and it's time you began using its features. Tap the Internet icon, go to whitepages.com, and type in Slice of Heaven, Woodford Harbor. The number will come right up! If we decide to have another treat later in the week you can go to 'recent,' and pull up the number from there!"

He smiled like a kid with a new toy, went through the steps, and successfully ordered our sandwiches. Pleased as a puppy with an open door, he was. Mr. Stanley and I are a great combination.

I took the short walk to Slice of Heaven, and took the opportunity to chat with the owner and several friends who were there. When our order was ready, I paid for it and returned to the funeral home. Through mouthfuls, Mr. Stanley and I discussed the upcoming service for Mrs. Arthur.

"I spoke with the girls, and they have scheduled the service for the day after tomorrow at ten in the morning. Apparently the sun is best in the garden at that time of day. I'm helping them with a speaker for the music, and baskets for the flowers," he reported. "I found one large basket for people to leave their flowers in at the end of the service; it should create a lovely bouquet. They are going to serve refreshments in the house afterwards. It should be a nice gathering."

"Good. That get-together after the service is so important," I said. "It's a time for everyone to remember Mrs. Arthur as a mother, a friend, and whatever else she was to each person there. It's also important for the girls to see all these ladies from the garden club, and other folks around town, and to understand that their mother mattered to so many. All those shared memories will be a great comfort to them."

"Actually, the girls did say they were wrestling with one last problem. They didn't tell me what it was, but I imagine it has to do with that ridiculous ring. They'd like to meet with you tomorrow. Is there a good time I might suggest to them?"

"Oh, for heaven's sake!" I suddenly snapped. "Make it early. I'm driving to the university in Orono tomorrow and that will take a good part of my day."

"Will do," said the unflappable Mr. Stanley. It's a shame I can't transplant some of that agreeable DNA into my own bloodstream.

CHAPTER FORTY

I wiped up the barbeque sauce that had spilled on my desk and Mr. Stanley left to complete his arrangements for Mrs. Arthur. I needed to place the order for the photo cake, so I stepped out and delivered the photo of Archie and his friends to the bakery. They smiled at the shot, and promised the cake by five. I felt good about providing some fun for the group that would soon gather. Next I stopped at the Apple store, where I picked out a bright green iPod for the birthday boy. Charlie was sure she could teach him to use the little thing and Bode was certain he would enjoy the world of music it would afford him.

It's just amazing what kindness to others does to raise one's own spirits. I stopped at the local hardware store on my way back to the office, and picked up 14 paint sticks for the Archie masks. Unfortunately, the only unpleasant clerk in the place happened to be behind the counter when I requested them. Scowling, she told me in no uncertain terms, "I can't just give you all these paint sticks."

"Well, then, I'll buy them," I replied.

"You can have a dozen, but it will be five cents each for the others."

I dug out a dime, wondering to myself just how much bad will a person can buy for ten cents. I had learned long ago, though, that it's important not to let another person's attitude affect one's own. Just because she scowled didn't mean I had to do so in return.

Back in the office I enlarged an adorable photo of Archie's face, cropped it, and printed out fourteen copies. I cut them out so only the outline of his face and hair remained, and then glued them onto my ill-gotten paint sticks. What a great surprise I had in store for Archie! I half-heartedly wrapped up a few more pieces of business at my desk, then left early in anticipation of the big party that evening.

Stopping at Brown's, I picked up two-dozen hot dogs, hamburger meat, buns, chips, baked beans, paper plates, lemonade, and ice cream to accompany the cake. Ice cream is nothing without blueberries, especially in Maine, so I grabbed a few pint boxes of one of our state's delicacies. Impulsively, I stopped at Mud Puddle Toys for some balloons—the ultimate accessory for any festive occasion.

Once home I patted the hamburger into patties, buttered buns, sliced hot dog skins, and arranged it all on the outdoor table. The balloons flapped around in the breeze and the paper plates and napkins provided additional spots of color. Plucking a handful of vibrant yellow daffodils, I arranged them in a pitcher that I set in the middle of the table. Much as I enjoy paper party hats, I had suppressed the urge to include them tonight. Archie, after all, was turning seventeen, and might feel a bit foolish. Otherwise, I was almost frighteningly pleased with myself.

Just then Charlie waltzed through the back door; rather wisely, I thought, she complimented all my efforts. Bode called soon after to report on his whereabouts. I told him I was off to pick up the cake, and would be ready for wine shortly. I could feel his grin over the phone when he promised to be right over.

The anticipation of picking up a photo cake is similar to the feeling I used to get when I went to the drug store to pick up pictures I'd left for developing. You have an idea what you'll get, but the reality—when you actually *see* it—is always so much better. I couldn't wait to see the look on Archie's face!

Returning home, I found Bob stretched out under the picnic table; Bode sat nearby, holding out a glass of wine. It was another one of those little moments that make my life so special. The Duncans' van rumbled in with all the boys just as Doctor Wilson and Trudy pulled up in their black Mercedes. Trudy had no doubt done her best to dress appropriately for the occasion, which is all you can really ask of a person, but had failed rather spectacularly. Hopefully, her heels would not sink into the grass. Likewise, I could only pray that the ketchup wouldn't find her cream linen pants. Uncle Henry and Pepper arrived simultaneously, but in separate cars. They seem to make a regular issue of not being seen as 'a pair.'

I hid the cake in the kitchen, and joined everyone outside. I was relieved to see Archie interacting with everyone like the Archie of old. Bode lit the grill and people were piling their plates with sizzling dogs and burgers. Folks had piled gifts for Archie on a rock ledge and I suggested to him that he open them. He was a bit shy, but looked pleased with the attention.

Ben and Karen Duncan had organized a card signed by all the boys, and presented him with a Dustin Pedroia T-shirt. Archie lit up, and stammered a heartfelt thank you that pleased the other boys immensely. Gifts are like that: they have such a nice way of sharing affection. Next he opened the iPod from the three of us. His expression looked a bit puzzled, but when Charlie assured him that she would help him with it he seemed happier. Uncle Henry and Pepper each offered him a gift card from iTunes to supply music for his new device.

I stood to get the cake when suddenly Doctor Wilson stepped forward, offering Archie a small, square package. When Archie unwrapped it, his face turned crimson and his eyes nearly popped out of his head. He looked at the doctor with a combination of awe and gratitude. There was an awkward silence. I stepped forward and looked at the gift. It was an official major league baseball signed by David Ortiz. I looked at Archie and he nodded his assent to pass it around. People held it like a hot potato, so amazed were they. Ben Duncan held the ball himself to show the boys, deeming it too precious to be sullied by sticky fingers.

"Doctor!" I exclaimed. "What a remarkable gift! Oh, my word, awesome! How did you ever get that?"

"Well, if you go online these days you can find most anything." He smiled. Archie hesitated, not knowing quite what to do. Livingston, upon first seeing Stanley in Africa, couldn't possibly have mustered a bigger smile than the one Archie bestowed on the good doctor. It was a great moment and the doctor blushed with pride. Suddenly Trudy came out of her reverie, and made a somewhat disgusting sound. She was clearly not as enamored with the gift as the others.

"Whatever will the boy do with that?" she fairly spat. She looked like she was ready to retreat to the Mercedes, but caught herself and sat back down. The black frown on her face might have been enough to dampen the festivities had Archie not yelped and jumped up to hug the doctor. The evening had turned out better than even I had expected and I had had high expectations.

I asked Charlie to subtly hand out the Archie masks, and went inside. I popped seventeen candles on top of the cake, being careful not to skewer any of the boys in the photo. I lit it up, and walked out singing "Happy Birthday." At the signal, everyone raised his or her mask, surrounding Archie with a gaggle of his own face. His own visage shown bright in the twilight, so great was his joy.

The young man who had been through so much for so long was engulfed by the moment.

Bode cut the cake, managing somehow to give each boy his own face. What remained was a bit of a hodgepodge, but no one seemed to mind; it tasted just as delicious. Walking over to give the doctor his piece, I smiled at him with a new respect. "That baseball is quite something. I don't think there's anything that could have pleased Archie more. It is so thoughtful."

"Well," he replied, "sometimes it's just nice to give a kid a boost."

I gave him a quick, spontaneous hug, and disappeared into the shadows to hide the tears welling up in my eyes.

Karen and Ben Duncan shepherded their charges into the van and one by one the other guests offered their thanks and said their good byes. I suggested Charlie go up and work on her homework and she was gone in a flash.

All the disposables found their way to a big trash bag, making the cleanup, while not exactly environmentally friendly, at least easy. The night air had just the perfect chill to warrant a fleece, and the clear sky was carpeted with stars. Bode grabbed a last beer, and brought me a small glass of wine. We propped ourselves up on a ledge next to the house and did the next best thing to having a party: discussing it in a post-mortem. The biggest thrill, we both agreed, was seeing Archie so comfortable with everyone, and so pleased with the attention.

"I don't know why those photo cakes tickle me so much, but they do," I told Bode. "They're just such fun!"

"All those Archie faces singing to Archie was priceless," added Bode.

We sat in contented silence for a bit. Finally, I brought up what had been on my mind since morning, recounting what Uncle Henry had said earlier.

"All this attention on April finding her real father has gotten Uncle Henry to thinking about Charlie and *her* father. I'm almost embarrassed to say that it has never occurred to me. The similarities seem distant, to be perfectly honest, but maybe there *are* some parallels. Then, of course, I started thinking about you, and how you would feel," I said quietly, taking Bode's hand.

"I have never felt that Charlie lacks for anything in her life, so Uncle Henry's intimation that a part is missing really upsets me. Initially, I was angry with him for bringing it up. It's not that I don't love my father and understand what he has contributed to my life. I do. But everything has been on such an even keel with Charlie and me. Why mess it all up by dredging up her father?"

"I think I've always had an underlying awareness of the issue, Z. Charlie and I have a great relationship; you know that. I may not be her father, but she feels like family to me. I've never needed to define it any differently."

"Our relationship is secure," I said, "and nothing will change that; we're as solid as can be. I can't imagine that whatever might come of a discussion like this with Charlie would change anything between the two of you. It's just, for lack of a better word, awkward."

"Ha! Now there's one of your classic understatements," said Bode, grinning. "I don't think we need high drama to deal with this, just a good, honest conversation."

"Bode, it's amazing how helpful it is to give words to a worry. As soon as I spoke my concerns out loud, they acquired definition, and with definition I feel better able to handle them. I am *so* lucky to have a friend like you."

Bode pulled me up from the ledge with a grin. "Prove it."

Bob led us in.

CHAPTER FORTY-ONE

When the sun hit my eyes Bode was gone and I felt a jolt of energy in anticipation of my day ahead. I swam almost frantically, showered, and dressed in record time. My wake-up call to Charlie was enough to get a "Calm down!" from her up on the third floor. I had covered her English muffin with peanut butter before her feet hit the first floor. I handed it to her, and suggested she eat it in the car. And we were off. The drop at school was seamless, and Charlie walked into the high school barely knowing where she was.

I stopped for a quick bite at The Driftwood, but was there longer than I had anticipated. Pepper led the barrage of questions about my discovery of Martha. All ears were on me. I related all I knew, with the exception of the ring, as I needed to keep something to myself. I then shared the fact that I had invited Martha to the memorial service for April.

"Well, that's nice Lizzie, but I don't know what real difference the discovery of Martha has made," said Trudy.

Tommy was leaning over Trudy's table, handing her a bag of some sort of goodie, when Glenda came flying out of the kitchen and declared. "Well I think it's fascinating that you found the missing Martha! Good for you, Lizzie!"

I wasn't sure whether to accept the purported compliment or see it as the reality is was—a rebuttal to Trudy's comment. What Trudy saw as black, Glenda saw as white. And vice versa. At some point it almost seemed as if the doctor ignored these vocal altercations and took them for granted. Not nice on anyone's part.

I finally made it out with just enough time to rush to my office and meet with the Arthur girls. Sure enough, Mr. Stanley had them seated around my desk when I dashed in. We traded good mornings and I braced myself for the next challenge they would throw my way.

Josie and Miranda deferred to Meg, who said, "You know Lizzie, we have had a very nice few days going over Mother's photos and putting a nice collection together on a board. We have had a chance to meet with Mother's friends in the garden club and have been so pleased with their affection for her. However, we still have the somewhat ludicrous problem of the ring. We just don't know what to do with it, and wonder if you have any suggestions."

I knew immediately. "Ladies, this ring has caused nothing but unpleasant feelings for all of you. I think the most sensible solution would be to bury it with your mother. The sooner the ring is gone, the sooner all the wounds associated with it can truly and thoroughly heal. It was an unfortunate episode in your lives. I say bury it with her, and be done with it. Focus on all the other aspects of her life.

"Listen to her friends at the memorial service. Recognize all the good she did for the three of you in your lives. Let her have her ring, and don't dwell on it. I think by the end of the service tomorrow you will have many more pleasant memories of her life to think about."

There was a moment's hesitation, but gradually all three seemed to embrace the idea. Meg looked at her sisters for assent, then smiled and nodded to me.

Another chapter closed in Mrs. Arthur's life. And I was on the road.

CHAPTER FORTY-TWO

I picked up 295 North, and set my cruise control for 65 mph. I had brought along an iced tea and some cookies, so I was well prepared for the two-hour drive. I hoped it wasn't a fool's mission, but I wasn't sure what else to do. Uncle Henry had been subtly skeptical; it certainly wasn't the first time he had questioned my judgment. Bode and I had googled all the colleges and universities around the Portland area and only the University of Maine in Orono had a Sigma Alpha Epsilon chapter. I headed there, hoping that—like all frat houses—they would have framed group photos of each pledge year hung throughout the house. The boards generally had individual photos of each member, along with their names. Alumni returning for homecoming and other special events usually made a beeline for their individual frat houses to re-live memories of 'the old days.' University fundraisers knew this, and used it as a great opportunity to tap the old boys for donations.

It was a pleasant drive north and the sun gave an almost neon green tint to tree leaves just beginning to bud. I cruised along, stopping only for the occasional tollbooth. Ever since the concept of practicing random acts of kindness has come into vogue, I am always slightly disappointed when the car ahead of me doesn't leave money for my toll as well. Then again, had I ever left a payment for the car behind me? Goodness, life is challenging.

I found it impossible to drive past Waldoboro without a stop at Moody's Diner. It is quintessential Maine, and nearly world famous. Their pies make life worth living, so I grabbed a blueberry and a banana cream and was quickly—and happily—on my way. I loved being on this road, and let my real mission slip from my consciousness as I drove. I remembered so many other wonderful trips up this same route. I had vacationed on Vinalhaven in the summers with my parents and Charlie and Bode and I always managed a few days there each summer. We grab the ferry in Rockland, and look forward during the brief crossing to the magic that awaits us at our destination.

It was almost lunchtime when I entered Orono. I had eaten so many cookies that I was more sick than hungry, so decided to postpone lunch. Instead, I entered the address of the SAE house in my phone, and began following the purple line of my GPS. I arrived to find a large, dignified white building; 60 or so young men lived here. I knew from experience that fraternity houses are at their best when seen from a distance, for the interiors inevitably disappoint. The universal smell of stale beer coupled with ratty furniture holding its ground atop stained and ragged rugs is the norm. In that regard, this SAE house did not disappoint.

A nice-looking young man in shorts and a T-shirt—one featuring a beer unknown to me and a jungle of palm trees—passed me on the porch. He eyed me suspiciously; I guess I no longer look like a co-ed. I did, however, pass the terrorist test. "Can I help you with anything?" he asked.

"Thanks! Do you hang pictures of past pledge years in the house?"

"Yeah. The most recent are in the dining room; the older ones are in the study area in the basement."

"I'm looking for the one from 1990," I told him.

"Whoa! I don't know if they go *that* far back, but you can have a look."

I quelled an urge to tell him that 1990 was not ancient history. He held the door open as I exercised a nonjudgmental mantra in my mind. The basement smelled horrible, and looked worse than the upstairs, which was itself pretty bad. I circled the room's perimeter until I found a light switch. Once flipped, it exposed a somewhat disheveled room in its fluorescent glow. The framed photos descended in year from left to right. I found 1997, and worked my way back. Five frames into my search, I found a pile leaning against the wall.

It was so dark in the corner and I wished I wasn't there. Uncle Henry would be amused if he could see me now. I dragged two of the five away from the wall, cursing as they deposited a line of dust down the front of my shirt. They were surprisingly heavy, and extremely awkward. I pulled out the one from 1989, and inspected the bright young faces. The glass was so dusty that it was neither easy, nor pleasant, to discern most of their features. I thought of going upstairs to get paper towels to clean them off, but it sounded like too much work, so I thought the better of it.

I dragged out 1990 next, but still couldn't discern anything worthwhile. Like a good Girl Scout, I returned them both to the pile. As I dragged out 1991, I scraped a knuckle against 1992, which added a splotch of blood to the dust already on my shirt front. This was getting old fast. Propping the thing against the moldy basement wall, I began to methodically look at the faces. The third photo from the left in the fifth row stopped me in my tracks. I stared at it, willing it away. But when I read the name beneath it, there was no denying the facts. The youthful, unlined face of Dr. Ronald Wilson smiled back at me.

My drive home was a blur. As soon as I reached the car, I called Uncle Henry. I desperately needed someone with whom to share the weight of this discovery; he was my obvious choice for so many reasons. No matter how old I become, Uncle Henry will always be older—for just that reason, I perceive him to be wiser. He took the news in his predictably unruffled manner.

"Let's sleep on this, and meet with the doctor in the morning. And since you seem to be up to your neck in this investigation, I think you should come along with me. I'll call, and set up an early appointment in his office."

"Do you think he'll have Trudy there?" I asked.

"Hmmmm," was Uncle Henry's response. We'll just see what the doctor does with this request for a meeting. That in itself should be telling."

That seemed an understatement to me. My brain was exploding with the news. I wanted Uncle Henry to arrest him, and chain him to the most public lamppost in town while he interrogated him. What, my mind screamed, did this 'hmmmmm mean'? My first thought was that Uncle Henry felt the doctor had murdered April. It suddenly occurred to me that I was not watching *Perry Mason*, but was dealing with life—real life—in color, and not in black-and-white. Obviously, I had no way of knowing if poor April had even found her biological father. How *could* she have found him without understanding the meaning of the ring? This was the clue that had brought *me* to him. But maybe there was another path through the labyrinth that led to the same end.

This only opened up another round of questions. If she had found him, what was his reaction? Did he bundle her in his arms, and take her home to Trudy? I had a real hard time imagining this scenario. Trudy's attitude toward Archie didn't bode well for a long-lost, illegitimate child of her husband. Did he offer her money? Shoo her away? It could very well be that she never found him. That left tomorrow's meeting with him even more traumatic.

Would we be informing him of a situation from his past that would impact him forever? Why had I gotten involved with this at all? A kernel of curiosity had led to a mountain of knowledge. Maybe some things are left better alone. And yet, with April's death, the entire situation had a much different flavor. It seemed highly unlikely that April had wandered into Woodford Harbor, and randomly met with her demise. Possible, but not probable. The secrets within such a small, and seemingly benign, little town are extraordinary.

I had a quick thought then. I was thankful that no one was delving into *my* past quite so diligently.

CHAPTER FORTY-THREE

I pulled into the Bainbridge Funeral Home a little after three. The burden of my newfound knowledge had shifted my perspective on even the most mundane things. My desk looked smaller, my bills appeared bigger, the view out the window seemed different, and I felt like I had been gone for weeks. The sound of Mr. Stanley's voice went a long way toward bringing me back to reality.

"I called the Chelsea Crematorium and they will take care of April when the body is released."

"Thank you, Mr. Stanley. I'm going to put in a call to Detective Daniels to tell him about April's Aunt Martha. I hope he'll release her possessions to me so I can give them to her. I have learned over many years that each death and the situations that arise around them are unique, but this one seems especially so."

"You are so right, my dear. Any case involving a child is difficult. This one, however, appears to be murder. A mysterious young woman on the cusp of life wanders into our town and meets her demise. It is almost inconceivable. Breathtaking, really."

It felt good to hear Mr. Stanley give my feelings credibility—and he was not yet aware of one of the most bizarre aspects of the case.

"Mrs. Arthur's daughters were in earlier," he continued. "The service is set for 10:30 tomorrow morning in the garden. The weather seems to be cooperating, and should be lovely. They dropped off a copy of the program so you can review it and pull your thoughts together. There will be electricity for the music and flowers will be handed out at the beginning. I've arranged four rows of twelve chairs for seating, a table at the front for notes, and a beautiful, large, woven basket in which to set the bouquet at the end. A table right outside the back door will hold all the seedlings, each planted in a small cup. The caterer has everything under control for the reception in the house afterwards."

"Thank you so much, Mr. Stanley. I'm afraid I have been distracted. You have done a wonderful job organizing this event. It should be a lovely and meaningful time for everyone."

With that, Mr. Stanley left me. I immediately called Bode to confirm he was coming for dinner.

"Hi, Z! Just pulling up to the dock. We had a great haul today. As soon as I get them over to The Lobster Company I'll clean up and be over. Are you all right?" asked Bode.

I guess there was something off in my voice. He certainly knows me to a T. "Well, something has come up that has thrown me for a bit of a loop," I confessed. "I am really looking forward to seeing you, and getting your thoughts on it. And maybe Archie will be better off eating with the Duncan clan tonight."

"I'll be there by 5:30. Have a cold one ready for me!"

I smiled and said good bye. Just then my cell phone rang. I was sure it was Charlie checking in.

"Hi, Mom! Lacrosse practice was awesome, they served great pizza in the cafeteria for lunch, I think my white shirt needs to be bleached, and I have a bunch of homework."

"Well, I'll be home soon, and Bode is coming over around 5:30, so we're all set."

And you know what? Normal felt good.

People often assume that, living in Maine, we eat lobster on a daily basis because we're surrounded by it. But we don't, in much to same way I bet ranchers don't eat hamburger every night, or farmers eat chicken day after day. Too much of a good thing, at times, can be anything *but* good.

Meat loaf seemed a good choice for dinner, so I drove straight to the market. I love Ritz crackers so much that sometimes I worry my meat loaf is nothing more than a vehicle for the buttery things. I think the same could be said for lobster and drawn butter. In any case, I loaded up with hamburger, eggs, onions, pre-made mashed potatoes, and green beans. I knew I had at least seven sleeves of Ritz crackers at home.

The only familiar face I saw was Glenda's. She was examining a counter filled with fancy cheeses and caviar. An expensive bottle of champagne was already in her cart. I tried not to be too judgmental, but really—who buys that assortment of food for oneself or one's girlfriends? I tried to rein in those negative thoughts, but I must admit I could not totally obliterate them.

I arrived home where Charlie was playing music and purportedly doing homework. Bode and Bob arrived at the stroke of 5:30. Clothed in jeans and a T-shirt, I felt more at home in my body, and somewhat less overwhelmed by my discovery.

After receiving my customary whack on the butt, I requested a glass of red wine. Bode seemed to sense my excitement and gave me a curious look, but did as requested. I had my hands in a bowl covered with hamburger meat, raw egg, onion, and Ritz crackers, so Bode brought the glass to my lips and gave me a sip. It seemed a bit decadent, but I needed it. Bode then grabbed the meat loaf pan and I spread the mess into it. I crumbled more crackers on top, and completed it with four strips of bacon. I put the pre-made potatoes in a casserole, as I think everyone enjoys them more when they haven't seen the box. Bode grabbed the green beans, and started washing them and snapping off their ends.

"I stopped by and saw Mom just now. She is just amazing—always cheerful, or at least it seems so. But sometimes I wonder what she thinks about with all that time on her hands.

"She started reminiscing about you again today. She talked about all the ball games we used to play in the backyard, and the little boats we sailed around the cove. She even recalled that we hadn't gone to the senior prom together. She never mentioned it before, but all of a sudden she seemed curious as to why we hadn't gone together. I told her I thought it was because we were such good friends we were afraid we might ruin it if we went the boyfriend/girlfriend route. What do you think? Why *didn't* we go together?

"Then she asked me how I feel about you now. I have to say it was a bit awkward. I feel things, you know I do, but putting them into words is not what I do best. I tried, but I don't know what she heard. Anyway, it's nice to be right here with you."

I gave him a hug, and suggested we go outside for a chat as I had news for him as well.

Just as we sat down on the glider, Charlie came dancing out and sat down on the top step with her favorite drink, half diet Coke and half lemonade. We had never set up a routine for adult time versus family time and I momentarily wished we had. I was bursting to talk with Bode about the doctor. Looking over at Charlie, though, I suddenly recognized that she was no longer a little girl, but was indeed a young adult. Perhaps I could discuss April and the doctor with her; her insights on the subject might be interesting.

"Okay, you two," I said. "Here's what I dug up." I began to describe my day. When I got to the punch line, a young Ronald Wilson among all the fraternity pictures, their reactions were not dissimilar. No matter how you came at the story, the idea of the doctor being a father was as incredulous to a sixteen-year-old as it was to one of the doctor's contemporaries. Bode, of course, didn't squeal quite the way Charlie did. There are few more effusive souls than teenage girls, and although Charlie is not a drama queen she does express herself with abandon. I felt as though she was giving voice to my own personal amazement.

The persona of the doctor was ingrained in all of us as a late-middle-aged doctor, childless, and married to Trudy. His extra-curricular activities were common knowledge. But a twenty-three year-old girl in search of her father arriving in Woodford Harbor and finding him in the person of Ronald Wilson? Mind-boggling. Staggering. Borderline ludicrous. Even Bode was at a loss for words. Not so Charlie.

"That is radical! Unbelievable!" Of course anyone over the age of thirty having sex was astonishing to her. "And I met her! She was real. And really nice. Actually pretty cool. I thought she had a lot of guts to come here alone to try to find her real father. But her whole life was kind of bizarre to me. She and her mother wandered all over the country, living in each spot as long as her mother wanted. She didn't really have a home. Or even a best friend. I can't imagine.

"She seemed normal," continued Charlie, "like someone who should have lots of friends. But she didn't. The only friend she had here was that woman who visited her. April said it was an odd situation, but I never got the details. I only saw her once at the laundromat. Maybe I should have gone back, and been nicer to her. We could have had her over for dinner. Oh, why didn't I do more for her!"

"Charlie, calm down. You had no way of knowing what she was doing here. We all meet people and have passing interactions with them. We can't act on every chance meeting. Relatively speaking, she really was much older than you. Her life experiences were a world apart from yours. It's nice that you had a chat with her and I'm sure it made her time that evening more fun than it might have been."

"Can we talk about the implications for the doctor?" asked Bode. "What does this mean for him? We don't even know if he knows about April. And how in the world does a grown man with a wife like Trudy handle an illegitimate daughter? Illegitimate sounds so harsh. There should be another word."

"Let me look it up on my iPhone thesaurus," offered Charlie. "Here we go. Unlawful. Illegal. Illicit. Dishonest. Criminal." That brought a terrible pause in our conversation.

"Let's leave it at out-of-wedlock," I said.

"So you and Uncle Henry are meeting with the doctor tomorrow morning," said Bode. "You don't even know what the poor man knows! Did April find him? She must have been on to something to have been in Woodford Harbor. But if she didn't understand the significance of the ring, how else could she have located him? And if she didn't, you could be dropping quite a bombshell on him. I wonder if he'll include Trudy in the meeting."

"If she's *not* there it might mean that Dr. Wilson knows what's going on, and doesn't want her to know," I said. "Oh, brother. What if he doesn't know and she *is* there? I'm not sure I'm ready for that moment."

Bode smiled. "'Oh, brother' is an understatement." Even Charlie had the beginnings of a smile on her face. This was all at my expense and I wasn't best pleased.

"Knock it off, you guys! This is serious," I said.

"OK, Z, you're right. It is quite a dramatic conversation one way or the other."

"I am not a big fan of drama," I lamented.

"Well, you'll be up to your eyeballs in it tomorrow!" said Bode.

CHAPTER FORTY-FOUR

I suddenly knew the moment was right to introduce 'the subject'. I had already reconciled myself to it, so I said a little prayer, took a big breath, and said, "So, honey, what do you think about *your* biological father? Is it something that seems important to you? Do you think about it?" I'm almost sure there was not a quiver in my voice.

The drama of the moment was lost on her as she answered in what I can only believe was complete honesty. In a level tone, she said, "You know I have always wondered about it. Sometimes it seems important, and then other times I couldn't care less."

She looked over at me as if to read my take on this. I smiled and gave her an encouraging look.

"When I was really little I had a kind of imaginary daddy in my head. Like when you would tell me I couldn't have something I wanted, I was always sure that my 'real' daddy would make sure I got it. Of course, that never panned out. Then when I was a bit older I started noticing fathers walking hand in hand with their little girls. And I would wonder what it would feel like to have a big hand holding mine. Now when I think about it I have mostly curiosity. Would he have curly brown hair? Would he be smart? Funny? Have long legs like me? So yeah, I think about it. And this whole thing with April has made me think about trying to find him. Maybe. I don't know. It's like wanting to know something, and yet not being sure you really want to know."

I had tried to teach her that giving a problem 'words' sometimes lessens the intensity of a highly emotional problem, and that honesty was paramount. I was so proud of her at this moment for having taken these words to heart. Her answer was completely honest, and objective. Even Bode looked impressed.

I jumped up and put the potatoes in the oven to warm, and turned on the water under the beans. I started breathing again. I wasn't sure this made everything all right, but at least it was out on the table.

We piled our plates with the meat loaf, beans, and potatoes, and retired to the living room with our trays. *Wheel of Fortune* morphed into *Jeopardy*. Charlie got up and did the dishes and Bode and I started watching a dismal Red Sox game. Pedroia hit into a double play with the bases loaded, retiring the side. I pleaded a headache and Bode and Bob went home. Charlie was still doing homework when I said good night and fell into my bed with relief.

It was then I started to cry. My chest ached with the hurt and disappointment I was feeling. The betrayal. The frustration, and the guilt. Who was I to think that Charlie didn't need a father? Weren't Bode and Uncle Henry and the whole town and me enough for her? What more could I have done? The thought of her wishing for someone in addition to me was awful.

To think she was fantasizing about an imaginary man all these years was so hurtful. I knew I was overreacting, but the pain was real. I started to feel paranoid. Had people been looking at me for years, wondering why I had withheld a father from Charlie? Fresh angst. I was just a self-centered, selfish bitch who had no right to feel good about much of anything. I wanted my mother to hold me and tell me everything was okay. I wanted tonight's conversation not to be a part of me. I wished April had never landed on my embalming table. My misery was escalating geometrically, but I had to live with all these thoughts and feel the emotions to fully process them.

It was well after midnight when I crawled out of bed, unable to sleep. I slipped into sweats, walked across the street to the water and sat looking out at the harbor. The sound of the water on the rocks and the smell of salt in the air enveloped me like a comfy blanket. The full moon splayed a beautiful swath of moon glow across the water. Nature was once again working its magic. I felt a peace start to flow back into my veins and I breathed in the gentle night air.

My emotions began to take a more rational form. No, Charlie did not lead a miserable life without her biological father. She was surrounded by caring people with healthy, moral standards. And Bode, while not her *real* father, was a hell of a good influence. Uncle Henry and my parents *were* real family and loved her. And me? I couldn't imagine anyone loving another human being more than I loved that girl. The true importance of the father figure Charlie was missing still wasn't entirely clear to me. But the big picture had come back into focus, and it was not a bad one.

CHAPTER FORTY-FIVE

Morning seemed to arrive a few hours later. I managed to pull myself out of bed and across the street for my morning swim. The extra half hour under the covers seemed awfully inviting, but I knew the dip in the cold water was more pragmatic, and indeed it was. By the time I ran into the house from the outdoor shower, life was on a much more even keel. I checked on Charlie, and dressed in black pants with a crisp white shirt, pulled my hair back, put on a hint of blush, and was in my 'as good as it gets' mode for the day.

The phone rang and it was Uncle Henry. "We're on with the doctor at 8 o'clock in his office. Must admit to being a mite uneasy." This from the unflappable Uncle Henry. I had a knot in my stomach.

"I'll meet you at your office, and drive over with you," I said.

I packed up Charlie and dropped her off at the high school. I kind of wished I could follow her in. Anything was better than the meeting coming up.

"Here I am, Uncle Henry," I called upon arrival. "Oh dear, what are we doing? This is just nuts."

"Nuts. Now there's a word. I'm sure I could be more articulate, but it wouldn't really change this scenario. Nothing to it but to do it, I guess. Let's go, Lizzie."

Uncle Henry suggested we take my car so as not to attract undue attention at the doctor's office. We walked down his hallway at precisely eight o'clock, and found the door open. We entered the empty reception area, and the doctor came out immediately to greet us—sans Trudy. "Come on into my office," he said.

We sat down, and without hesitation the doctor said, "I imagine you have discovered that the young murder victim and I are related."

"Yes, sir," said Uncle Henry. "We have. Quite something. How long have the two of you been in touch? This is quite a surprise to me."

"Well, multiply that times a hundred and you can begin to imagine what a surprise it was for me. Young April came to my office about two weeks ago, on a Monday when Trudy was not working. I assumed she had come as a patient, but when she told me the story of her and her mother Sarah, I was baffled. Shocked, really. Of course, I remembered Sarah, but those college days seem like a lifetime ago.

"To have this beautiful young person present herself to me in such a fashion was, I must say, earth-shattering. I felt we should act sensibly, and begin with a DNA test. I took samples from us both, and sent them off to the lab in Portland. She returned the following Monday and we sat down together as father and daughter."

"The initial shock wore off after a bit and I began to contemplate the enormity of it all. I cannot say I was entirely displeased with the revelation. Here was a person who shared my genes, after all. I guess I finally understood Peter Ustinov's observation that 'children are the only form of immortality that we can be sure of.' And here she was, standing in front of me. I must admit I felt incredulous at first. There was certainly no instantaneous surge of love. The news was, by turns, problematic, tricky, and awkward.

"I tried to put those feelings aside as we got to know each other over the next few days. Twice I picked her up at the laundromat and we drove to Freeport for lunch. It was an interesting dynamic. As she told her story I realized that Sarah had raised a strong and independent little being. April was bright, despite her lack of a college education. Her passion was to become a nurse, like her mother. To fulfill that dream, she needed to go to school. Helping her do so, I felt, was the least I could do for her and we began to work out the details.

"Fortunately, she was not looking for a new home for herself. I explained that my wife would probably not be the stepmother of her dreams. She smiled, and graciously agreed that our relationship need not be one of an adoring father embracing his long-lost daughter. I felt affection for her gallant little soul, and a very healthy respect for her ambitions. I have sufficient money, so assisting her would not have been a hardship. What is money for if not to make the world a better place? The addition of a noble and compassionate nurse would certainly improve the lives of many. I felt our relationship was just the thing for both of us.

"I knew she was staying with Duke, and although I was not thrilled with the idea, she assured me that Duke had been reasonably kind to her, and she felt safe. The hoodlums that were part of his life I hadn't anticipated, though. I had the feeling she might somehow have become involved in foul play while she was with Duke, but that's awfully difficult to prove. What a waste people like Duke and his ilk are."

"Doctor Wilson, this is fascinating," I told him. "How did April find you?"

"Ah, such an enterprising little thing. Apparently her Aunt Martha equipped her with funds and a bus ticket to Portland. It was the place where Martha assumed Sarah had gotten pregnant. April followed a crooked and rather winding path with great tenacity until she found her answer.

"Her aunt told her that her mother had been involved with an intern during her time in Portland, so April wisely started at the Maine Medical Center. Knowing that her mother had been employed there between 1991 and 1998, she found someone to look up the hospital's old personnel records. That individual discovered several nurses whose employment went back at least 24 years. One of them, Karissa, told April all she remembered. Her recollection was that Sarah had been involved with an intern before she left town. Karissa then went the extra mile, and searched through the files from those years. The name Ronald Wilson rang a bell, and she suggested April try to find me. I was quite easy to find through Google."

"My goodness, doctor," said Uncle Henry. "That is quite a story. Life does seem to happen sometimes while one is busy making other plans. I can understand the positive feelings you experienced. As for myself, I can't imagine how I would feel."

I almost fell off my chair. Men were creating families everywhere I looked. Uncle Henry could understand Doctor Wilson's feelings? Uncle Henry has no children, and no wife. I assume he never will. What thoughts does he carry to which I am not privy? The world was starting to feel like an uncertain and scary place. Even people you thought you knew well were more three-dimensional when you dug deeper.

"You must know, Doctor, that as ludicrous as this sounds, you are a potential suspect in this case. You would certainly have the provocation to want her out of the way. The autopsy report should arrive today; hopefully, it will clarify things a bit," said Uncle Henry.

"Her body is being transported to the crematorium soon. I'll go over to identify her, and take possession of her belongings. That might shed some light on things as well," I added.

"We will keep you in the loop, Doctor," said Uncle Henry.

"My goodness," said Wilson suddenly. "I guess I need to have a chat with Trudy before all this gets out."

Ha! If I didn't like the idea of this meeting, at least I didn't need to be a part of *that* one.

CHAPTER FORTY-SIX

I think Uncle Henry and I were equally relieved to have that chat over.

"You just can't write real life," said Uncle Henry. "Never in my wildest dreams did I think I would ever have a conversation like that with the doctor. Imagine my telling him he is a suspect in a murder case.

"And to top it all off I am going to have to contact Detective Daniels with this piece of news. I dread having to speak to him and I loathe his inevitable genius deduction that the doctor is now a person of significant interest in this case."

"I'm sorry, Uncle Henry. Really. April's body should be at the crematorium by now so I'll need to get going. Poor, poor dear. Good luck with your unpleasant task, and let me know what you find out from the autopsy. But first, run down to The Driftwood and fortify yourself with two eggs over easy before you do anything!" At least I knew how to care for Uncle Henry in the gastronomical department.

I drove off, once again not feeling much pleasure in my next task. The director of the crematorium had the pine box ready when I arrived. He opened the lid and there she was. Someone at the coroner's office had gone through her possessions, and dressed her in a nice pair of pants and a tie-dyed T-shirt. I wanted so badly to just touch her, and see those eyes open.

"Yes, that's April," I said. "God bless her."

I touched the top of the lid, and left with her few things in a cloth sack. I felt as though I had grieved the end of her life on so many occasions already.

I raced back to the funeral home just in time to see Mr. Stanley leaving for the memorial service.

"I have the programs and I think everything else has already been delivered to Mrs. Arthur's garden. The seats are set up, the sound system arranged, the cut flowers are in order, and the big basket is set up next to the lectern in the front. The seedlings are looking lovely. And what a beautiful day it is. Very nice for the Arthur family," he observed.

"Thank you so much, Mr. Stanley. I could never have pulled this together myself. I will explain what has come to light with the murder after the service. It just sucks my mental capacities and leaves little room for anything else. I'll go over my notes for this service and be with you shortly.'

I sat down at my desk and took a big breath. It was time to give my entire attention to Mrs. Arthur's memorial service. To do less would be unfair to her and to her three daughters.

After half an hour of dedicated meditation, solely focused on the event before me, I was in the right frame of mind to give my best to the Arthurs.

It was still forty minutes before the service was to begin, but there were already so many cars that I had a hard time finding a parking spot anywhere near the house. It was a pleasant day for a walk, though, and this helped clear the final cobwebs from my mind.

The white bamboo folding chairs were in orderly rows. The lectern was white wicker, with a large empty white wicker basket on its left. There were name cards on the chairs set up behind the lectern; I put my notes down on mine.

A number of photo boards were set up on easels behind the chairs. They revealed a younger Mrs. Arthur, but not a different Mrs. Arthur. She held her chin high with a formal air. Most consistent, however, was that her three girls were always gathered around her. She obviously adored the trio, and was quite pleased when they encircled her.

As promised, the ladies had put small wooden signs with sayings throughout the garden. I walked among them slowly, letting their messages fill my mind.

the earth laughs in flowers from ee cummings

Play in the dirt because life is too short to always have clean fingernails.

Gardens are a form of autobiography.

I greeted the three girls. Meg had on a well-tailored black suit, Josie was dressed in a rather limp A-line skirt and peasant shirt, and Miranda and her three little girls were in pastel dresses with ruffles protruding at all angles. The husband/father stood to the side as almost a condiment. Paramount was that they all stood together as a family.

Ladies of all shapes and sizes began arriving. It was clear these were friends from the garden club. They almost *smelled* like dirt. Each mourner was offered a single cut flower to take to his or her seat.

Pachelbel's "Canon in D" started playing over the speakers and the chatter was instantly muted to a respectful murmur. Mr. Stanley invited the guests to sit and I moved forward.

To begin the service by talking about the weather seemed like such a cliché, but to have ignored the topic was to not recognize the elephant in the room. It was a stunning spring day, and whether the universe had created it to honor Mrs. Arthur or not, why not take the credit? After I recounted some biographical details we sang the old hymn, "In the Garden." The recorded piano accompaniment was almost strident, but it felt right.

I introduced Mrs. Arthur's good friend, who was also the president of the garden club. She recounted Mrs. Arthur's contributions and service to the club, and then shared memories that were both touching and humanizing. She remembered coming upon Mrs. Arthur as she was stomping her hoe on the ground in anger because a hydrangea had bloomed pink instead of blue. It brought a few sympathetic giggles from the ladies. But then she went on to relate another time when Mrs. Arthur was almost in tears when one of her aged perennials did not come back one spring. To some that might seem an overreaction, but not to this group.

Josie then stood and read Rudyard Kipling's "The Glory of the Garden," which concluded thusly:

Oh, Adam was a gardener, and God who made him sees
That half a proper gardener's work is done upon his knees,
So when your work is finished, you can wash your hands and pray
For the Glory of the Garden that it may not pass away!
And the Glory of the Garden it shall never pass away!

It was daunting to follow those lines, but I read my prepared remarks equating gardens to human lives. It is not a stretch and was a perfect metaphor. I felt pleased as I finished up.

Mr. Stanley then brought the speakers to life again and we all sang "For the Beauty of the Earth." Familiar music is powerful in these situations.

Meg then delivered her remarks. Moments like these can bring out the very best in people, and Meg was indeed at *her* best. In her short remarks she said that to her, Mrs. Arthur was a mother, first and foremost. Whatever else she did with her life was secondary to that role for Meg. She knew her mother loved her, there was never any doubt in her mind. Therefore, her mother's life had been a complete success as far as she was concerned. And what greater accolade can a woman be awarded?

Miranda and her three girls then stood in front of the group, and explained that they would like each person to put their cut flower in the wicker basket next to them. To the strains of "Amazing Grace" everyone came forward and deposited a flower. It was a beautiful arrangement when completed.

We all reveled in its beauty while we sang "All Things Bright and Beautiful." Meg then graciously invited everyone into the house for tea.

Conversation in the house was animated and lively. The gathering after a memorial service is where much of the real healing begins. On this day, folks shared their memories of Mrs. Arthur and the girls were bolstered knowing that their mother mattered to other people as well. I excused myself after a half hour, thanking Mr. Stanley again for all his hard work. My office felt anticlimactic after the emotions of the previous hour. In the end, Mrs. Arthur had been treated well and I felt that Meg, Josie, and Miranda had behaved nobly. Nice.

CHAPTER FORTY-SEVEN

As I walked into my office the phone was ringing. I answered, and was greeted by an excited Pepper, assaulting me with questions.

"The doctor? The doctor is April's father? Her illegitimate father? How, oh how, can this be? How did she find him? Do you really think it's true? Holy Toledo!"

"Slow down, Pepper, you're making me crazy! How did you get this information so fast? Apparently it's true, according to the doctor, anyway. He claims they did a DNA test to confirm the facts."

"Does that make him a suspect? Can you even imagine the doctor killing someone?"

"Pepper, stop! This is ridiculous. Yes, it makes him a suspect, but only because of police protocol. A man in his position would always be suspect. But we all know the doctor. He certainly doesn't seem like a likely candidate to me."

"Well, you can't be so sure of that," said Pepper. "It's a pretty big surprise that he has an illegitimate daughter. Nothing can be more shocking than that!"

"Pepper—" I said. I just could not dignify this argument with any more words or energy. We agreed to disagree, and ended the conversation.

I sat back in my chair, and picked up a piece of mail. The phone rang again.

I saw Uncle Henry's number, and braced myself.

"Lizzie, dear, I just heard from that pompous Detective Daniels. You would think he had single-handedly done the autopsy, performed the lab work, and then ascertained the cause of death. At any rate, it appears she was poisoned. Cyanide was found in the crumbs."

Hearing this added one more layer to my despair. I had always held out hope that this whole thing had been a dreadful accident, and that somehow some natural aberration had taken April. There was no doubt anymore.

"That's dreadful. Awful. It sounds like something out of an Agatha Christie novel. Are you sure?" I asked.

"Seems so," answered Uncle Henry. "It does make everything worse."

"How would anyone gain access to cyanide?" I wondered aloud, speaking what my mind was thinking.

"Actually, Lizzie, cyanide can be found in many of the foods we eat every day: Think lima beans, almonds, and the pits of apricots, apples, and peaches. It's found in certain bacteria and mushrooms as well. Seems to me that this whole thing was premeditated.

"Mind you, I'm not implicating the doctor, but it would take a certain sophistication to pull this off."

How awful. How can people let a lifetime relationship with someone like the doctor go right out the window as soon as something out of the ordinary happens?

"That is so unfair, Uncle Henry."

"I know it is, Lizzie, and I'm sorry. Right now, though, I think we need to figure out who it was who had befriended April. Charlie remembers April telling her that she had been grateful for this unknown woman's attention. Do you think it could be that the interest this woman had in April wasn't of an entirely affectionate nature?"

"I want to know who did this to April," I seethed. "I feel like we're close to finding this woman; just a few more pieces of information, and I think we'll have her. Think, I tell myself!"

"Take care, Lizzie. Sometimes these things have a way of sorting themselves out on their own."

I could think of little else. Pepper called back, wanting to know if I would speak at April's memorial service. I readily agreed and we ended our chat on a much friendlier note than previously—on the surface, that is. I was still incredulous that she would throw the doctor under the bus for being the newly-discovered father of April.

It was impossible to concentrate for the remainder of the afternoon. The mysterious woman owned my mind. I could think of little else.

Mr. Stanley announced a new client. We hopped in the hearse, and picked up the body of an 89-year-old man who had been in hospice care at his home for a few weeks. It is always easy to feel that a death of this sort is a blessing that puts an end to suffering, but it is much more than that for his loved ones. We allowed his family to sit with the body until they were ready to let it go, then made an appointment to meet at noon the next day to begin arrangements. For now, they were fortunate to have seemingly close relationships with each other. Their journey with grief was just beginning.

I bid Mr. Stanley good night when we got back to the funeral home, and headed to Brown's. I had a lot of nervous energy coursing through my veins, and was anxious to talk with Charlie to see if she had forgotten any details about this 'friend' of April's.

I impulsively called Captiva, and was greeted with my father's wonderful voice.

"Well, hello, Lizzie Ann!"

I filled him in on the doctor's role in all this and he was as shocked as I had been. Maybe more so, as the doctor was closer to my father's age than mine. Everyone's perspective held equal shock, but for different reasons.

I explained Charlie's involvement with April; fortunately he didn't question Charlie's presence at the laundromat.

"This mysterious woman sounds as though she could figure quite prominently in the solution to this mystery. Why don't you invite your Uncle Henry to dinner tonight, and have Charlie retell her story? Encourage her to remember every detail. Having Henry there might be good for her, and an extra set of ears, especially Henry's, can always be helpful."

I thanked him, avoided asking about his dinner plans to avoid another attack of jealousy, and called Uncle Henry.

"Uncle Henry! Would you like to come by for dinner tonight? I want to ask Charlie again about any recollections she has about April and her mysterious visitor. I would love to have you there."

"Well, that is a kind offer. Can't say as I often pass up a free meal, and you and Charlie and Bode are some of my favorite company, so yes, dear. What time?"

"If you come at 6:30, it will give me time to start dinner and let Charlie get a head start on her homework. I haven't spoken with Bode today, but will give him a call. Thanks, Uncle Henry!"

I clicked my cell phone closed, and felt instantly better. More heads are certainly better than one. I tried Bode, but had to leave a message as he was still out on the water. The thought of having all my favorite people together for the coming meal was comforting.

What to eat? Ha! Pork, the other white meat, seemed like a good idea. Of course it really is just an excuse for applesauce, but that's not so bad. I picked up a double pork tenderloin, broccoli, and baking potatoes. Impulsively, I grabbed a delicious-looking blueberry pie and chocolate chip ice cream. Vanilla ice cream is always good on pie, but little chunks of chocolate definitely improve it.

Charlie was, predictably, upstairs listening to twanging sounds and doing homework when I walked in. I gave her a peck on top of her head, and told her about our dinner guests.

"Sounds good," she said, not knowing we were all about to pick her brain. I wondered if she would recall anything new. I was pondering this, and spreading Dijon mustard and brown sugar on the tenderloin, when my phone rang.

"Hi, Bode! Uncle Henry is coming for dinner. Does 6:30 work for you?"

"Hi, Z. How are you? How was your day? Oh, how was my day? Nice you should ask. Am I free for dinner? Sure. I'll check in with Mom, and be there around 6:30 if that works," said Bode laughing. He doesn't always appreciate my habit of cutting to the chase on the phone.

I smiled. "Yes, 6:30 is perfect. Can't wait to see you," I said.

"That's more like it, my friend." And we both hung up chuckling.

CHAPTER FORTY-EIGHT

I finished preparing the broccoli, and popped the potatoes in the oven. I did all this on automatic pilot, as the mystery of April's lady friend was on spin cycle in my brain.

I actually set the table. Uncle Henry seemed like a good excuse to break up our routine of eating in front of the TV. It felt good to pull out placemats with matching napkins. Of course, I was the only one who would notice, but hey—I count.

Bob, Bode, and Uncle Henry arrived simultaneously, and caused such a commotion that Charlie came down in no time to join the party. Bode had found some new designer beer and Uncle Henry was all over it. He has simple tastes, but when offered a new beer he is on cloud nine.

Bob was wound up in all the excitement, and barreled around the kitchen, his his tail swiping everybody and everything. Sometimes I forget that Bernese mountain dogs are extremely large, and can cause havoc in small spaces. And that fish breath! Poor animal, having that flavor in his mouth! I gave him a dog cookie to help counteract it.

Bode poured me a glass of wine, he and Uncle Henry twisted the tops off their beer bottles, and Charlie settled for a diet Coke and lemonade. We retired to the backyard.

Uncle Henry asked Charlie about her lacrosse team, and Bode followed up with questions about school. I let the conversation go as long as I could bear, then interrupted. "Charlie, remember you said that April had mentioned a woman who had befriended her? Do you remember exactly what she said about her?"

"Didn't I tell you, Mom? April said that some woman from town had come to visit her a couple of times. I didn't quite get it, but April had seemed pleased to have someone pay attention to her. She said Duke had been nice, and so had this woman."

"Did she mention anything about her? Her age? What she looked like?" I asked.

"Well, let's see. She said the woman was very nice, but that she didn't really seem to understand where April was coming from— like maybe she had never had children, or at least not a girl. I couldn't quite understand what April and the woman had in common. Maybe just a lonely lady wanting to be nice. I don't know. My feeling was that she was probably a little older than you, but not really old."

"Good to know I'm not close to 'really old'," I said during the chuckles that followed her reply.

"That's it? No mention of a name, or anything else at all?"

"Sorry, Mom, no. Why is it so important?" asked Charlie.

"Well, I'm just feeling very defensive about the doctor. People seem to jump on a bandwagon pretty quickly when they want a problem solved. They want to be done with worrying about who killed April, and the doctor is an easy target. I just feel that it's all wrong; I want to find a better, more reasonable solution."

"You can only look so hard before you begin inventing solutions that are quite unlikely," said Uncle Henry. "The most obvious answer can be the correct one, but I'm keeping an open mind. We just need one critical piece of information to clarify everything. Maybe we'll find it in the pork tenderloin."

"Oh," I said. "Are you hungry, Uncle Henry?" I smiled and went back into the kitchen to check on the broccoli, and pull the tenderloin and potatoes out of the oven. Bode followed me, grabbed two more beers, and retreated to the yard. I sliced the meat, squished open the potatoes, slathered them with butter, and poured the water from the steamed broccoli. They looked a bit lackluster so I added some butter to them as well.

"Come on in, kids," I called. "Let's have at it!"

We enjoyed a lively conversation around the table, covering all the news that school, traffic incidents, lobster counts, and new deaths could offer. My mind, though, was like a broken record, replaying the same nagging question: who was the mystery lady?

There was a round of applause when I pulled out the warm blueberry pie that had been hiding in the lower oven. I brought it to the table along with ice cream, a spatula, and an ice cream scoop. It was a quiet crowd that savored dessert.

Charlie cleared the table. Bode offered to do the dishes for her so she could retire upstairs to finish her homework. Uncle Henry sat back, and let a contented burp escape, then announced his intention to call it a night. He gave me a perfect 'uncle hug' and walked out to his car.

I wanted to feel equally content with my full belly, but my brain was still in high gear. Who, who, who was the woman? I felt she was the last chance for a clear resolution to this crime.

"Shoot! I forgot to give Uncle Henry April's bag of possessions from the coroner. I'll bring it down to The Driftwood tomorrow morning," I said.

Bode looked at me and I think he could almost feel the blood racing through my veins as my mind whirled.

"How about some ping-pong, Z?" We each grabbed a paddle.

Bode easily hit the ball to my side, but my returns were inevitably overzealous and off course.

"You are wired, kid. You can't stop thinking about that woman, can you? Let's go for a walk, and see if we can slow you down bit.

"By the way," he said as we headed out, "Mom had a bunch of ideas today for the house. She asked me again about cleaning the living room rug, so I'd better do it. Then she began talking about the two chairs on either side of the couch; she said they're getting a bit worn after all these years. She asked if I would ask you to choose some fabric, and see about having them reupholstered. And maybe add a few new throw pillows for the couch. I guess you are being allowed indoors!"

I smiled to myself, secretly thrilled at my new relationship with Thistle. She had always been a sort of aunt to me. But I felt we had just taken a giant step further.

CHAPTER FORTY-NINE

B ode was gone before I opened my eyes. I had that heavy feeling in my bones from a night of fitful sleep. It took me a moment to remember what had me tossing and turning and then it started all over. Who was the mysterious woman who had befriended a lost April? It seemed a great kindness. What had gone wrong?

I dragged myself out of bed and brushed my teeth. I made myself put on my bathing suit, grab a towel, and go downstairs. As I was about to walk out the front door I noticed April's bag. Impulsively, I knelt down and opened it. It seemed terribly intrusive to look through her possessions, but I found what I was looking for. Her cell phone. Of course it was dead, but I plugged it into my universal charger and went across the street for my swim.

Upon my return I showered, jumped into some clothes, and returned downstairs to the phone. I clicked it on, and was met with what appeared to be a selfie of April with her mother. They were smiling and looked like two peas in a pod. Again I found myself grieving her death. This photo was hitting much too close to home. I wanted desperately to find out what had happened to her.

She had stored no other photos. Or music. Or games. She didn't seem to use the phone much as there were no contacts listed either. Recent phone calls seemed to be the only information the phone held. I quickly scanned the numbers she had called here in town. There was one that had been dialed five or six times, but I didn't recognize it. I wondered to whom her last phone call had been. There was that number again. It seemed like a terrible invasion of her privacy, but it might be important—or not. I was grasping at straws now. None of the numbers rang a bell with me.

I gave a last glance around the kitchen and was looking for the Jeep keys when I sensed, rather than saw, Charlie in the room. I looked to the bottom of the stairs and there she was in Bode's big old Red Sox T-shirt, which served as her nightgown. I was surprised to see her, as it was Saturday and she usually didn't emerge from the third floor until closer to lunchtime. Her somewhat expressionless face was disconcerting. I moved toward her, gave her a hug, and motioned for her to follow me over to the couch.

After a brief silence, Charlie began, "Mom, we are all so caught up in April and her terrible death and the doctor and some missing woman. There was also all this talk of the doctor having an illegitimate child. I was thinking about all this in bed last night and I realized that I guess I'm illegitimate. Am I? I mean, I don't know who my father is. I've thought about it, and it never bothered me, but with all this talk about April it sounds like a bad thing. Like almost a dirty thing. Mom…" And she began to cry.

If you haven't been a mother it might be difficult to understand that your child's pain is your pain. You own it, you feel it. I felt the weight of a stone in my chest and it was frighteningly painful. I held Charlie, pushing against the pain, and realized that I was taking her to a worse place. I knew I had to get a grip, and be the adult, something that's not always easy. There is a part of everyone's soul that is a child and I was feeling the pain in that place. I had to give these feelings words, make them manageable.

I didn't let the sobbing escalate much further. I sat up, and pulled Charlie up with me until we were eye-to-eye. The mushroom cloud of emotion settled down, and we each took a breath and tried to recuperate.

"Honey, you're right. It's a nasty word, a nasty label. People often say things thoughtlessly, and use a word without clearly understanding not only the meaning, but the power it holds.

"I guess a so-called 'illegitimate child' is defined as one born to a mother and father who aren't married. But that definition is driven by custom, what society currently embraces as a truth at the time. Some laws are absolute throughout time, but there are also traditions that are fluid and change.

"The definition of family has evolved over time. It takes a man and a woman to create a child, but from that moment on the family of that child is unique. Women used to be 'given' to men, along with a trousseau, and thus began the family. Times changed and people were allowed to choose their mates. It was expected that these people, especially as parents, would stay together forever. For whatever reasons, this isn't always the case in the twenty-first century.

"Children don't necessarily live with a father and a mother anymore. They can have two men as parents or two women or, in cases like ours, just a mother. And Bode? Is Bode a part of our family? That's a question I don't want to overanalyze. Some questions can be answered with cold, hard numbers. Feelings? Not so much. Life is full of realities that cannot always be understood through society's rules. As time goes on, though, both rules and customs change. Change, as they say, is the one thing you can count on.

"I was in Michigan when I got pregnant with you. I was living in a world I had created for myself and I was loving it. I was learning about life, love, and embalming. The people around me were my friends and we were all learning together. We had everything in common on those counts. Having a child seemed like fun at the time, kind of like having a little brother or sister around. Fun to be with, probably a little needy. When you were born I was so consumed by my own little world that I didn't even want Grandma to come out and help me. My girlfriends and I could handle it.

"Ha! It was the first time I understood what family really meant to me. The feelings you have for a little baby of your own cannot be described in words. And neither can the responsibility you have suddenly assumed. My girlfriends were amused by the novelty of it all for awhile, but that faded fast.

"I began to understand that the feelings I was having for you were incredibly powerful. The same powerful love, I recognized, that I had for my own parents. And I quickly understood where I needed to be. I wanted my mother. I wanted my father. I wanted what was real family to me, Woodford Harbor. It was clear as a bell, and since then we have both been blessed to have each other and live here.

"Now here we are, sixteen years later. You are my daughter. You are Grandma and Grandpa's granddaughter. You are Uncle Henry's niece. You are Pepper's goddaughter. You have a very special friend in Bode, and so many of the folks in Woodford Harbor are a sort of extended family. You are a loved person. I hope you have a little girl someday so you can understand how much I love you."

Charlie was somewhat subdued and I realized belatedly that I had probably overwhelmed the poor thing—like killing a mosquito with a baseball bat. But it was a big subject, and I wanted to address it adequately.

"Okay, Mom, I think I understand some of that. It's a lot, but I'll think about it. Can we make an appointment at the registry to get my learning permit?" It was hard to believe my little girl would be driving soon.

"Sure," I smiled. It was good to know she had moved on to other things.

CHAPTER FIFTY

I gave Charlie a big hug, and jumped into the Jeep. I had arranged to meet Uncle Henry at The Driftwood to give him April's bag. I arrived first, and sat at the little table to the right of the door. It wasn't packed, but there was a good buzz going. I gave Pepper a wave, and let her continue her monologue about people who don't pick up their dog poop. The latch on the front door made its familiar sound and I felt a rush of aftershave precede the couple who entered. The buzz muted. I felt as though the room—and everyone in it—had suddenly been plugged into a 220-volt socket. People didn't shift their positions, but their bodies tightened perceptibly. Doc Wilson and Trudy came in, and stood for a second as if frozen in place.

It was Trudy who moved—waltzed might be a better description— first. She lifted her chin a bit higher, flipped her hair back, and led her husband to an empty table. I marveled at how an entire town could learn a few facts about a fellow citizen they'd known for years, and arrest, try, and convict him—in their minds—all before breakfast. Doctor Wilson was the same man who had walked through that door hundreds of times, usually in a coat and tie, and usually accompanied by Trudy. On this morning, however, his friends and neighbors saw in him a murderer; worse yet, a man who had killed his illegitimate daughter. I wanted to come to his defense, but was strangely paralyzed by the weight of the room. The doctor and Trudy were not people I'd normally choose as breakfast table mates, but my gut felt protective of them this morning.

Even Tommy was subdued. He peered out the pass-through, and gave me a quick wink, but he seemed to prefer the protection of the kitchen this morning.

The Wilsons sat down quietly at a table near the kitchen. The awkwardness was broken by Archie's arrival, big plastic tub in hand.

"Hello, Doctor!" he sang out. Ever since receiving the Big Papi baseball, Archie had practically tripped over himself in his enthusiasm for the doctor. "Did you see Big Papi last night? Did you? That double off the Green Monster scored Pedroia from second and that was it for the Yankees! Ha! Did you see it?"

"As a matter of fact, I was surprised to see him take that ball to the opposite field...," began the doctor.

"Archie, dear, we're here for our breakfast. Can you please wipe this table down? It seems a bit sticky." Trudy's abrupt and less-than-warm attitude toward Archie only heightened the tension in the room.

Uncle Henry arrived, and joined me. The fresh air he brought in with him eased things a bit—that and the gravitas of his solid girth. He gave me an inquiring look while the scene continued to play itself out.

Jenny arrived with coffees for the pair, and conversation resumed, although at a more reserved level.

She then delivered coffee and iced tea to the two of us. She looked pleadingly at Uncle Henry, as if he could do something. Trudy's piercing voice cut through the air as she spoke to her husband in a honey-soaked voice, put a napkin in his lap, and wiped his mouth.

She seemed to feel a real need to prove her undying love and loyalty to this poor man whom the town had suddenly branded with a big red A. She continued cooing to him until a loud voice suddenly distracted the room.

"Oh, please, Trudy. Give it a break!" I recognized Glenda's piercing voice without having to turn around. "Are you suddenly Tammy Wynette standing by your man? *Your* man? You hold that fake blond head a bit too high for me! You can clutch him all you want, but he's not with you at night, is he now? Do you even know where he was the night April was killed? Do you?"

The long-anticipated confrontation was at hand. Although it seemed inevitable, the reality of the hostility finally being out in the open was appalling. It intimated a violence that made me want to flee.

An ashen-faced Trudy retorted, "With me, of course. He *is* my husband, you know!"

"Wrong. In your dreams he was with you. He was with me!" It hit me like a brick. Only one of these women could have been with the doctor that night. That clearly meant that one was not. These three were the only ones who knew. The doctor, Trudy, and Glenda. And then I knew. I knew what to do.

I had April's bag with me. I reached into it, and pulled out her cell phone. The conversation I had had with Mr. Stanley just a few days ago replayed in my head. 'Mr. Stanley, you don't need to look up a number every time you call it. You can go to 'recents,' and press the number again without re-dialing.'

I stood, and lifted the phone from her bag, turning it on as I did so. The screen popped up and I quickly hit the phone icon. I punched the last number called.

And sure enough I heard an old-fashioned telephone ring coming from the corner that held Trudy, the doctor and Glenda. I held my breath, waiting for one of the women to move. It seemed like an eternity before I heard the doctor say, "Trudy dear, answer your phone."

CHAPTER FIFTY-ONE

Uncle Henry's voice cut through the electrified air as he headed to the table at which Trudy sat. Instinctively I followed him. "Come along, Trudy," he said. "Let's go have a chat."

The couple seemed frozen in a still-life pose. She sat ramrod straight and he just stared at her, moving neither toward nor away from her. "I have done nothing," said Trudy. "But I would like some privacy to discuss this situation."

Uncle Henry led the three of us out of a silent Driftwood. I rode in the police car's passenger seat; the couple awkwardly got in the rear.

"We'll just go down to my office, and see what we can figure out, Trudy." Then silence. Silence for the remainder of what seemed like an hour's drive to the sheriff's office, only a block away.

The moment was a combination of old friends gathering around Uncle Henry's desk, and a moment laden with anxiety.

Uncle Henry began. "This is so very sudden, Trudy. Certainly a shock to all of us, and so terribly difficult for you. I am at a loss as to how to proceed, to be perfectly honest. Do you feel comfortable explaining this?"

"As I said, I don't feel I have anything whatsoever to feel guilty about. Yes, I was visiting with April that night. She had given me a call to say she was home, and to come over. And yes, dear," she turned to her husband. "I knew who she was long before Nancy Drew here found your photo up in Orono." I felt slightly bruised at that, as I was quite proud of my detective work.

"I discovered April's relationship to you through the blood work you sent to the lab," Trudy said. "I always check and double-check everything that goes in and out of that office. When the results came in I was curious about a DNA test, so I opened the envelope and looked at it.

"I was shocked—just dumbfounded. I hated the thought of you having a child. We were never able to have children and I felt betrayed—and not just by that male sex drive you seem unable to control. This was different. This was walking, indelible proof of your infidelity. Even though it was before I even knew you I found it disturbing. And now, of course, everyone will know unequivocally that it's my fault we have no children. I just found the whole situation quite overwhelming.

"I peeked at your cell phone; it wasn't hard to figure out which phone number was hers. When I discovered you were meeting her secretly for lunch I didn't know what to do. We all have our secrets, of course. But this? I followed you when I knew you were going out for lunch, and learned that she worked at the laundromat.

"Then I began to look at the big picture. Maybe there was a chance this could be handled in a civilized manner. That depended, of course, on this girl, April. It all hinged on her attitude and expectations. I wanted to get to know her on my own, without the added baggage of a 'step' relationship.

"I went down to the laundromat, and struck up a conversation. She was a lonely thing, and quite anxious for company. She mentioned that she and her mother had experimented with exotic teas, so I offered to bring some over for her to try. We met a few times and, you know, I liked the girl. I liked her very much. She had an extraordinary amount of gumption to come to a strange town to locate her biological father. I'm sure many people would applaud that. To my way of thinking, though, it was a bit troubling.

"But beyond that, she was a lovely thing. Her ambition to become a nurse certainly hit a chord with me. She explained that her newly-discovered father had offered to help pay her tuition, but the two didn't seem to be planning on going down any primrose path holding hands. After awhile I began to think that the three of us might be capable of having a very nice relationship.

"I must also admit that I very much enjoy being married to you, Ronald. Some might call it blind loyalty, but, dear, I love being with you. Certainly I want nothing to destroy that."

This was getting to be a bit much for me. The doctor did not rush to embrace her, but did put a kindly hand on her knee. My judgments had turned into an absolute cyclone in my brain, but I forced myself to focus on what was playing out before me.

"What exactly went on that evening, Trudy?" asked Uncle Henry gently.

"Well, I brought a new, exotic flavor of green tea to her. She boiled water, and set out a pleasant arrangement of cups, milk, and sugar. I had brought her one of those hideous Big Blues that Tommy had given me that morning and she found an un-chipped plate."

"Did you share it?" asked Uncle Henry.

"Heavens, no! I don't eat those things!"

"Trudy, why didn't you come forward with this information? You were one of the last people to see April alive and you must know the investigation has to include you."

And then it happened. Trudy not only choked up, but tears began to fall down her smooth and perfect cheeks. Her mascara smudged.

"I felt sorry, and frightened, and embarrassed all at the same time. I was terribly sad the girl was dead, and quite frightened at the idea of being involved in a murder investigation. I was humiliated that everyone would know I had been sneaking around meeting my step-daughter.

"And now I *am* part of a murder investigation! I have done nothing! Nothing," she said plaintively, looking at her husband, "but try once again to be your wife."

That was when she really cracked. It was awful to watch the woman crumble. She appeared unable to hold herself upright, so the doctor held her. Their relationship seemed to be based more on loyalty than love, so it was a bit uncomfortable seeing him hold her, as even in that position there was a distance between them.

At that point Uncle Henry made eye contact. We had the same thought simultaneously. The Big Blue. That had been intended for Trudy. From Glenda. Oh, my!

"I'm going to call Detective Daniels right now," he said to the couple. "I'll wait here with you until he comes, then we'll go down and meet him at The Driftwood."

Uncle Henry took the phone into the other office for his conversation with Daniels.

I went down the street to The Bean, and got coffee for the four of us while we waited. Trudy had calmed down and the moment didn't seem to hold the drama it might have on TV.

The doctor and Trudy didn't understand the significance of returning to The Driftwood. They had enough on their plates, and didn't need an explanation. We chatted awkwardly about town politics until the return call came from Detective Daniels. Once again we piled into Uncle Henry's car to retrace our steps.

We all arrived at the same time. The detective entered ahead of us, and quietly asked everyone to leave. He asked the employees to sit at the two front tables. Tommy, Carly, and Archie sat at the table next to me and Glenda stood off to the side. When everyone was seated, Daniels and his officers began a search.

We sat in silence as they banged and clanked around in the kitchen and the back office. No one spoke; it didn't seem necessary. The tension in the room was almost paralyzing.

Finally Detective Daniels emerged from the kitchen, a triumphant smile spread across his features. He carried what appeared to be a bottle of vitamin pills.

"This is one of several four-ounce bottles of vitamin B17 we found. The powder, in sufficient quantities, is fatal when ingested. It does so by causing a reaction with human enzymes that creates cyanide, traces of which were found in April's body during the autopsy; it is believed to be her cause of death.

"How long have you been baking with vitamin B17, Glenda? We found the bottles with your spices. There would be no good reason for you to have such a large quantity of these pills. You put it in the baked gifts that Tommy gave Trudy, assuming Trudy would eat them, didn't you? You never intended for an innocent 24-year-old girl to die. And yet, Glenda, it seems evident that you *did* intend for Trudy to die."

We all looked expectantly at Glenda, waiting to hear some reasonable explanation to dispute his claim. She tightened her body, as if ready to pounce. Her mouth twisted downward as she finally spat out, "Damn straight I wanted to murder Trudy. I have wanted her dead for years! I have been spiking those infernal little delicacies Tommy insists on giving her every day for over a month. I thought at some point she would at least try one! But, no. The self-absorbed body-image queen wouldn't touch anything containing sugar. I thought she might relent at least once, then I would finally be rid of her!

"You're nothing!" she exploded, looking directly at Trudy. "You are nothing but a woman sucking the money and life out of the man I love! He wants to be with me. You are the only obstruction. My life was meant to be shared with him, not just on elicit evenings, but each and every day. He is all I want!"

Trudy looked completely stunned at the vicious diatribe directed at her. I wondered momentarily if she really had the same passion for the doctor as Glenda. But I put that thought way in the back of my brain for later examination. Much later.

The doctor was pale as could be, and looked like he might actually keel over. He remained seated, looking at neither woman, but intently studying the red-checked tablecloth.

Suddenly I heard my own voice break the silence. "This whole thing is awful. It's not just a dreadful accident, but a disgrace to Woodford Harbor."

Uncle Henry stepped to Daniels' side and together they took hold of Glenda's arms. The two lawmakers had put aside any unpleasantness between them, so pleased were they to have cracked the case. Uncle Henry looked like a different man in this, his finest hour.

Much as I dislike the word 'surreal,' I must admit that the scene we were witnessing seemed to be just that. Sure, Glenda was a pill. And Trudy could be utterly annoying as she strutted her imperious self about town. But Glenda as a murderer? Perhaps I had underestimated her loneliness. Her perceived scorn. Perhaps? No, unequivocally.

It was an awful situation all around. For Trudy. For the doctor. For Glenda. And, oh my, for poor April.

CHAPTER FIFTY-TWO

B ode and I sat at our favorite table at The Old Port later that
night. My red wine tasted particularly good for some reason
and its effect was the perfect antidote for my whirling mind. That
and Bode's arm around me.

The day had indeed been otherworldly. Glenda had been surprisingly passive when Detective Daniels approached her. Tommy
and Carly had instinctively jumped to their sister's defense, but the
look on her face subdued them both.

There had been a pregnant pause as each of us let this stunning
news filter through our minds. Glenda was unpleasant. Glenda was
rude, perhaps even vindictive. But this? What was this?

Everything else for the remainder of the day was a bit of a blur
until now. I picked up my glass and pressed a bit more heavily on
Bode's shoulder. I loved Bode and I loved the wine. Might be a
stretch in terms of the the wine, but not much. It felt good to stop
thinking, and just relax in the moment.

"I had kind of a bizarre conversation with Charlie when she got
home," I said to him. "She had already heard about Glenda, and
of course, had plenty to say. She seemed dumbfounded that it was

a woman who had committed the crime. Of course I have always tried to instill the idea in Charlie that women are just as capable as men. In a terrible twist, I found myself starting to defend Glenda, saying that of course a woman could commit murder. I couldn't believe what I heard myself saying. Sometimes these principles can get the best of you."

Bode expelled what seemed to be an amused grunt.

"My mom had a twisted take on it as well," said Bode. "I went over soon after we left The Driftwood to tell her about it; it seemed nicer than letting her hear it through the rumor mill. I found Gus and her in the library together. I explained the convoluted relationships the doctor had, and the awful consequences of Glenda's hateful act. I had anticipated she would be horrified and distressed by the story, but really, her reaction was almost inexplicable to me. First of all, she was practically jumping out of her chair with admiration for you when I explained your method of using the previously-dialed number trick to uncover Trudy's involvement. She seems to be one of your all-time fans at this point.

"My mother is such a romantic she seemed to almost admire Glenda's passion, especially that she would resort to such drastic measures to get her man. I think she's watching a few too many soap operas in the afternoon.

"And Gus was uncharacteristically silent. I was rather looking forward to his reactions as they are always so interesting. But he had very little to say. Maybe he's learned to just let my mom enjoy her dramas."

"And why not!" I mused. "But I must admit I like the part about her championing my resourcefulness." And I did.

There was a good crowd at The Old Port that night. Uncle Henry stopped by, beer in hand, to say hello. "That was certainly something this morning, wouldn't you say, my dear?" he asked.

"I still can't believe it actually happened," I said in reply. "We underestimated poor Glenda. As I've been thinking about this, I realize that she is almost always the one on the outside. She pretty much isolates herself in that office at The Driftwood and here she's usually solo at the bar. At social gatherings she primarily hangs out with her family, but still seems on the fringes in a way. Maybe the loneliness was too much for her."

"Mark Twain said it best," noted Uncle Henry, when he wrote, 'The worst loneliness is not to be comfortable with yourself.' I think that's her real problem."

I looked on amazed at my mother's little brother, and felt a wave of affection and gratitude that he was part of my life. A wise uncle is a real gift.

"Next beer's on me, Uncle Henry," I said. He winked and I think we were both pleased.

Pepper inevitably landed at our table as she made her rounds. "Guess I shouldn't have been so ready to tar and feather Duke. Or the doctor. Ha! I would have dunked Trudy in the drink before Glenda. Guess we'll never know what got her goat so badly."

I nodded, noting that Pepper wasn't in any condition to listen to a Mark Twain quote just now. We could have that conversation another time. For now, everyone was dealing with this in his or her own way.

Although neither the doctor, Trudy, nor Tommy was in evidence, I was sure they would all be fine. Their wounds, however, would need to heal before they could be comfortable with each other again—here and elsewhere. Trudy and Doctor Wilson had a number of things to settle between them. And Tommy not only had a tainted sister, but I suspect he was a bit hurt knowing Trudy never partook of his gifts.

Enough of this studious contemplation. "How you doing, Bode?" I asked.

"I just need a lot of beer, a lot of steak, and then a lot of you."

"Bingo," I said.

CHAPTER FIFTY-THREE

Sunday dawned a beautiful, breezy spring day. April's service was scheduled for one o'clock. It seemed natural to have the gathering in Norton Park on the harbor. Pedestal Rock would be the focal point. White bows festooned the park: on tree branches, in the evergreens, and on benches, signposts, and railings. The white ribbons fluttered like shimmering water. There was almost a festive air about the crowd as people gathered.

Martha arrived early in the morning and we took her to The Driftwood to introduce her to the town.

"I hope this won't be too hard for you," I said as I greeted her. "I'll be right near you, so let me know if you are uncomfortable, overwhelmed, or need anything at all. It has to be so difficult for you to be grieving April with so many unfamiliar faces around you."

"I'll be fine, Lizzie, but I do like knowing you'll be with me. I understand that everyone is doing this for a noble reason. I'm just not good at being the center of attention."

The old iron door handle clanked as we opened the door to The Driftwood. The place looked as though it had just been scoured and scrubbed. Perhaps for Martha's sake, perhaps to give it a fresh look after its recent shame. Carly came right over, and introduced herself to Martha with a welcoming hand.

Bode, Uncle Henry, Charlie, and I sat at a window table, giving Martha the seat with the harbor view. We fell into a comfortable conversation and I could see Martha visibly relax. Tommy's blueberry pancakes were a hit and Carly would not hear of her paying. Martha was taking in this little town that her niece had discovered, and seemed to approve.

We wandered down the street and up the hill to Norton Park, where we took a seat on one of the benches overlooking the boats. I found Mr. Stanley, who was busy setting up his outdoor sound system. As I approached he leaned into a tree to take a break.

"This is quite something, Miss G," he observed. "Never in my memory has anything like this taken place in Woodford Harbor. I'm very proud to be part of it.

"It's a terrible shame, though, that that young girl lost her life in such a useless mess. Much as I would like to simplify things and put Glenda in an evil box with no forgiveness, I just can't do it. She had her reasons. And misguided though they were, I'm afraid they were very real to her."

I nodded, feeling a pain in my chest.

The town hall clock struck one and Mr. Stanley moved off to turn on the pre-recorded hymns. It was spectacular to hear such lovely organ music in this setting. It seemed to cast a spell over the hundred guests in attendance and the park became—for a short while at least—a sacred spot.

I was initially surprised, and then impressed, to see Duke sitting on the fringe of the gathering. He was clean-shaven and wearing a white shirt and clean jeans. Credit where credit is due. Duke was paying his respects to the girl he had befriended.

I stepped up to the rock, thanked everyone for coming, and read the 23rd psalm. The ancient words struck a common chord, and brought the group together.

I began. "April and her mother Sarah's lives were entwined and each depended on the other to give it hope and meaning. They traveled together as a unit, from town to town, and from state to state. Sarah's free spirit rubbed off on April, as did her love of nursing and her calling to care for others. When her mother passed away last month, April felt a need to fill in some unresolved details in her life. With creativity and perseverance, she found Woodford Harbor and was blessed to discover that our own Doctor Wilson was her biological father.

"She shared her dream of becoming a nurse like her mother with him and the two were working together to enable her to follow that dream when her life was tragically taken. Perhaps her time on earth was too short, but April lived it well. She was strongly independent, and when she had a passion she followed it to the end. This young lady had both a mother and father who loved and respected her. She led a short, but noble life. I know that had she lived she would have been a great addition to the world."

Pepper then rose, and read the Henry Van Dyke poem I had suggested, "Gone from My Sight." Read at harbor side, it was stunning.

I am standing upon the seashore. A ship, at my side,
spreads her white sails to the moving breeze and starts
for the blue ocean. She is an object of beauty and strength.
I stand and watch her until, at length, she hangs like a speck
of white cloud just where the sea and sky come to mingle
with each other.

Then, someone at my side says, 'There, she is gone'

Gone where?

Gone from my sight. That is all. She is just as large in mast, hull and spar as she was when she left my side.
And, she is just as able to bear her load of living freight to her destined port.

Her diminished size is in me—not in her.
And, just at the moment when someone says, 'There, she is gone,'
there are other eyes watching her coming, and other voices ready to take up the glad shout, 'Here she comes!'

And that is dying...

Mr. Stanley began the accompaniment to "Amazing Grace," and the gathering's collective voices joined in on the old hymn, their uplifted harmony carrying across the placid water.

I had asked Dr. Nielson, the minister of our local Congregational church, to say a few words in closing. His low, melodic voice filled the park.

"I think the story of April goes back to the ancient traditions found in the first chapter of the book of Ruth in the Old Testament, Ruth 1:16," he began. "After her husband died, Ruth followed her mother-in-law, Naomi, back to Bethlehem, leaving her blood relatives behind. Ruth loved and admired Naomi, and made her decision based on love rather than familial ties. Speaking to her mother-in-law, she said, 'Where you go I will go, and where you lodge I will lodge. Your people shall be my people, and your God my God.' Not all allegiances are based on blood," Reverend Nielson continued. "They can also be directed by love. The community of Woodford Harbor is embracing April as one of their own. She may not have been born and raised here, but we choose to honor her as one of our own. So be it."

Finally, the high school choir gave a heartfelt rendition of Woodford Harbor's town anthem. Martha had tears on her cheeks, but she held her head high and proudly. Woodford Harbor had behaved well. I like to think that April's spirit was felt that day at Norton Park.

Following the service, I joined Martha off to the side. She took my hand, and gave it a squeeze. Her eyes were filled with tears and I could tell it was all she could handle. We embraced for a few seconds and then she pulled back. We smiled into each other's eyes, I nodded, and she was off. We both knew this would not be the end of our relationship.

As people broke off into groups, Uncle Henry stopped to say his good byes. "Thanks so much for doing this, Lizzie. It's been a very difficult chapter in the town's history, but I feel we have dignified it with a positive ending."

"Thanks, Uncle Henry," I said. "You're a good one." The poor thing blushed as I gave him a big kiss on the cheek.

The Duncans came over to grab Archie, who had sat with Bode and Charlie. He had seemed relatively unperturbed by all the goings on. I don't think he understood why Glenda would want to inflict such a dastardly fate on Trudy, but it wasn't a part of his world so he wasn't overthinking it. His part had been a blessedly short chapter. He joined the other boys, and seemed relaxed and at peace now that the final chapter of the story had been written.

Charlie, Bode, and I helped Mr. Stanley collect the speakers and sound equipment, and put it in his car. I gave him a quick hug, and noticed his body was becoming a bit frail.

I turned from that farewell, and from seemingly nowhere the doctor stepped up with Trudy by his side. She, of course, was perfectly outfitted for the day, with nary a hair out of place. Her face looked a bit worn, but it seemed softer somehow.

"Lizzie," said the doctor, "there are no words for the gratitude I feel for what you have done today. You brought April alive. She had a family here in Woodford Harbor, even though she didn't know it. Her short life ended here, but it ended with dignity. I feel a real loss, even though I knew her such a brief time. But I will always carry a bit of her with me, and I feel like I am a better person for having known her." I hugged him, hoping he could feel my warmth and find some comfort in it.

Trudy gave me a tired smile, and trundled off behind the doctor.

Pepper was pontificating to a small group gathered around her. It took the two of us no more than a nanosecond of eye contact to thank and congratulate each other. It was moments like this that let me know I had chosen the perfect godmother for Charlie; I so hoped she was aware of the true worth of her godmother.

I stood with Charlie by my side as Bode and Bob joined us. Bob brought his bad breath and bouncing body and Bode knocked us around a bit, adding that masculine energy that balances the human teeter-totter.

"Let's go sit over there for a minute," Bode said to Charlie and me, pointing toward a big rock overlooking the water. So often it's not the words that Bode says, but his instinct to do what's meaningful in the moment that defines him.

We settled in to look out over the water for a moment. The harbor was starting to fill up with boats for the summer, and held an air of pleasant anticipation. Charlie snuggled in next to me. Actually, we snuggled into each other. The story that had just played out made us appreciate more than ever our wonderful lives and relationships. "You guys," Charlie said, "I think I might want to find my real father someday—or at least the man who shares my actual genes. But that doesn't dilute any of my feelings for either of you. Bode, I love you. And Mom, I adore you."

I was grateful for so much at that moment. And I was anxious to get back to my "succession of ordinary days."